GERONIMO'S GOLD

ISBN: 1542912040
ISBN 13: 9781542912044

ALSO BY TED RICHARDSON:

Imposters of Patriotism

Abolition of Evil

To my parents

GERONIMO'S GOLD

A Novel

Ted Richardson

"If we lose the virile, manly qualities, and sink into a nation of mere hucksters, putting gain over national honor, and subordinating everything to mere ease of life, then we shall indeed reach a condition worse than that of the ancient civilizations in the years of their decay." — Theodore Roosevelt

Prologue
Early 1880s
Mogollon Mountains in Southwestern New Mexico

The small band of Chiricahua Apaches had evaded the U.S. Cavalry yet again. Their warrior leader, Geronimo, had driven what was left of his ragtag collection of followers, half of whom were women and children, relentlessly. He had little choice. He had to gain separation from the more than four thousand pursuing U.S. troops. Two days earlier they had crossed the border from Mexico back into the newly designated territory of New Mexico in the United States. After their third successive all-night march, they were finally in range of their homeland.

After years of press exposure, Geronimo's name had become synonymous with lawlessness and savagery in the minds of the American public. East Coast newspapers branded him a butcher and sensationalized the many raids he and his Apache warriors had conducted throughout the Southwest. But for Geronimo and his followers, the raiding and plundering of ranchers, prospectors, and anyone else with food, supplies, or horses to steal was simply a matter of survival.

Geronimo finally relented and let his small party of sixty people pause to rest. They had reached the Gila River valley at the base of *the Mogollon Mountains. Geronimo knew that only the rugged mountains of his homeland would provide his people with the secure refuge they so desperately needed. During the brief respite, Geronimo and a handful of his warriors rode on ahead to scout the best route up into the towering peaks that rose imposingly in front of them. With a large Bowie knife strapped to his side and rifle slung across his shoulder, he cut an imposing figure. The sun glinted off the silver-washed barrel on his Winchester Model 1876 lever-action rifle as he led his men forward. Although he was not tall, he was powerfully built and had a grim determination that both intimidated and impressed his followers. He was also believed to possess shaman-like powers that only added to his mystique.*

This land was familiar territory for Geronimo. He had been born nearly sixty years earlier not far from the valley they had just entered. With green peaks that reached ten thousand feet high, steep canyons, and rocky ravines, it could be an unforgiving place—but not for Geronimo. He knew this place better than most men; perhaps better than anyone else alive. In his youth he had hunted elk, buffalo, and deer here. And he fished and trapped along the Gila River that flowed in a looping southwesterly direction toward the neighboring territory of Arizona.

This is the place where he had learned how to fight and been initiated into manhood. At the age of seventeen, after successfully participating in a number of raiding parties, he had been formally accepted as a full-fledged warrior. Since then, he had led more raids and killed more men than he could count. He knew he was nearing the end of the line—that the army of soldiers chasing him would not give up until his head was at the end of a pike. But he forced these thoughts from his mind and set his sights on the terrain in front of him. He had an uncanny knack for reading the land, so it didn't take him long to locate the best route around the cavernous ravine that lay just ahead.

A few hours later, Geronimo and his followers had snaked half-

way up the first peak, leaving behind them the prickly cactus that clung to the lower slopes of the Mogollon Mountains. Still not satisfied, he pressed his people forward. It wasn't until he noticed that Douglas fir and aspen had replaced cactus and oak as the predominant vegetation that he eased his pace. He only relented because the changing terrain signaled to him they had reached an elevation at which they would be safe. He dismounted from his horse and signaled to his people this was where they would make camp for the evening. They had arrived not a moment too soon. Flashes of lightning from a fast-approaching late summer storm lit up the dusky sky and large drops of rain began splattering noisily on the rocky ground.

The next morning, Geronimo arose at dawn. He needed to visit a special place from his youth—and he needed to do it in secret. He slipped quietly out of camp, moving as if his feet never touched the ground. Geronimo was a master not only at reading the land but also at traveling without leaving a trail. If he didn't want to be tracked, then no man alive could follow him.

On foot, he moved swiftly through the thick forest, following natural landmarks that had meaning only for him. Five miles later, he came upon a confluence of two rivers. He paused and breathed in deeply. He knew he was close. His mind raced back to a time before all the raids, the killings, and the running. He couldn't have been more than ten or eleven years old when his mother had brought him here. The memory of his mother, who was murdered by Mexican soldiers during a raid thirty years earlier, brought back anger as raw for him as the day she had died. But that anger was quickly replaced by sadness—at her death and the deaths of so many of his people over the last half-century. What was once a thriving and proud tribe of more than three thousand now numbered in the hundreds.

Before entering the mouth of the hidden cave, he reached into a bundle strapped to his belt. He carefully removed a still smoldering ember he had wrapped in damp tree bark back at camp. He proceeded to assemble a makeshift torch by wrapping a resin-soaked cloth around a large stick he found on the ground nearby. He blew on the smoldering ember until it sparked, and touched it to the cloth. The cloth erupted in flame. With torch in hand, Geronimo entered the sacred place.

He followed a route from memory that took him more than four hundred feet deep into the subterranean cave. The rough, naturally carved sidewalls dripped with moisture as he made his way further into the abyss. His heart pounded in anticipation as he remembered the spot he had seen only once before, a lifetime ago. Suddenly, the tunnel angled sharply to the right and widened into a vault-like chamber. Geronimo knew he had reached his destination.

The only sound he could hear was water weeping from the walls of the cave—and his own breathing. He extended the torch out in front of him. As if by magic, the room was instantly bathed in a golden yellow glow. A smile crept slowly across his normally grim face. He took one step closer so he could see the source of the reflection more clearly. There were veins of gold as big as pack mules embedded throughout the quartz-filled walls of the chamber. In awed reverence he reached out and touched the golden treasure with the tips of his fingers. He felt a familiar energy surge through his body.

Somehow this golden cave had escaped discovery by both the Spanish conquistadores in the 1500s and those who had sought their fortunes in the centuries since. In the late 1850s and early 1860s, prospectors from the East Coast began arriving in the hundreds to the new town of Pinos Altos just south of Chiricahua country in the new territory of New Mexico. Their arrival was precipitated by a large gold strike just north of an old Spanish copper mine. For a time, the prospectors respected Apache territory. But eventually the lure of riches drew them further upstream. Their infringement upon Apache land led to inevi-

table confrontation and eventually an all-out war that lasted close to a decade. Ultimately, the flow of prospectors subsided—partly because of the threat of Indian raids but mostly because the initial gold strike near Pinos Altos was never replicated.

As Geronimo exited the cave and began walking back to camp, the words of his mother reverberated in his mind. This sacred golden place, she had told him, would endow Geronimo with great Power. To receive the Power, his mother had said, all he needed to do was reach out and touch the golden wall. The Apache Indians believed in the concept of Power—and that a chosen few were endowed with more Power than others. The source of this Power could come from the natural or supernatural world. He had listened to his mother that day years before and placed his hands on the largest vein of gold embedded in the wall. Afterward, she made him swear to never tell another living soul about their special place. If he did and the golden chamber was unearthed, Geronimo's Powers would be destroyed forever.

His mother had spoken the truth that day. He touched the golden walls and they had helped him become a great warrior and fearless leader of men. His followers revered what they believed to be his supernatural Powers. They believed he could make it rain; that no bullet could ever kill him; and that he could heal the sick. The Power had worked. And Geronimo had never revealed its source.

This latest journey home had been long and arduous. But Geronimo had come for a reason. He was desperate. He needed to visit the golden chamber one more time, because he needed the Power of invincibility now perhaps more than at any other time in his life.

1

Present Day
New York, NY

The fluorescent lights in the drop ceiling above his desk hummed like a nest of angry wasps. The air-conditioning in the forty-two-story Wall Street office building had automatically switched over to its warmer overnight setting more than two hours ago. It wasn't particularly hot, but the back of his blue button-down oxford was wet with perspiration. He leaned back in his chair and loosened his tie a notch further.

A door slammed at the end of the darkened corridor. He glanced down at his Rolex—it was almost eleven o'clock. He got up nervously from his desk to have a look. But it was only the night janitor emptying wastepaper baskets from under the desks of his coworkers on the trading floor. The wheels beneath the fifty-gallon garbage can squeaked noisily. Headphones planted firmly in the janitor's ears made him oblivious to the noise. The man continued on down the hall, head bobbing up and down to the music.

"Pull yourself together, man," Adam whispered to himself. He took a deep breath to calm his nerves before returning to his desk.

Adam Hampton was the thirty-nine-year-old director of the

Commodities Trading Group at Morton Sinclair, one of the largest investment banks on Wall Street. The firm actively traded in most of the major commodity markets, but its primary focus was in the oil and gold sectors.

Adam had been recruited heavily by Morton Sinclair because he was confident, aggressive, and brilliant. He had worked for two other blue-chip investment banks prior to landing at Morton Sinclair a decade earlier. Since then, he had made countless millions in profits for the firm. His efforts had been rewarded with a promotion to the head of the commodities desk. He was very good at what he did and he loved his job—at least until recently.

When he stumbled upon some irregularities in a series of commodity trades a few months earlier, he had thought nothing of it. But then those same irregularities popped up a few weeks later. After some digging, he noticed a distinct pattern to the timing of trades that dated back more than two years. But his curiosity turned to outright suspicion when he got stonewalled trying to determine the name of the client for whom the trade orders had been executed. The account in question was known as a "shadow account" because the identity of the client was hidden behind a series of ambiguous shell companies.

Undeterred, he dug deeper and began to uncover a financial conspiracy so massive that at first he didn't believe it. From what he could determine, not just his firm but at least five other major U.S. investment banks were complicit in the scheme. But much of what he had uncovered was circumstantial evidence. He knew he couldn't blow the whistle unless he had ironclad proof.

After some internal debate, he made the decision to enlist the help of a computer hacker. He needed to gain access to the commodities trading history of the other investment banks he suspected of participating in the conspiracy. He paid the hacker to surreptitiously breach the computer database systems of the firms involved so he could prove their wrongdoing. With this decision, he had reached the point of no return.

He knew what he was doing was illegal, but he had no choice. The men behind the scheme were corrupt and he couldn't just look the other way and let them get away with it. He was raised on the principles of fair play. There was a right way to live your life and a wrong way. If someone was cheating the system, it was your obligation to call them out. In the three weeks since he hired the hacker, he had secured enough evidence to make his case. But he also received something he hadn't counted on.

For the last two hours, he had been sitting at his desk reading and rereading the latest set of encrypted files. They had been sent to him earlier in the evening from his diligent albeit less-than-principled hacker friend. He ran a nervous hand through his hair because he still couldn't believe what he was reading. *This was a game changer.*

He knew right from the start he had stumbled upon a widespread financial conspiracy. But with this latest information, it had become clear the endgame was much more insidious than simple fraud.

This revelation not only scared the shit out of him, it also made him realize he was in way over his head. He needed help. The question he had been wrestling with for the last hour was what to do about it. Finally, he picked up the phone and dialed the number of a man in whom he had recently confided—a man he believed he could trust.

Adam finished his call quickly and rode the elevator down to the lobby. He exited the building. It was approaching midnight and the streets of downtown Manhattan, comprised mostly of office buildings, were deserted. He walked two blocks west to the Wall Street subway station to catch the Uptown 4 train to the Upper East Side. He found himself walking faster than usual and looking over his shoulder at the slightest sound. He knew he was probably being paranoid, but he couldn't help himself. A lot of people were involved in the conspiracy he had uncovered. And, as he had startlingly discovered that evening, some of those people were very powerful. He would be glad when this whole thing was over. Maybe he'd finally get a good night's sleep again.

He made his way down the steps beneath the streets of lower Manhattan. The oppressively humid updraft from the depths below hit him like a summer gale. Far from fresh however, this breeze was a stale-smelling mélange of urine, dirt, steel, and the sweat from tens of thousands of straphangers that rode the trains every day. He remembered when he first arrived in Manhattan. He couldn't imagine how anyone could stomach the smells and the claustrophobic confines of the New York City subways. Seventeen years later he knew he couldn't survive a day without them. In fact, the subterranean sights and smells barely registered with him anymore. He had become a true New Yorker.

He swiped his disposable subway card through the electronic reader and hurried through the turnstile. The loudspeaker announced that the train below was preparing to leave. He ran down the last set of concrete stairs, two steps at a time. But by the time he made it to the lower platform the train had already started to pull away from the station.

"Damn it," he cursed his bad luck. He looked up and down the length of the platform and discovered he was the only person in the station.

He spotted a wooden bench nearby and sat down to wait for the next train. He realized his heart was racing again. He'd visited his doctor the month before because he hadn't been sleeping and had lost more than ten pounds. The doctor advised him these were classic symptoms of work-related stress. *If only he knew.* He prescribed antianxiety medicine and told Adam to take some time off.

Unfortunately, the patient had done just the opposite. He spent the ensuing days running the frenetic commodities trading desk at Morton Sinclair and evenings attempting to discreetly unwind a financial conspiracy of growing proportions. As a result, he hadn't gotten more than three hours of sleep any night since his initial discovery of the trading anomalies.

He reached into his jacket pocket, pulled out a bottle of pills, and popped one in his mouth. He hoped it would settle his racing heart and jangly nerves. He found it hard to sit still so he got up and began to pace. He walked to the edge of the platform and craned his neck to peer down the tracks.

There was still no train in sight.

He heard a noise coming from the far end of the platform. He could see the tops of a pair of men's black dress shoes slowly descending the concrete stairs.

Five minutes later, the shattered body of Adam Hampton lay lifeless on the tracks.

2

Present Day
Fairfield, Connecticut

There was something incongruous about a funeral taking place on such a beautiful day. The dogwood trees were in full bloom, their delicate pink-and-white colored blossoms clashing resplendently against a cloudless cerulean sky. The two-hundred-year-old white clapboard New England church sat proudly atop the highest hill in the bucolic seaside town. Its four-story iconic steeple reached majestically toward the heavens. Horses grazed in an open pasture across the street. The smell of freshly cut grass assaulted the senses and signaled the arrival of spring. Everything was bursting with life. Yet it was death that had brought the more than three hundred friends, family, and coworkers of Adam Hampton together that day.

The service had been equal parts beautiful and gut-wrenching. The minister, a long-time family friend who had both baptized and married Adam, delivered a heartfelt eulogy. Members of the family provided warm and amusing remembrances of the deceased, doing their best to hold their emotions in check. Adam's younger sister delivered a particularly poignant tribute to her only brother. But there was no escaping the crushing reality that a life had ended far too prematurely.

Matt Hawkins first met Adam as a freshman at Brown University in Providence Rhode Island. The two had come from different sides of the tracks. But that hadn't stopped them from becoming fast friends. They even roomed together during their final two years of college. Adam was from a wealthy Connecticut family. His mother had a New England bloodline that dated all the way back to William Bradford and the arrival of the Mayflower in 1620. His father was a successful New York banker who, like thousands of other men along this waterfront commuter corridor, spent their workweeks dutifully commuting to jobs in Manhattan and their weekends playing golf and tennis at leafy country clubs in the suburbs.

Although Adam had come from money, he made no outward showing of it—which is one of the reasons he and Matt became friends. They met busing tables at a local Providence restaurant during the spring semester of their freshman year. Matt needed the job, Adam simply liked to work. Raised in a blue-collar town north of Boston, the closest Matt had ever come to a country club had been a failed attempt at caddying one summer. But as he got to know Adam better, he discovered their work ethic wasn't the only thing they had in common. Both were passionate about sports—the only difference was that Matt excelled on the field whereas Adam's lack of athleticism forced him to the sidelines. They were also both very smart with an insatiable appetite for learning. In fact, Matt's academic scholarship was the only reason he had been able to matriculate at the pricey university.

Matt made his way inside the memorial reception hosted by the family at a local yacht club. A collage of pictures showing Adam at various stages of his life hung on an easel just inside the front entryway. Matt smiled as he scanned the montage. There was a picture of Adam and him, carefree arms slung over one another's shoulders and got-the-world-by-the-tail grins on their faces. It was taken just after graduation. Right before Matt started his bond-trading career at Goldman Sachs and Adam started his first banking job. *God that seemed like an eternity ago.*

And it was. Matt had long since left his Wall Street career behind. He now lived in Savannah, Georgia, trading antiques instead of municipal bonds. He had converted a mid-nineteenth century mansion in the town's historic district into his shop. He also called the sixty-eight-hundred-square-foot mansion home after converting the third floor of the once grand old house into his residence. In a way, Matt had also left his friendship with Adam behind when he relocated to Savannah more than a decade earlier.

Life for both of them had taken a series of unexpected turns since college. Both their marriages had come to an end. But the circumstances had been quite different. Matt's breakup had been mutual. He and his wife simply grew apart and, truth be told, they had never been right for each other from the start. For the most part, Matt had landed on his feet and moved on from his failed marriage. Adam, on the other hand, never quite came to terms with his split. In large part due to the way the relationship ended.

Adam had come home unexpectedly one day to find the love of his life in bed with a neighbor—more accurately, the wife of one of his neighbors. He was understandably devastated at the time and for a number of years afterward. After much counseling he finally seemed to have gotten his life together. At least it had seemed that way to Matt, based on their last phone conversation. But that had been more than a year ago, and apparently everything hadn't been alright. Matt shook his head in disbelief that his one-time best friend had committed suicide—and in such a gruesome fashion.

Matt grabbed a beer from the bar and made his way outside to an expansive flagstone patio overlooking the Long Island Sound. On a clear day like this one, the faint skyline of Manhattan was visible some sixty miles to the south. It felt good to be outside, away from the pall of sadness that clung to the room inside like a bad stench. Matt had gamely offered awkward hugs and condolences to Adam's parents. They had tried to put up a good front, but they were clearly torn apart by the death of their only son. He had made small talk with the few people he recognized from his time living in Manhattan. But now he just wanted some time alone.

He breathed in deeply to clear his mind of the myriad emotions bombarding his psyche. He felt guilty for not making an effort to call Adam more often, sad for the loss of a good friend, and angry for the waste of it all. He kept returning to the same thought. *Damn it, Adam, why the hell did you kill yourself?* It was the last thing he would have ever expected from his old friend. The act just didn't fit the man he knew.

"Excuse me," a voice sounded from behind him. Matt turned around. "It's Matt, isn't it? Matt Hawkins?" the woman said, holding out her hand. "Remember me? I'm Kate Hampton, Adam's younger sister." Her forced smile did a poor job of masking her grief.

It took a moment for Matt to respond. The last time he had seen Kate Hampton was back when he and Adam were in college. She couldn't have been more than fifteen or sixteen years old at the time. She was just a skinny kid then with a mouthful of braces and frizzy blond hair tied up in braids. The woman standing in front of him looked nothing like that little girl. The braces were gone, the body had filled out, and the thick blond hair was now fashionably blunt cut at the shoulder.

Matt shook her hand. "To be honest," he said, "if I hadn't seen you speak at the service today I wouldn't have recognized you." He released her hand. "Last I heard you were playing professional tennis?" Matt thought back to the few times he had visited Adam's childhood home in college. Kate was always racing out the door with a duffel bag full of rackets slung over her shoulder.

"Oh, that. Well, you're information is a few years out of date," she said. "I did turn professional right after college and played on the Tour for a couple of years. But I wasn't good enough to crack the top tier of the sport, so I retired. The grind just wasn't worth it."

She looked beyond Matt's shoulder at a sailboat making its way out of the harbor. "It's a beautiful day, isn't it?" She tucked a strand of hair behind her ear as she spoke. Her green eyes were tinged with red. She had clearly been crying a good part of the day and was still raw with emotion. She was trying to keep it together, but Matt could see was teetering on the edge.

"You gave a beautiful talk at the church today," he said. "It took a lot of strength for you to get up there. I know Adam would have been proud."

She wiped a tear from her eye, catching it before it streaked down her cheek. "Thanks," she said, and sniffled. "I can't seem to stop crying, you know?"

Matt thought about reaching out and comforting her, but it seemed like an awkward thing to do. They weren't really friends, just acquaintances from a very long time ago. Instead he said cheerily, "Hey, would you like to take a walk? It's so nice out and I'm feeling a little restless."

"That sounds perfect," she said, glad for the distraction.

They walked slowly along a narrow wooden pier that jutted thirty yards out into the water. The wind had freshened and there was a slight chill in the air. Matt saw that Kate was shivering. After living in the South for so long, he had forgotten the sun didn't pack a lot of warmth this far north in mid-April. He stripped off his suit jacket and placed it around Kate's shoulders.

"Here," he said. "Looks like you need this more than me."

"Thanks," she said distractedly, her voice barely above a whisper.

They walked in silence for a while. Finally, she spoke up, "You live in Savannah now, right?" Matt nodded, and she added, "How do you like the South?"

"Actually, I love it. I sure as hell don't miss the New York traffic or the Northeast winters," he said, smiling, attempting to lighten the mood. "But I still haven't acquired a taste for sweet tea or collard greens." He chuckled. "Guess I'll always be a Yankee down deep."

He looked over at Kate. She was staring trancelike at the water, lost in her own thoughts. He wondered if she'd even heard him.

She stopped walking and leaned her elbows on the rail of the pier just as the sun dipped behind a cloud. Matt could see she was still shivering. "Hey, let's get you back inside," he said. "You're freezing out here." He turned to head back toward the clubhouse.

Kate didn't move.

"I don't think he did it," she blurted out suddenly.

"Who...did what?" Matt asked, confused.

She turned and faced him. The look of vulnerability and sadness that marked her face just a moment earlier had disappeared completely. It was replaced with determination, even anger.

"I don't think Adam jumped in front of that train," she stated evenly.

Matt stared at Kate in stunned silence.

"I think he was pushed," she said. "In fact, I'm sure of it."

3

Present Day

Fairfield, Connecticut

A seagull swooped in low before landing on the rail of the pier not more than ten feet away. It squawked loudly, black eyes darting left and right in a never-ending search for discarded scraps of food. Finding nothing, the gull hopped along the rail flapping its wings agitatedly before finally lifting off again. A healthy gust of wind sent ripples racing across the water. Bright orange moorings bobbed up and down in the harbor like lottery Ping-Pong balls. The rigging on a forty-foot Morgan Cruiser sailboat rattled noisily against its aluminum mast.

Matt shivered involuntarily, but not because he was cold. "Kate, I know this has been a traumatic experience, but..." he began to say.

She held up her hands. "No, Matt this isn't my grief talking. I know Adam wouldn't hurl himself in front of a subway train. He just wouldn't do that," she stated emphatically.

Matt knew he better tread carefully so as not to upset her any further. He leaned his back up against the railing. "I'll be honest, I didn't believe it either when I first heard about it," he said. "It just seemed so out of character for him—at least the Adam I knew." He paused before adding delicately, "But people change, Kate. And he *had* gone through some pretty rough times."

Her expression softened slightly. "The way his marriage ended was pretty shitty, I know that. But one positive thing from his divorce was that afterward we became much closer; closer than we ever had been. We talked all the time. And I'm telling you, he had really turned a corner." She started to tear up again.

Matt felt like she had more to say so he gave her a moment. She took a halting breath and pulled Matt's suit jacket tighter around her shoulders.

She said, "I talked to him the day before he died. And I'll admit he wasn't himself. But he didn't sound down, just the opposite, in fact. He was hyper. I think maybe even a little scared."

"Scared," Matt said taken aback, "why?"

She seemed to be second-guessing whether she wanted to share the next part with him. After a moment's hesitation, she said ominously, "He told me he had found something." In a slightly hushed tone she continued, "He said he had uncovered a financial conspiracy. And that it was big—big enough to cripple the economy."

She stopped and waited for Matt's reaction.

"Cripple the economy? You mean like some sort of financial terrorism?" he asked, confused.

"I don't know. He wouldn't say any more than that. And the day after we talked, he was...gone." She looked away, shaking her head in disbelief that her brother was dead. Then she said with a glimmer of hope, "You used to work on Wall Street so I thought maybe you could help somehow. Maybe you could talk to some people."

Her request for help caught him off guard.

He was still trying to reconcile the fact that Kate had just told him in no uncertain terms that someone had murdered her brother. If that wasn't shocking enough, Adam had stumbled onto some massive financial conspiracy.

"I don't know, Kate. I mean, even if Adam had found something, I wouldn't know where to begin. I haven't worked on Wall Street in over ten years. My contacts are a little out of date," he reasoned.

Kate felt suddenly foolish. She wouldn't blame Matt if he thought she was nuts. She smiled sadly. "I shouldn't have asked you. I'm sorry, I just..." She let the thought pass. "Hey, it was great seeing you again," she said, smiling weakly. She slipped his jacket off her shoulders. "Thanks for listening. I should get back inside and see how my parents are holding up." She handed over the jacket and started walking back toward the clubhouse.

Matt stood alone on the pier, staring at his feet. He felt awful. Adam was dead and there was no changing that. Even though Kate was probably acting out of desperation, didn't he owe it to her to at least offer his help? If nothing else, to give his friend's grieving sister some closure.

"Kate," he called out.

She stopped and turned around.

"Let me make a few calls."

Matt rode the Metro North commuter train into Manhattan the next morning. Before flying home to Savannah he decided to pay a visit to a friend in the city. He walked from Grand Central Station a few blocks west to the *New York Times* office building in Times Square. He got off the elevator on the eleventh floor and made his way down the hall to David Becker's office.

Matt had gotten to know Becker right after he unearthed a secret surrender letter penned by George Washington during the Revolutionary War. Becker helped Matt out of a jam back then, and a few others since. As a result, the two had become good friends. Becker was a Pulitzer Prize–winning journalist for the country's most venerable paper. And with his shoulder-length brown hair, faded jeans, and horn-rimmed glasses, he looked the part.

"Matt," Becker shouted, coming out from behind his cluttered desk.

"Hey, David, I see you're still using the same filing system," he joked, nodding at the paperwork piled high on Becker's desk.

In among the clutter were two laptops, both in use, a pathetic-looking African violet plant in desperate need of water, and no less than six discarded cups of coffee. A Mr. Met bobblehead doll sat on the corner of the desk—a childhood memento. Becker was a native of Queens, New York, and lifelong suffering Mets fan. On the credenza behind the desk were pictures of his beautiful wife, Trish, and their three teenage kids.

His numerous awards, accumulated over two decades of exemplary reporting, were stuffed in a drawer somewhere. Becker wasn't in the investigative journalism business for the accolades. He was an idealist and motivated by making sure people who did bad things were brought to justice. And luckily for Becker, people in the financial world, his particular area of expertise, were always doing bad things.

"Yeah, filing is definitely not my thing," he said and laughed, pumping Matt's hand. "Come on in."

He reached down and removed still more files from a nearby chair so Matt could sit. "You look good," Becker said, "but then again you always do, you son of a bitch," he joked. "I swear, combine your looks with my brains and we'd be unstoppable."

Matt had always been considered handsome. He had the kind of looks and easy-going manner that made women want him and men want to be like him. The tall, lean, and athletic frame that served him well in his days of playing college baseball had for the most part been maintained. He ran a few times a week and did push-ups and sit-ups to stay in shape. Now that he was approaching forty years old, however, he thought he might finally have to give in and join a gym.

After catching up for a few minutes, Becker said, "I'm really sorry about your friend. That's a tough way to go."

Matt had called Becker the day before to tell him he'd be stopping by. He filled him in over the phone on Adam Hampton's death, as well as Kate's belief it wasn't a suicide.

"She really thinks someone pushed him in front of a subway train?" Becker asked.

"She does."

"Do you?"

"I don't know, David." Matt shook his head skeptically. "Adam was a brilliant guy with a high-paying job. But he'd also been through a difficult divorce that had thrown him for a loop. I guess he could have jumped. But I have a hard time seeing him doing it."

"People change, Matt."

"I know, I said the same thing to Kate yesterday."

Becker shrugged. "Unfortunately, I've come across more than a few people over the years that chose to check out rather than face their demons."

"But that's just it, David. According to Kate, Adam had turned a corner recently and was actually excited, or at least energized, by what he had uncovered."

"You mean the financial conspiracy you mentioned? If I remember correctly, I think the word you used yesterday was *scared*."

"Yeah, that too," Matt replied. He leaned back in his chair and exhaled before continuing, "Look I don't know what to believe. If the conspiracy he allegedly uncovered was as big as he claimed it was, then maybe it's possible someone murdered him. Either way, I promised Kate I'd do a little digging. She's understandably devastated by the whole thing. Maybe this will help give her some closure."

"Fair enough," Becker said. He turned on one of his laptops around him and cracked his knuckles, like a concert pianist getting ready to launch into the first movement. "Let me tell you what I found."

Matt seemed surprised. "You found something already?"

Before his friend got too fired up, Becker warned, "Don't get excited, Matt. It isn't much. I ran some cursory searches and made a few phone calls to some of my Wall Street contacts."

"And?"

"Since Adam was head of the commodities desk at Morton Sinclair, I figured whatever he stumbled across would likely be related to the commodities markets. So I asked around to see if there'd been any anomalies in the past twelve months in the major sectors."

"Anomalies?"

"Yeah, like strange buy or sell patterns or wild price fluctuations—stuff like that," he explained. "Anyway, two things came back. The first is related to the energy sector—more specifically, oil—and the second occurred in the metals sector, related to gold."

He looked up at Matt who nodded for him to continue.

"Evidently," he forged ahead, "oil prices have dropped by more than sixty percent over the last six months—that's more than a seventy dollar a barrel decline. One of the most precipitous drops in recent history." He paused. "Like I said, the second aberration involves gold. Apparently, out of the blue last month, Switzerland requested that all of their gold being held on U.S. soil be repatriated back to their country."

"Oil and gold," Matt interrupted. He got up and walked to Becker's huge plate glass window that overlooked Times Square. "Those are two pretty valuable commodities; certainly valuable enough to kill for."

"True, but before you go any further," Becker cautioned,

"each of these events can be explained. The drop in oil prices is the direct result of classic supply and demand dynamics. Demand has decreased pretty significantly recently, because of a weakening worldwide economy. And on the flip side, the discovery of new shale formations in the U.S. and new deposits in other countries has spiked supply. It's kind of like the perfect storm—and it caused the price of oil to drop like a rock."

"What about the Switzerland gold situation?" Matt asked.

Becker explained, "During World War II, the U.S. became a safe haven for most of Europe's gold caches. But it seems after seventy years of relative peace and stability, Switzerland wants their gold back. It isn't unprecedented—Germany did the same thing a couple of years ago," he concluded. "It's just unusual."

Matt glanced at his watch and sprang from his seat. "Shit," he said, "I've got to get to LaGuardia. My plane to Savannah leaves in less than ninety minutes." He reached for his coat.

Becker walked him to the door.

"Thanks for trying, David. I really appreciate it."

"Not a problem. I'm glad to help. I've still got a few more calls to make. I'll let you know if I come across anything else."

The two friends shook hands and Matt hurried out the door.

4

March 4, 1905
Washington, D.C.

Theodore Roosevelt won the 1904 presidential election handily. He carried thirty-two of forty-five states and won fifty-six percent of the popular vote. That was almost twenty points higher than his closest opponent. The enigmatic bull of a man, who had overcome so much in his life, had at last been elected to the highest office in the land. He had already ascended to the presidency in 1901 by virtue of being vice president when President William McKinley was assassinated. But this time the American people, who were equal parts enamored of and fascinated by Roosevelt, had elected him president. It was in this accomplishment he took the greatest satisfaction.

The weather on the day of his inauguration mirrored Roosevelt's personality—blustery, tempestuous, and unpredictable. During his inaugural address the wind blew so hard, caps and bonnets were ripped off the heads of spectators and American flags snapped against their metal stanchions like horse whips. As if daring the elements to challenge him, Roosevelt stuck his chest out defiantly on the stand that had been set up on the East Portico of the Capitol building. He thrust his fists into the air and practically shouted out his brief—by his stan-

dards—six-minute address.

After his swearing-in, Roosevelt lunched with hundreds of invited guests at the White House. Then it was on to a reviewing stand that had been set up for the forty-six-year-old president, from which he could view the inaugural parade. Among those marching in the event that day were miners, soldiers, students, army veterans, cowboys, and countless marching bands. For Roosevelt, however, the highlight of the procession that lasted more than three and a half hours was the six mounted Indian chiefs riding side by side. They were adorned in native paint and sported colorful feathered headwear. The tribes that had been invited to participate included the Blackfeet, Comanche, Ute, two tribes of Sioux, and the Chiricahua Apaches. The latter tribe was represented by perhaps the most famous warrior of them all—a man known by only one name, Geronimo.

Upon sighting the approaching spectacle, the president leapt to his feet and began to clap and wave his hat exuberantly. Earlier that day, Roosevelt had eschewed the glass-enclosed reviewing booth that had been specially constructed for him. True to his hardy character, he preferred to join the throngs of onlookers braving the elements. So as Geronimo rode past and let out a hearty whoop, Roosevelt could hear him clearly. In another bit of theatrics, after catching the president's eye, Geronimo dramatically brandished his spear high above his head. Roosevelt loved it, as was evidenced by his trademark toothy grin that could be seen clearly by the adoring throngs below him—all of whom were jockeying to catch a glimpse of the larger-than-life figure.

A few days later, the president invited Geronimo to visit him at the White House. Roosevelt had grown up enthralled with stories of the fierce warrior who had once been the most feared of all Indians. By this time, however, the Apache leader was more than eighty years old and had been a placid prisoner of war for close to twenty years. Even so, Roosevelt yearned to meet the man who at one time had held the imagination of the American public.

Upon Geronimo's entrance into Roosevelt's office in the White House, the president bounded from behind his desk to greet his guest. At first he had a hard time reconciling the slightly stooped, old man standing in front of him with the cunning and ruthless warrior he had read so much about in his youth. Even so, he pumped Geronimo's hand vigorously and grasped the old warrior's shoulder in a welcoming clutch. Roosevelt had a profound respect for men who fought bravely and it was clear he believed Geronimo fit into this category. For his part, Geronimo, who was wearing simple, dark clothing and clutching a well-worn broad-brimmed hat, appeared a bit perplexed by the president's manic energy.

Sensing his trepidation, Roosevelt grinned warmly and offered a seat to his guest. The men talked for a short while. The president did most of the talking, which was the usual course of events when one conversed with Teddy Roosevelt. Geronimo did the best he could, in broken English, to answer as many of Roosevelt's queries as he could. When there was a brief lull in the rapid-fire questioning, Geronimo seized upon the opening to say something to the president on his own behalf.

"Before I die," Geronimo stated haltingly, "I must return to my homeland. I have been gone a long time."

Roosevelt's face darkened. "When you were free you had a bad heart and killed many of my people. We keep you at Fort Sill so we can watch you and keep you from doing bad things again."

Geronimo did not relent. "The ropes have been on my hands many years. I am old man now. Please take me back to my homeland. That is where I want to die." Tears welled up in his eyes.

Roosevelt looked at the third man in the room, Commissioner of Indian Affairs Francis E. Leupp, before responding. Leupp shook his head from side to side as if to say "no chance." Roosevelt turned back to Geronimo and insisted, "I cannot grant you the request for yet a while. We will have to wait and see how you act."

Geronimo's eyes flashed with anger momentarily. It did not go unnoticed by the president. The long-feared warrior had returned, at least in his eyes, and it had an unsettling effect on the cowboy president.

Geronimo could see by the president's guarded reaction that Roosevelt was not going to grant his request. He decided it was time to play his final card. "I speak to the great father in private?" The malice had disappeared from his steely eyes, but Roosevelt remained on guard.

Never one to show fear or to back down from a confrontation, however, Roosevelt promptly turned to the commissioner of Indian affairs and politely told him to wait outside. Commissioner Leupp reluctantly left the room and slowly shut the door behind him.

The two old warriors sat silently, sizing each other up. While Roosevelt was only forty-six years old, he had many physical ailments of his own—the by-product of a life of nonstop action. Although he hid his shortcomings from public view, Roosevelt was extremely nearsighted, had hardening of the arteries, and was going blind in one eye from a blow to the head during a recent boxing match. He also carried with him Cuban fever from his time famously leading the Rough Riders during the Spanish-American War.

Finally, Geronimo spoke up. "I make trade for my freedom," he said solemnly.

"Trade?" Roosevelt answered. He looked skeptically at the old prisoner of war, silently wondering what he could possibly have to trade that would merit his release. His curiosity was piqued, however, so he motioned for Geronimo to continue.

"When I was a boy, I found a cave," he began.

Geronimo was ashamed at himself for defying his mother's explicit instructions to never tell another living soul about the golden cave. He knew it meant the loss of any powers he might still possess. But he didn't care anymore. He was old and he was tired—and he wanted to die in his homeland. Not on an army base in Fort Sill, Oklahoma.

He told Roosevelt of a cave buried deep inside the mountains of his youth, near the confluence of two rivers. He claimed there was so much gold in the cave that in the light of a flame it shone so brightly one had to shield his eyes from the reflection. He claimed there were veins of gold the size of the president's writing desk, literally spilling out of the cave's crystal sidewalls. When Geronimo finished telling his story he finally got around to making his offer.

He would trade Roosevelt the gold for his freedom.

The president remained stoically silent. Finally, he pushed up out of his chair and walked to a bookshelf across the room. A few minutes later he returned with a recently printed map of the territory of New Mexico. He laid the detailed map out on the table and asked Geronimo to show him exactly where the gold could be found.

Geronimo hesitated only momentarily. He knew even if Roosevelt was within one hundred yards of the hidden cave, he'd never find it without his help. So he picked up the map and examined it closely. It took him less than a minute to locate the mountain range that represented the rugged Mogollon Mountains from his youth. He lifted a hand slowly and planted a crooked index finger firmly on that spot.

"Geronimo's Gold," he said decisively.

Before ushering Geronimo out the door, Roosevelt promised to consider his offer.

5

Present Day
Shanghai, China

Smog belching from coal-fired power plants and the legions of factories in the congested Yangtze River Delta choked off the midday sun. The Pudong district was teeming with activity, as it was every day. No one would have ever have guessed that just two decades earlier the city's expansive financial district was a track of open farmland. Now its impressive skyline, filled with skyscrapers of every imaginable size and shape, rivaled the scale and beauty of any urban panorama in the world—including Manhattan or Tokyo.

The city of Shanghai had become the epicenter of China's transformation from an isolated communist regime to an economic world power. It was the richest city in the communist nation, largely because it was home to the country's biggest port and its stock exchange. China's expansion had come at a furious pace over the past decade with annual GDP growth rates that dwarfed any Western nation. Of course, the country's vast supply of cheap labor and government control over a large proportion of national assets had fueled most of that gain.

One of the by-products of China's astounding growth was an

enormous trade surplus with the West—particularly the United States. As a result of this trade imbalance, China had accumulated more $4 trillion in total foreign reserves including a staggering $1.5 trillion of U.S. Treasury securities. This considerable exposure to U.S. debt, however, had become a major political issue. The prevailing belief within the upper echelons of the Chinese government was that the long-term value of the U.S. Treasuries held by China was anything but guaranteed.

"I'm afraid our calls to the executive board of the International Monetary Fund to step in and supervise the overissuance of U.S. dollars fell on deaf ears a long time ago," Xi Liang decried angrily. "The United States continues to issue billions in additional U.S. Treasuries to cover their mounting debts, with no concern for how dilutive it is to the value of the treasuries already held by their trading partners. If they remain on this current path, the dollars we own will be severely marginalized."

Xi Liang was the director of the Shanghai Investment Consortium, the largest of the country's Sovereign Wealth Funds. The Chinese government had created a number of these investment funds over the previous decade to help manage the country's burgeoning reservoirs of foreign currency reserves. The SIC had been charged with coming up with a plan for converting what was viewed inside the government as increasingly worthless U.S. dollars into assets with more intrinsic value.

"The American politicians and bankers are reckless and greedy. They continue to issue more debt because they spend far more than they can collect," replied Xiang Wu, Commerce Minister to the Chinese government.

The two men were sitting in a private dining room atop the tallest building in Shanghai. The recently completed Shanghai Tower topped out at a staggering 121 stories. It stood at more than 2,000 feet high, making it the second tallest building in the world. But the Shanghai Tower was only one of three newly erected skyscrapers in the ever-expanding Pudong district. These latest engineering marvels were considered the crowning jewels in the Chinese government's ambitious plans to someday soon have Shanghai usurp New York's Wall Street as the world's preeminent financial center.

"The end of the road for the U.S. dollar is closer than the world realizes," Wu said as their lunch plates were removed from the table by the scrupulous and unobtrusive waitstaff.

When the attendants were out of earshot, Minister Wu continued, "We continue to execute against our plan of diversifying out of U.S. dollars." He paused. "But we must be careful not to tip our hand," he cautioned. "This cannot appear as a dollar dump. That would crash the bond and currency markets and jeopardize our long-term goals."

"Understood, sir. We will continue to quietly pursue the current strategy using our U.S. currency reserves while they still retain at least some value," Liang said.

It had begun to rain outside. Water tinged brown by the ever-present pollution in the air cascaded in sheets down the massive dining room windows. Their conversation was interrupted once more as tea was served. Wu waited again until their servers disappeared back into the kitchen.

"I must commend you on the secrecy with which you have operated these past few years," Wu complimented Liang. "Thanks to your efforts, when we finally do play our hand, it will take the world by utter surprise. And of course, have its intended effect."

Liang bowed his head slightly. "Thank you, sir. We are simply following the plan you laid out. The shadow banking network you suggested has allowed us to maintain complete anonymity."

Liang then added with pride, "By my estimates, the buying network we have set up with our New York banking partners combined with our own production will enable us to reach our goal by the end of this year." He removed the thick cloth napkin from his lap and carefully wiped the edge of his mouth before boasting, "One year ahead of schedule."

Wu took a moment to blow on his hot tea. When the Commerce Minister responded, his voice was measured, "I can assure you, Mr. Director, your good work has not gone unnoticed by my superiors." His eyes narrowed. "But the job is not done yet," he cautioned firmly. "We are entering the most critical stage of the operation. The sequence of events over the next two months must happen exactly as planned. Or we risk exposing our intentions before we reach our objective."

Wu got up to leave. "And if that happens, we will all suffer the consequences," he warned.

Liang stood and bowed his head deferentially as the superior government official left the room. Once Wu was gone, Liang sat down heavily in his chair. He stared hypnotically at the dreary weather on the other side of the plate glass window. The Commerce Minister's words had unsettled him. He certainly didn't need Wu to remind him his future, let alone the future of their country, hinged on the success of the plan currently being carried out by the contacts he had put in place in the largest commodity banks in New York. He knew better than anyone how high the stakes were—and he could ill afford any mistakes this late in the game.

6

Present Day
New York, NY

Today was the day. She had put it off long enough.

Her brother had been dead for more than two weeks and Kate had yet to visit his apartment. It was time to begin the process of cleaning out his things. Her parents had informed her they didn't want any of their son's belongings—it would simply be too painful for them. They left it in Kate's hands to decide what to sell, donate, or keep. She would most likely hang on to a few items that held sentimental value for her. But his furniture and clothing would all go to Goodwill. She just didn't have the stomach to hold an estate sale and watch the ten-cent-on-the-dollar bargain hunters rummage through her brother's personal effects.

She hailed a cab from just outside her West Village apartment and gave the driver Adam's address on the Upper East Side. Fifteen minutes later she walked into the lobby of the pre-War building. The doorman immediately recognized Kate, as she had been a frequent visitor to the apartment over the years. He expressed his condolences and asked if she needed anything. She told him she had her own key and could let herself in. She pressed the elevator button for the fourteenth floor. The doors closed behind her. Adam's apartment was actually on the thirteenth floor, but in many older Manhattan apartment buildings, the numbering of floors superstitiously went from twelve to fourteen—skipping over the unlucky number thirteen. *Maybe it was bad luck to live on the thirteenth floor after all.*

After exiting the elevator, she walked down the narrow hallway to Adam's apartment. Reaching the door, she was alarmed to see that it was already ajar. That was odd because she knew she was the only other person with a key. That's when she noticed the splintered door frame. The dead bolt had clearly been jimmied. Her heart began to race. She thought about bolting down to the lobby to get the doorman, but she didn't.

Curiosity got the better of her. She slowly pushed the door open.

What she saw terrified her. It was as if a tornado had ripped through the place. Furniture was overturned, stuffing had been torn out of cushions, and the contents of drawers were strewn across the floor. She took a step back in shock. She turned to run, but again she stopped.

She stood frozen in place just outside the entryway. She listened for any sounds coming from inside the apartment. After a minute or two, it became apparent whoever did this was long gone. Her fear dissipated slightly. Even so, she remained on alert as she made her way through the spacious one-bedroom apartment.

She had to step carefully so as not to stumble over her brother's brutally discarded belongings. After making a thorough inspection, she collapsed on the cushionless couch. She began to sob uncontrollably. Her brother was gone and now even his memory had been violated. She felt as if she were reliving his passing for a second time—and it was just as devastating. She didn't know how long she sat there crying, but when she looked up the sun had started to set. The thought of being alone in the ravaged apartment after dark spooked her. So she got up and wiped her face dry with the palms of her hands.

Her initial pain and shock at finding the apartment in such disarray had slowly morphed into a state of numb disbelief. She sat there struggling to make sense of what had happened. She knew this was no ordinary robbery. It had to be connected to the conspiracy. Whoever had come here was clearly looking for something. *Had they found it?* Then a thought occurred to her—*Adam's laptop.* She began a frantic search for it. After ten minutes of sifting through the wreckage, she realized it was gone.

It was time to leave. On her way out she spotted a framed photo lying on the kitchen floor. It was taken of her and Adam a couple of years earlier at a rock concert in Central Park. They were happily mugging for the camera. She slipped the photo out of the splintered glass frame and pocketed it. With tears in her eyes, she pulled the door closed. Somehow she was able to get the dead bolt to reengage. She would call the police, but that could wait until the morning— there was probably nothing they could do anyway. At the moment she just wanted to go home.

Back in her apartment, Kate sat curled up on the couch with a glass of wine. She tried to relax, but images of Adam's plundered apartment kept running through her mind.

"What had you gotten yourself into, big brother," she said out loud.

The fat Bengal cat purring loudly in her lap lifted his head at the sound of her voice. Kate stroked his back. The cat stood, stretched, and hopped down off the couch. He padded across the room to find his bowl. A few seconds later, he began to meow loudly. Kate looked up and realized she had forgotten to refill the cat's automatic food dispenser.

"Okay, Mac, I'm coming," she said.

She had named the cat after the famous tennis player, John McEnroe. Her feline roommate was feisty like the former number one player had been in his day. And McEnroe had also been Adam's favorite player growing up. Mac leapt up onto the kitchen counter and began sniffing around for food.

That's when Kate saw it—sitting under a pile of unopened mail next to the microwave.

She had completely forgotten about the package she had received a few days earlier. She knew the box contained personal items the police had retrieved from Adam's body after they removed it from the tracks. But she just hadn't the stomach to open the package the day it had been delivered—her emotions were still too raw. Given what she had seen earlier that day in her brother's apartment, however, her resolve had stiffened.

She put her glass of wine down on the coffee table and hurried into the kitchen. *Maybe Adam had been carrying something important with him when he died. Maybe that's what the thugs who tossed his apartment were hoping to find.* She pulled open the lid on the shoebox-sized package.

The first item she removed was Adam's prized gold Rolex. She remembered the day he had purchased the watch. He used his very first end-of-year Wall Street bonus to buy it. It was way too expensive, but he had been so proud at the time. She smiled wistfully at the memory. Remarkably, given the circumstances, the watch didn't have a scratch on it.

His wallet was also inside the box, along with his cherished St. Christopher medal. He had worn it on a chain around his neck ever since his confirmation into the Catholic Church as a teenager. Finally, at the very bottom of the box was one last item. She reached in and pulled out a yellowed piece of paper folded into thirds. Perplexed, she unfolded the sides and laid the paper down on the counter, flattening it carefully with the palms of her hands.

It was a map. And it was very old.

She knew this because the state represented on the map, New Mexico was still designated as a territory. Kate's brow furrowed in confusion. She had never seen it before and, for the life of her, couldn't imagine why her brother had been walking around with an old map of New Mexico in his suit pocket.

She pulled out a bar stool from underneath the kitchen island and sat down to contemplate its significance. The mystery deepened when she saw that a section within the New Mexico territory had been circled.

And written inside the circle were two words: *Geronimo's Gold.*

It was a beautiful spring day in Savannah. With the oppressive summer heat still a month away, Matt decided to go for a run in Forsyth Park. He ran for two reasons. It helped clear his head and it allowed him to drink as much beer as he wanted. The latter proved to be his primary motivator. He had finished two laps around the perimeter of the park when his phone rang. He debated letting the call go to voice mail, but his hamstring was a little tight, so he stopped to take the call.

"Hi, Matt, it's Kate Hampton."

There was no reply, just heavy breathing. "Matt? Did I catch you at a bad time?" she asked hesitantly.

"Hi, Kate. I just finished running," Matt finally replied, wiping sweat from his brow. "What's up? Is everything okay?"

"Yes, I'm fine. I was just calling to follow up on our conversation about Adam. You know," she hesitated, "about the conspiracy he mentioned to me the day before he died."

"Of course, I'm sorry I didn't get back to you sooner," he apologized. He spotted an empty park bench and sat down. He cradled the phone between his chin and shoulder so he could massage the back of his right thigh. "Unfortunately I haven't been able to turn up anything promising."

"That's okay, I'm actually calling to tell you about something that's happened up here in New York," she said.

She went on to apprise Matt of how she had discovered Adam's apartment in shambles the day before. She also told him about the map she had found inside the box of her brother's personal effects.

"Geronimo's Gold?" Matt said in confusion. "What the hell is that?"

"I have no idea, but maybe this is what the guys who broke into Adam's apartment were looking for," she offered.

"Maybe," Matt commented. "What did the police say?"

"I spent all morning with them up at Adam's place," she said.

"Did you share your theory about Adam being murdered?" He asked gently.

"I did," she sighed, "But I could tell by the looks on their faces they think I'm just a hysterical sister who hasn't come to terms with her brother' suicide. They insisted these types of robberies are not uncommon. Evidently there are sickos out there who target vacated homes of the recently deceased—ripping them off before the families have had a chance to settle the estate."

She paused before adding, "I'm telling you Matt, what happened in his apartment wasn't a random robbery."

He could hear the challenge in her voice. "I believe you," he said quickly.

"You do?" she seemed surprised.

"I don't believe in coincidences, Kate, and there are just too many surrounding your brother's death." Then he added, "But I'm also not willing to go as far as to say he was murdered or there is some huge conspiracy behind all of this. At least not until we find some proof."

"Does that mean you're going to help me try to get to the bottom of this?"

He paused for an extra beat before saying, "Yes, Kate, I'll help."

"Thank you, Matt," she said, relieved that someone believed her, at least enough to lend a hand. Then she added, "There's one other thing."

"What's that?"

"One of the detectives I talked to at the station shared something interesting with me. He told me in his original statement to the police, the conductor of the train said there might have been another person on the platform with Adam."

"Seriously?"

"He said he thought he saw someone duck behind one of the pillars. But he couldn't be sure if it was a person or just a shadow."

"Not exactly an ironclad eyewitness. I'm not sure that gives us much to go on, Kate," he said soberly.

"It's enough for me, Matt," she answered with conviction. "My brother didn't jump in front of that train. And somehow I'm going to figure out a way to prove it."

7

Present Day
New York, NY

Matt was most of the way through his second half-dozen order of Long Island Cherrystone clams. He had landed at New York's LaGuardia Airport about an hour earlier and taken a cab straight to P.J. Clarke's. He hadn't eaten since breakfast and was famished. The reason for his visit to the Big Apple was to try to help Kate determine the significance of the old map she found in the box of her brother's personal effects.

Once dubbed the Vatican of Saloons by the *New York Times*, P.J. Clarke's was truly a survivor from a bygone era. Built in 1884 in what was once a squalid section of Manhattan, the little brick building was now dwarfed by skyscrapers. An elevated subway train, the Third Avenue El, had been torn down in the mid-1950s making way for real estate developers to move in. Somehow the popular saloon had survived demolition and continued to thrive.

He chuckled as he spotted "Skippy" the stuffed dog. The dog was once the bar's mascot and had evidently met an untimely death after being run over by a car. According to the story, the regulars had him stuffed and mounted so he could continue to keep vigil over the old establishment—albeit through sightless glass eyes.

It was mid-afternoon and the vintage mahogany bar where Matt was seated was relatively empty. The lunch crowd of businessmen, tourists, and locals from the neighborhood had departed and the dinner crowd had yet to arrive. David Becker had called the meeting that day. He wanted to share some more information he had uncovered regarding Switzerland's gold repatriation request. But in return, he insisted they meet at his favorite watering hole.

Matt glanced toward the front entrance just as the door swung open. Kate Hampton walked in. She spotted him at the bar and offered a quick wave of acknowledgment. Matt was taken aback again by the stunning transformation of the scrawny little sister he remembered from his college days to the striking woman walking his way.

Kate was in better spirits than she had been at Adam's memorial service. Her cheeks had a healthy glow and her smile was much less strained than a few weeks earlier. She was dressed casually in yoga pants, sneakers, and a sweatshirt. Her hair was pulled back in a tight ponytail. Matt stood up to greet her. This time they embraced like old friends.

"Sorry for my casual getup," she said apologetically. "I didn't have time to change after teaching my yoga class."

Matt couldn't help but notice Kate's athletic figure. There didn't appear to be an ounce of fat on her. Not many women could pull off the outfit she was wearing and still look amazing. She had clearly kept in shape after her professional tennis days.

He waved away her apology. "Don't worry about it, you look great." He pulled a barstool over and she sat down. "So how long have you been teaching yoga?"

"About five years. I have a little studio near my apartment in the West Village," she said. "It helps pay the bills between shows."

"Shows?" He asked confused.

"Oh, sorry, I'm an artist, too. A painter to be exact. At least I aspire to be one," she joked. "I sell my art out of my yoga studio. And I do one or two shows a year," she explained.

"That's terrific. Congratulations," he said, impressed.

"Yeah, well, like I said, the yoga studio pays my bills. I'd be living on the streets if I relied on the income from the sale of my paintings," she smiled self-deprecatingly.

"I'm sure they're amazing. Can I see them sometime?"

"Only if you promise to buy one," she kidded.

"Deal. When's your next buy-one-get-one sale?" he deadpanned.

"Oh, you're one of those types, huh?"

"Not at all, I'm a big spender." He smiled devilishly. "And just to prove it, I'll buy you a beer."

She returned the sarcasm. "A whole beer?" she said.

He laughed and motioned for the bartender. "Well, actually I think they're running a buy-one-get-one special, so I'm getting off easy."

"Better make it two," a voice sounded from behind them.

They turned around and saw David Becker approaching. Matt pulled a third stool over as the bartender promptly delivered their round of beers.

After he introduced Kate to Becker, Matt dived right in. "So what did you find out, David?"

"Evidently the U.S. has been dragging their feet over Switzerland's request. In fact, they've established an eight-year schedule for returning all of Switzerland's gold."

Matt turned to Kate and quickly filled her in on his prior conversation with Becker regarding the somewhat unusual demand by Switzerland. He explained how, out of the blue, they had suddenly asked for their gold to be returned to them.

To Becker he said, "Eight years sounds like a hell of a long time for a country to wait for their gold."

"Yes, it does," Becker admitted. "And this lengthy repatriation schedule has only reignited some age-old speculation about Fort Knox."

"Fort Knox?" Kate said, confused.

"Yeah, you know, the world's most famous vault located just outside of Louisville, Kentucky," Becker said. "It seems some people believe it's empty."

"Empty?" Matt said.

"That's ridiculous, right?" Kate added.

"Not if you're a conspiracy theorist," Becker answered. "You see, Fort Knox is supposed to be the most secure sight on earth," he pulled out his yellow legal pad and referred to his notes: "For starters, the vault itself is located on a 109,000 acre U.S. Army post. It's protected by video cameras, minefields, barbed wire, electric fences, and armed guards—and supposedly they've even got a few unmarked Apache helicopter gunships on hand. On top of that, it's encased in 16,000 cubic feet of granite and 4,200 cubic yards of cement."

He continued, "The vault door weighs 22 tons and is made of a 21-inch-thick material that's resistant to drills, torches, and explosives. And oh yeah," he added almost as an afterthought, "it's bombproof, too."

"Okay," Matt interjected, "that just proves nobody could ever get inside that place."

"That's just the conspiracy theorists' point," Becker said cagily.

"I'm not following, David," Matt admitted.

"It's exactly what you just said, Matt. Nobody outside of the military has ever been anywhere near the place. The government hasn't allowed an independent physical audit of Fort Knox since 1953, right after President Eisenhower's inauguration. And that makes people believe the government is hiding something. That's why some people think the vault is empty."

"Seriously?" Matt asked. "I'll agree it's a bit strange an audit hasn't been done in over half a century, but what makes people believe there's no gold in there?"

"Because," Becker replied, "for the past fifty years the U.S. government has been a net seller of gold. According to their own reports, they've reduced their holdings from about 20,000 metric tons in the 1950s to a current level of 8,000 tons."

"It still sounds like a lot of gold to me," Kate interjected.

Becker held an index finger aloft, pantomiming like Sherlock Holmes, "Ah, but therein lies the problem. Many believe the figure of 8,000 tons is way overstated. And I'm not just talking about the fringe conspiracy nuts. There are some well-respected financial analysts who think our actual gold reserves are much lower than the government claims. And furthermore, they believe whatever cache of gold is left inside Fort Knox isn't wholly owned by the U.S. government anyway."

"It's owned by other countries like Switzerland," Matt said, beginning to catch on.

"Exactly, many countries, before and after World War II, gave their gold to the United States for safekeeping. The subsequent lengthy timetable for repatriating Switzerland's gold is proof—the conspiracy theorists say—we don't have the gold we say we do inside Fort Knox. If we had it on hand, then why would it take eight years to fulfill Switzerland's request?"

"Jesus," Matt exclaimed. He grabbed his glass of beer off the bar and took a swig. He passed around a plate of French fries that had come with his clams. Kate declined but Becker grabbed a handful.

"Sorry, David, but what does any of this have to do with my brother?" she asked.

"Honestly, I'm not sure any of it does," Becker admitted. "But I told Matt I'd let him know if I discovered anything out of the ordinary. So when I came across this story about gold repatriation, I thought I'd better share it. One thing I've learned over my years as an investigative journalist is that one loose end can oftentimes lead to another. And if you can connect enough loose ends it eventually leads you to the truth."

"It's as good as anything else we've got at the moment," Matt said.

"It's better than nothing, I guess," she replied skeptically.

Matt was lost in his own thoughts. Finally, he said to Becker, "Why do we care how much gold is in Fort Knox, anyway? I mean, I know at one point in time the world operated on the gold standard, but not anymore."

"What's the gold standard?" Kate inserted, feeling out of her element when it came to the world of finance. "Sorry, but I have trouble enough balancing my own checkbook." She smiled sheepishly.

Becker explained, "Up until 1971 the world's currencies were tied to the price of gold. This meant all governments had to have enough gold in their bank reserves to back their respective country's currency. But the Nixon administration did away with the gold standard. Ever since then the U.S. dollar has served as the world's reserve currency."

Becker turned back to Matt. "And as to your question, I don't know why it matters," he said. "For some reason, every country still carries gold reserves even though nowadays it's nothing more than an asset on a balance sheet, not an integral part of the international monetary system."

"I hate to sound like a broken record, guys, but I'm still struggling with what any of this has to do with the conspiracy Adam uncovered." Kate said, becoming frustrated.

Becker looked at Matt and both men shrugged as if to say, "We don't either."

Finally, Matt spoke up. "I'm not sure exactly what any of this means, but it appears as if whatever Adam got mixed up in involved gold. All roads keep leading back there." He counted off a number of facts as proof he was onto something: "One, Adam's firm, Morton Sinclair, traded heavily in gold; two, he was carrying around an old map with the words *Geronimo's Gold* written on it; three, Switzerland wants their gold back; and four, evidently there seems to be some question about the amount of gold left in Fort Knox."

Becker seemed unconvinced but was willing to play along. "Alright," he said, "so what do we do next?"

Before Matt could answer, Kate, who had been quietly listening to the exchange, said, "Morton Sinclair."

Both men turned their heads in unison.

"Why don't we go see Adam's old boss," she said. "Maybe my brother spoke to him about what he was working on."

Matt smiled at the idea. "Sounds like a good place to start," he said enthusiastically.

8

Present Day

Near Johannesburg, South Africa

The small Chinese delegation had arrived in Johannesburg the night before. The weather in South Africa this time of year was characterized by chilly evenings and cool, sunny days. Two factors contributed to the temperate climate in this part of the sub-Saharan country. The first was that it was early May and the winter season had just begun. The second was that the city of Johannesburg was situated in a range of mountains with elevations that topped out close to six thousand feet. The Chinese contingent had arisen early that morning and driven forty-five kilometers southwest of the city to the Witwatersrand Basin—the spot where gold had first been discovered in the region more than a century earlier.

In the early 1880s less than three thousand people lived in the area surrounding present-day Johannesburg. After gold was discovered on a local farm, however, it didn't take long for the gold rush to begin. Miners poured into the region. Tent camps became settlements and settlements became villages. Within ten years the sprawling boomtown had more than one hundred thousand inhabitants, and it also had a name—Johannesburg. Today there were close to ten million people living in the city and surrounding area. Seventy-five percent of the population was black, approximately sixteen percent white, and about four percent were of Asian origin. This last group was comprised mostly of descendants of immigrants from southern China.

Chinese immigrants had first arrived to work in the gold mines just after the Second Boer War in the first part of the twentieth century. Known at the time as "colored" people, they established a close-knit community in Johannesburg—one that still remained.

Now, a hundred-plus years later, another Chinese delegation had arrived in South Africa. But they had not come to perform backbreaking labor. They were part of a far-reaching covert operation, and their mandate was to take ownership stakes in the largest gold mining companies around the globe.

The mine they had come to visit that day was the largest in South Africa and the third largest in the world. At more than two miles deep, it was also one of the deepest mines ever excavated. So deep, in fact, it took more than an hour to reach the bottom via specially constructed underground elevator shafts. The surface area of the mine site covered more than ten square miles. Beneath the surface lay proven reserves totaling more than forty million ounces, enough gold to be continuously mined until the year 2050.

Over the past four years, the Chinese had invested heavily in the mammoth mine project. The funds from their investment had been used primarily to construct a new shaft system that would increase annual production of the mine by more than thirty percent. Within two years, they fully expected to be extracting more than one million ounces of gold annually. They were already the majority shareholder in the Johannesburg mine project, but they had been in serious negotiations with the current owners to buy the mine outright.

This would be the Chinese delegation's third such investment in South Africa and eighteenth investment throughout the world.

They had taken financial positions in mines in India, Peru, Australia, and Indonesia. But the largest of these investments had been made with their newest favorite trading partner, Russia.

Earlier that month the same Chinese delegation had paid a visit to the Magadan region in Russia's Siberia, home to one of the largest gold mines in all of Asia. Recent U.S. economic sanctions against Russia had forced their government to step up business cooperation with China. As a result, China was on the verge of obtaining large minority share positions in a slew of Russian gold mines, all containing world-class orebody.

All of these investments had been made as quietly as possible. The Chinese government had no intention of letting the world know the extent of the ownership positions they had taken in mines around the world. This simple yet elegant leg of China's overall strategy involved taking ownership of the ore and ingot as it came out of the ground—before it ever hit the open market. That way they could bypass the London Gold Exchange, the entity that set the price of gold, and ship raw gold directly to refineries in Switzerland and the increasing number of refineries being constructed in mainland China.

The price of gold was "fixed" twice daily by the five member banks that comprised the London Bullion Market Association. These banks monitored the supply and demand for gold around the world and set a price for settling contracts among themselves. The benchmark they set twice daily was then used by the international financial markets to price the majority of gold products and derivatives across the globe.

If the London Bullion Market knew how much gold was in demand by China, they would simply raise the price to prohibit them from hoarding too much supply. To avoid interference from London, the Chinese government developed a plan to secretly buy raw gold from the mines in which they had ownership stakes on terms they negotiated directly. That way the exact quantities of refined 1kg bars of gold that would eventually line the walls of government-controlled vaults in China would be effectively concealed from international reporting.

The delegation was on a tight schedule and could spend only two days in Johannesburg. Their superiors had ordered them to accelerate their plan. They had to finalize as many ownership deals as possible in the next sixty days. There was no time to waste. Once their business was concluded in South Africa, their private jet would depart immediately for Canada. There they would ink a deal giving them a fifty-one percent ownership stake in the largest mining company operating in North America.

9

May 1918
Lawton, Oklahoma

"This is going to be the most spectacular 'crook' ever," Preston exclaimed to his buddies. He swung his pickax forcefully into the hard-packed prairie earth. "Crook" was their code word for the theft of a trophy item that would eventually be brought back to their clubhouse in New Haven, a place known as the Tomb.

It was well past midnight and the six army captains had already broken open the iron door of the burial vault. They were now digging for their prize—the skull of Geronimo the Terrible. The man who had reportedly taken more than fifty white scalps while leading countless raids a half-century earlier. Earlier in the week they had paid a local Apache woman to lead them to the old Prisoner of War Cemetery. The unmarked grave was located in a remote corner of the Fort Sill army post and had become quite overgrown in the nine years since Geronimo had been interred there. It didn't look like much, but the woman swore this was the final resting place of the notorious Apache warrior.

"Shit, Hamlet, can you be a little quieter with that thing?" The man who stood sweating next to Preston cursed as the ping of metal against rocky earth reverberated in his ears. "You're going to wake up the whole damn post." It had been an unusually warm spring and even though it was the middle of the night, the temperature remained stifling.

"Oh, pipe down, Hellbender," Preston replied with an excited grin, "there's nobody within a half mile of here. Besides, Long Devil is keeping watch out by the road. He'll alert us if anyone's coming."

The men referred to each other by the nicknames given to them by the secret society they had all been handpicked to join in college. Their alma mater was Yale University, the third oldest institution of higher learning in the country located back east, in New Haven, Connecticut. The society into which they had been initiated was known as Skull and Bones. Members of the secretive organization had developed a reputation over the years for stealing keepsakes from around the Yale campus. It was the goal of each class to outdo each other's "crooks."

Bonesmen were predominantly white Protestant males from wealthy East Coast families. These six young men were no exception. They had grown up the privileged sons of bankers and industrialists, and had attended the best prep schools in the country. Once they had achieved membership into the Skull and Bones society, their futures were equally secure. That's because the list of well-placed society alumni was impressive and extremely exclusive. Well-connected businessmen, politicians, and statesmen would not hesitate to pull a few strings to help advance their fellow Bonesmen's careers. For the time being, however, all that would have to wait. With World War I raging in Europe, their country required their services in the armed forces. And as part of that enlistment, the boys were required to perform a stint of training at the U.S. Army artillery school at Fort Sill.

"I think I hit something," Preston shouted out in heightened excitement. He dropped to his knees and began to feverishly dig with his bare hands. Hellbender joined in.

"What is it?" another Bonesman, nicknamed Thor, chimed in from above the darkened crypt.

It didn't take them long to hit pay dirt.

"I think it's a saddle horn," Preston called out breathlessly.

"The old-timers told us Geronimo was buried with his saddle," Thor replied, barely able to contain his excitement. "Keep digging."

A moment later Hellbender called out, "Here's a piece of the bridle." He held up a rotting but still recognizable horse bridle.

"No bones?" Another anxious voice could be heard from above them.

"Not yet...wait." Preston felt around in the moist dirt. "Give me a hand, Hellbender."

The two men dug until they excavated a large bone that looked like a femur. "Holy shit," astonished voices sounded as the leg bone was handed up to the young men now clamoring to get a glimpse inside the grave.

After a few more tense minutes of digging, Preston finally held up the trophy they had come to find—Geronimo's skull.

The captains quickly refilled the grave with dirt, shut the iron door to the tomb, and hurried back to Hellbender's bunkroom. Only when they reached the safety of their barracks did they take full inventory of their spoils.

In addition to the femur, they had come away with what appeared to be pieces of the pelvis and a host of other smaller bones. On the wooden barracks floor they spread out the bones along with the saddle horn, bridle, and assorted rotten leathers they had exhumed.

Preston sat with his legs crossed in the center of the room. Geronimo's skull rested in his lap. He had already finished cleaning the remaining flesh and hair from the skull with a liberal application of carbolic acid. As he looked around the cramped room, he paused and nodded at each breathless face staring back at him.

"Gentlemen, I give you, Geronimo the Terrible," he proclaimed, "the most feared Indian of all time." He dramatically thrust the skull high above his head with both hands and added, "Here's to the greatest

crook in the history of Skull and Bones."

The young men answered with exuberant hurrahs.

10

Present Day
New York, NY

Kate Hampton's apartment was located on the corner of Greenwich and Perry streets on the Lower West Side of Manhattan. She loved the cozy confines of the West Village because it allowed her easy access to one of the biggest cities in the world while still providing a quiet enclave in which to live. Matt could understand this. In a way, it reminded him of his own Savannah neighborhood—filled with charming architecture and tree-lined streets, and rife with history.

The one hundred-year-old painted red brick building was bathed in the late morning sunshine. Matt pressed the buzzer next to the name labeled *Hampton*. Evidently she lived on the top floor of the four-story building. A moment later she buzzed him in.

As in most of the older brownstones in Manhattan there were no elevators, but Matt didn't mind climbing the three flights of stairs. The burn in his thighs reminded him he hadn't run in more than a week. As he reached the top landing he saw Kate had left the door ajar for him. He knocked anyway and called out. She yelled from somewhere inside for Matt to come in and make himself at home.

As Matt entered the apartment the first thing he noticed was a huge plate glass window in the main living area. Matt guessed it must have been installed to let more natural light into the room to show off Kate's paintings, which seemed to be everywhere. At least he assumed they were hers.

Most of the paintings were cityscapes with local subject matter. There were brownstones, subway cars, public parks, taxis, and other iconic images that gave New York City its unique character. Matt took an instant liking to them. They almost seemed as if they had been painted in a different era. He took a closer look. The scenes were clearly present-day but they had a style more akin to the social realism captured in WPA paintings from the 1930s.

Kate came around the corner and saw Matt admiring one of her pieces. "Sorry, no buy-one-get-one sales today," she joked.

"I'll happily pay full price," he replied, eyes still glued to the painting. "These are really good, Kate," he added seriously.

"That's sweet of you to say, but as you can see," she said waving at the overabundance of paintings, "I have a fairly extensive inventory, so evidently not everyone agrees."

"You need a better agent," he said moving on to another piece.

"Is that an offer?" she joked.

"No, that's a little bit out of my league. But I'd be glad to sell some of these at my shop in Savannah."

"You would?"

"Absolutely," he said as he turned to face her. "I really think they'd do well there—we have a ton of New York transplants down our way."

"I might take you up on that." She looked down at her watch. "Hey, we better get going. I told Adam's boss we'd be there by noon. He told me the lunch hour was the only time he had free to meet with us."

"What's the guy's name again?" Matt asked.

"Barry Walker," Kate replied. "Ever heard of him?"

"Doesn't sound familiar," he said, "but like I said, my contacts in the financial industry have gone pretty cold after a decade in Savannah."

Twenty minutes later they walked into the lobby of the Morton Sinclair building just north of Wall Street in lower Manhattan. It was an impressive glass and steel monstrosity. Kate had visited her brother a few times over the years and it felt strange to be there without him. She almost expected to see him come bounding off the elevator to greet her. But sadly, that was never going to happen again.

Upon arriving on the thirty-second floor, the perfunctory receptionist pointed the way to Barry Walker's office.

At first glance, Walker looked like the stereotypical Wall Street trader. He appeared confident and was athletically built, despite the extra twenty-five pounds around his midsection that undoubtedly hadn't been there in his younger days. His full head of black hair was combed straight back and held in place with a styling gel that probably cost a few bucks a squeeze. He was dressed in an expensively tailored dark suit. His starched white shirt was loosened at the collar and rolled up at the sleeves—and the red-and-black striped tie screamed Ivy League all the way.

As they entered, Walker came around his desk to meet them. "I'm sorry for your loss," he said to Kate. He took hold of her outstretched hand in both of his. "Adam was a great guy; everybody here loved him."

Matt felt the double-hand grab was unnecessarily over the top. For some odd reason, the gesture seemed disingenuous. Even though he had yet to speak one word to Walker, Matt took an immediate disliking to the man. Upon closer inspection, Matt noticed some cracks in the veneer of the middle-aged trader's slick appearance. He had dark circles under his eyes, the expensive suit looked like it could use a dry cleaning, and the Ivy League tie was stained. There was also a hyper quality about him that was off-putting. It wasn't a go-getter, positive energy, but rather a shiftiness Matt couldn't quite put a finger on. And to top it all off, his handshake was clammy. All of these things put Matt on high alert.

Walker offered them seats before retreating to a large black-leather chair behind his desk. He was outwardly courteous but seemed slightly uneasy with their presence.

"So, what can I help you with?" he addressed Kate. "On the phone you mentioned you had a couple of questions regarding Adam's work here?" he added guardedly.

"Well," Kate eased into the conversation, "we'd like to know if Adam was working on anything out of the ordinary at the time of his death."

"Out of the ordinary?" Walker said. He looked at Kate quizzically. "No, nothing unusual that I can recall. Why?"

Kate glanced over at Matt. He gave her a nod of encouragement. "You see, Mr. Walker..." she continued.

"Please, call me Barry. My dad is Mr. Walker." He winked at Kate. Matt rolled his eyes.

"Of course," Kate replied. "Anyway, *Barry*, we believe my brother didn't jump in front of that subway train...." She paused a few beats before finishing. "We believe he was pushed."

Walker's eyes went wide. "You mean murdered? But why would anyone want to kill Adam?"

Matt studied the slick trader, intently trying to read his response.

Kate took a deep breath before continuing, "We think it was related to something he recently uncovered—a financial conspiracy to be specific. And we were hoping he might have shared something with you. Anything that might help us to understand what he had gotten himself into."

Walker leaned back in his chair and whistled through his teeth. "Sounds like something out of a thriller novel," he joked.

Kate looked back at him with a stony stare.

"Sorry, I know this must still be very painful for you," he said as he tried to recover from making light of her brother's death, "but I'm afraid I have no idea what you're talking about. Adam never mentioned anything about a conspiracy."

The alarm bells in Matt's head got louder. His instincts told him Walker was hiding something. So he made a spur-of-the-moment decision. He decided to stretch the truth a little. "That's funny because he specifically told Kate that he'd shared his discovery with you." Matt stared at Walker with his best poker face.

Kate shot a look at Matt. Adam had never told her that. To her credit, she recovered quickly and didn't give Matt away.

"I don't know what you're talking about," Walker said gruffly, getting up out of his chair. He walked back around to their side of the desk. "Look, I'm really sorry about your brother, but I'm afraid I can't help you." He looked at his watch as if to signal their allotted time was up.

"Barry," Matt said without moving, "we know Adam talked to you. So either you tell us what you know or we'll have no choice but to go up the ladder." He stood up so he was standing eye to eye with Walker.

Walker's body language went from confident to agitated to nervous in a matter of seconds. "Jesus Christ," he finally blurted out. He quickly strode to the door. He closed it so their conversation couldn't be overheard.

Kate stood up to join Matt, having no idea what to expect next.

Walker walked slowly back to the desk. He ran a nervous hand through his hair and looked up toward the ceiling, as if deciding how much to say.

Finally, he wiped his sweaty palms on his suit pants and said, "Okay, alright, Adam did tell me something. But before I say any more, you've got to promise to keep me out of this."

Matt replied evenly, "Out of what?"

Walker seemed to be reconsidering. But then he relented and started to explain. "Adam came to me a little over two months ago. He said he had discovered some anomalies in a series of the firm's trades."

"Gold trades," Matt said. It was time to test his hypothesis that the conspiracy Adam had uncovered involved gold.

Walker nodded in the affirmative. "Look, I have no idea what put him onto it...and I never asked," he quickly added.

"Why the hell not?" Matt said, unable to hide his hostility. "You were his boss. Weren't you concerned about a massive fraud taking place inside your own firm?"

"Of course I was," Walker replied anxiously. "But I was nervous... and..." he stopped short. He had a panicked look in his eyes.

"And what?" Matt pressed. He'd had enough of the slick trader's evasiveness.

After an elongated pause, Walker exhaled loudly. "I was told to drop it, okay?" he said defensively, perhaps even with a touch of shame.

Kate inserted herself back into the conversation and asked more empathetically, "Who told you to drop it, Barry?"

His eyes dropped to the floor. He appeared to be mulling over a decision. Finally, he said in a hushed tone, "James Sinclair, the CEO of our firm."

"Why," she asked more forcefully, "was he involved?"

Walker looked more distressed than ever. "Look, I like my job here. It pays me a lot of money. So when the CEO told me to drop it, I dropped it. And I didn't ask any questions. If that makes me a bad guy, so be it."

Matt's stare was icy. Walker turned to plead with Kate. "You've got to believe me, I told Adam to drop it but he wouldn't let it go."

"That sounds like him," she said, feeling both proud and sad at her brother's stubbornness. It was probably what had gotten him killed.

Walker looked at his watch again. "Look, you guys really need to go," he said.

He hurried them out of his office and closed the door firmly behind them.

11

Present Day
Savannah, Georgia

Monday was always the slowest sales day at Hawkins Antiques. Slow but never quiet. Not when Matt's acerbic store manager, Christina, was working.

"Maybe I should put a 'going out of business' sale sign out front, eh, boss?" she said cynically. "That might motivate someone to actually walk through the front door."

"Mondays are always a little sluggish, Christina, you know that," Matt answered without looking up from the *Wall Street Journal*. Even though he had left his bond trading days behind him more than ten years earlier, he still couldn't break the habit of reading the Journal every morning.

"A little sluggish? It's like a morgue in here," she parried. "Why do we even open on Mondays? It's a money-losing proposition as far as I can tell. Or maybe you just like spending time with me?" She batted her eyes playfully.

Matt peered over the top of the newspaper and grumbled, "Yeah that must be it."

Not a week went by that he didn't rue the day he hired Christina. She had a cynical disposition, a petulant attitude, and a nasty streak when crossed. But she was also loyal to the core, had an incredibly strong work ethic, and trusted Matt more than any other human being on the planet. The truth was Matt had developed a soft spot for his underling, especially after she opened up to him one day about her dysfunctional family and abusive father. Over the years they had forged a sibling-like bond. A bond that allowed them to carry on their caustic banter without fear of hurting each other's feelings.

"How about we hire one of those sign spinners and put him out front," she continued, refusing to let the issue go, "or maybe we can get someone to dress up in a chicken suit and hand out fliers—that would be attention-grabbing."

"Are you volunteering your services?"

"You're bigger; you'd draw much more attention than me."

Matt had missed her last volley. An article had caught his eye. It was on page two of the paper and was related to Switzerland's gold repatriation request. Evidently Brazil had followed Switzerland's lead and demanded the immediate repatriation of all their gold from the United States as well. Brazil had taken it a step further, however. They demanded to visit the U.S. vaults holding their gold so they could perform an in-person inventory and confirm it could all still be accounted for. The U.S. federal government flatly refused their request. According to the article, the government cited "security" concerns and a strict "no visitor" policy. Eventually the Feds agreed to allow the Brazilians to examine a handful of gold bars as a good faith gesture, but that was all.

"What the hell is going on?" he murmured to himself.

Overhearing him, Christina shot back, "Nothing, that's my point."

Matt held up his hand. "I'm not talking about the lack of customers, Christina. It's something else…just be quiet for a minute, okay?" He buried his head in the paper again.

"Whatever," she huffed, "I'll be napping in the back if you need me." She disappeared into the back office.

He knew it was an idle threat. Christina liked working too much to ever snooze on the job. If she sat still for more than a few minutes she got bored. A moment later, he heard the printer start humming away. She was printing out price tags for inventory that hadn't yet made it to the sales floor. He smiled at her predictability before returning to the newspaper.

According to the article, additional countries, including India and Ecuador, had threatened repatriation of their gold as well. Although none of the countries demanding repatriation had issued public statements explaining why, it was speculated that perhaps they had been "spooked" by the U.S. government's refusal to allow Brazil to confirm their gold was still in the vaults at Fort Knox. The eight-year timetable given to Switzerland hadn't helped matters either. Apparently the other countries concluded the most prudent course of action to guarantee the safety of their assets was to bring all of their gold currently held by the United States back into their respective countries.

He put the paper down and stared out the window. His gut was telling him these successive repatriation requests were way too coincidental—it was almost as if they had been orchestrated. *The U.S. is being backed into a corner, but by whom...and why?* He mulled this thought over but couldn't seem to make sense of who would want to do such a thing or what their endgame might be.

The ringing of his cell phone pulled him back to the present. He looked down and saw it was David Becker calling. He answered quickly.

Becker told Matt he had been digging around trying to determine the meaning of "Geronimo's Gold." He explained that on a whim he had typed the search terms "Morton Sinclair" and "Geronimo" into an online search engine. That's when he came across a remarkable story.

"Evidently," Becker explained, "six members of Yale University's Skull and Bones society robbed Geronimo's grave at Fort Sill, back in 1918."

"They robbed his grave?"

"Sounds crazy, I know."

"Where the hell is Fort Sill, anyway?"

"It's in Oklahoma, and it's where Geronimo was buried in 1909," Becker replied.

"He was buried on an army base?"

"You've got to remember, Geronimo was the most wanted man in America back in the 1880s. So when the army finally caught up to him in 1886, they never let him go again. For the next twenty–three years he was held as a prisoner of war, mostly at Fort Sill. He was an old man by then, but he was also a legend. The government allowed him to make appearances in fairs and shows and he was even paid to sign autographs and sell his handmade trinkets. For a time, he was even one of the main attractions in Buffalo Bill's famous Wild West Show."

"I had no idea," Matt admitted. "So what did the Skull and Bones college boys steal from Geronimo's grave?"

"Allegedly they made off with his skull," Becker said.

"That's a little weird, don't you think? Wait a minute, what's the Skull and Bones society anyway?" Matt asked. "I think I've heard of it before. Isn't it some cloak-and-dagger fraternity?"

"Sort of. It's a secret society at Yale that you have to be asked to join—very exclusive and very reclusive. Its alumni tend to be wealthy and extremely well connected—both politically and finan- cially."

"So what were they doing robbing Geronimo's grave? And what does any of this have to do with Adam's old firm, Morton Sinclair?"

Matt asked, grasping for answers.

"I'm getting to that," Becker said. "When I first came across the story of the theft, I thought it was just an odd bit of history. I was about to ignore it until I noticed the name of one of the four tomb raiders."

He paused long enough for Matt to get impatient.

"You're doing it again, David," he chastised his friend who, like the writer he was, enjoyed the dramatic buildup of a story. "You're toying with me."

"Alright, alright. One of the raiders was a twenty-year-old kid named Preston."

"Sorry, but the last name Preston doesn't ring any bells for me."

"No, Preston was his first name. His last name was *Sinclair*," Becker said with emphasis. "And when young Preston grew up, he went on to start a very successful investment firm."

"Morton Sinclair!" Matt nearly shouted.

"Correct, the same firm where your friend Adam Hampton was employed on the night he was killed."

"Holy shit, David."

"I know, but there's more. Preston's grandson is a guy named James Sinclair. James is also a Bonesman, as they're called, and he also happens to be the current CEO of Morton Sinclair."

Matt silently processed this enticing new piece to the puzzle.

"Matt?" Becker spoke up after an elongated silence.

"Yeah, I'm here. I was just recalling something Barry Walker, Adam's old boss, said. He told me he dropped his inquiry into Adam's claims about a conspiracy at the request of his CEO, James Sinclair."

"He told you that?" Becker asked, surprised.

"Yeah, he did."

"Well it appears the Sinclairs, both past and present, are mixed up in this thing," Becker concluded. The investigative reporter then hypothesized, "My guess is Preston Sinclair somehow found out about Geronimo's Gold. And he and his Skull and Bones buddies robbed the grave looking for clues to its whereabouts."

"It fits," Matt agreed, "but there are still lots of unanswered questions. Like, how much does James Sinclair know about Geronimo's Gold? How did Adam find out about it? And where did he get that damn map?"

"And the biggest question of them all," Becker posited, "how does Geronimo's Gold tie back to the financial conspiracy Adam uncovered?"

Even with these unanswered questions, progress had been made. And both men agreed on one thing—James Sinclair was somehow at the center of it all.

12

Present Day
New York, NY

Sam Rothstein was a short man. At barely five feet six inches tall just about everyone towered over him, including his third wife. Rather than holding him back, however, his diminutive stature only fueled his desire to prove himself, time and again. From the self-imposed brutal training schedule that had once helped him become a high school state wrestling champion to the arduous fifteen-hour workdays he adhered to throughout his career, Sam Rothstein was never going to be outworked—or outhustled.

Rothstein knew the difference between being wildly successful and being just another chump on the street was razor thin. Advantages were gained on the margin. And the easiest way to gain an edge in the world of finance was to have more information than the next guy. When this information was obtained legally, it was considered a competitive advantage. When it was obtained illegally, it was called insider information. And if you were caught using insider information it could land you in hot water with the Securities and Exchange Commission. In extreme cases it could even land you in jail. For Rothstein it had done both.

Back in the high-flying 1980s, he had been a hotshot Wall Street trader specializing in high-yield bonds, known in the industry as junk bonds. He was so successful trading in these products that over one four-year period he was the highest compensated trader in the securities industry. His face had once graced the front page of the *Wall Street Journal,* and an extensive personal profile had been published by *Forbes* magazine. He had been labeled the new King of Wall Street. But his reign was short-lived.

In 1993 his world came crashing down around him. At the conclusion of a two-year government investigation, he was indicted for racketeering and securities fraud and for insider trading. The reality was he was not the only offender, probably not even the worst one. But he was the most well-known. And that had put a bull's-eye on his back. The chairman of the SEC needed a head to mount on his wall, so he went hunting for big game—and the biggest prize of them all at the time was Sam Rothstein. As the result of a plea bargain, Rothstein pled guilty to securities and reporting violations but not to racketeering or insider trading. He was sentenced to eight years in prison and fined more than a half-billion dollars.

After six years of incarceration he was released early for good behavior. An average person would have been finished for good, but Sam Rothstein never considered himself even remotely average. If anything, he left prison more driven than when he entered. Only this time he had a massive chip on his shoulder. He was a man who harbored plenty of grudges. He was officially at war with anyone who doubted him and everyone who had wronged him in the past. And at the top of his list of enemy combatants were the people at the SEC—and their employer, the U.S. government. He didn't know how it would happen, but he made a promise to himself that one day the government was going to pay for the six long years they had taken away from him.

When he first emerged from prison he was treated like a pariah.

His former friends distanced themselves and his Wall Street contacts wouldn't return his phone calls. Even though his face had long since faded from the news, his name remained a lightning rod in the industry. It turned out things on the outside weren't much different than on the inside. Even though he could now move about freely, he still found himself in a lockup of sorts—a prisoner of his tarnished past. The fortune he had amassed had been largely diminished. The high-priced lawyers who failed in their efforts to keep him out of jail had nonetheless eaten up a significant chunk of his savings. The rest had gone to pay off fines the government levied against him. To his credit, he remained undaunted. And almost twenty years later, he succeeded in returning to the top of his profession.

Rothstein had rebuilt his empire and then some. This time he had done it on the back of so-called alternative assets, including private equity and hedge funds. Most of the investments came from corporate and public pension fund clients, insurance companies, and even some university endowments. His first hedge fund was so successful he started two more. It had taken him years of hard work. But he painstakingly rebuilt his empire and rebooted his reputation. But he was far from finished.

His company, Eight Ball Investments, had become one of the largest private equity firms in the world. Publicly, Rothstein claimed the name of the firm came from the fact he had once been "behind the eight ball" and had come all the way back to prominence. Perhaps only he and a few white-collar criminals with whom he had served time knew the true meaning of the name. "Eight ball" was prison slang for an eight-year prison sentence. He took smug satisfaction in the secret behind the name and even more satisfaction in the fact that he had not only returned to respectability but he was now one of the richest men in America.

But all his accomplishments had done little to diminish his desire to settle old scores.

Rothstein was sitting in his purposely modest office at Eight Ball's Midtown Manhattan headquarters. Unlike the four lavishly appointed homes he owned in the U.S. and abroad, his corporate offices were unassuming—even austere—in comparison. He had been born into a middle-class Detroit family with modest means and a simple lifestyle. His father owned a delicatessen and his mother was a seamstress. He had inherited his father's work ethic as well as his belief that a workplace should resemble a place where work happens, not a museum.

It was late in the afternoon when his assistant alerted him his guest had arrived. A minute later she escorted a well-dressed and meticulously coiffed Asian man into Rothstein's office. She closed the door behind her on the way out. The two men couldn't have been more different in styles. In business and in life, Rothstein was like a bull charging a red cape, waiting for the right moment to impale his adversary. The man sitting across from him was unsettlingly calm, almost as if he were disinterested in the proceedings. But Rothstein knew the man could be ruthless when it came to getting what he wanted.

It wasn't long after the Shanghai Investment Consortium formalized their minority equity stake in Eight Ball Investments that the Chinese revealed their true and far-reaching intentions— and exactly what they needed Rothstein to do for them. They had done their homework before investing in his firm. His checkered past had done nothing to dissuade them from pursuing an arrangement with him. In fact, it was the reason they chose him.

He was the perfect fit. More than having the Wall Street banking contacts so critical to pulling off their scheme, they knew he had an ax to grind. They had chosen wisely. When they disclosed the sweeping scope of their proposal to him, Rothstein hadn't hesitated for a moment to throw in with them. That had been three years ago.

"We are close to initiating the next phase of our plan," the slightly effeminate Chinese national began.

"Already?" Rothstein replied. He was under the impression they were still at least six months away.

The man's hands rested calmly in his lap, long delicate fingers intertwined as if in silent prayer. His fingernails looked as though they had been recently manicured. Rothstein was also fairly certain the man's eyebrows had been plucked. They looked like tilted commas over each eye, making him appear in perpetual surprise. Both men wore expensively tailored suits, but Rothstein felt under-dressed compared to his Princeton-educated guest. Even this late in the afternoon, the man's suit pants were creased crisply down the middle and his blue oxford shirt looked freshly pressed.

"Yes, thanks in large part to the efficiency of the network you set up for us," he complimented Rothstein with a tight-lipped smile that showed no teeth.

Rothstein chafed inwardly at the false flattery. But he didn't let it show. He knew the man sitting across from him was neither a friend nor an admirer. He also knew he was dealing with danger-ous people and he needed to watch his step. So he bowed his head slightly in polite acknowledgment of the compliment.

"We've been able to buy more gold," the man continued, "more quickly than we thought. So we have accelerated our timetable."

"You're sure China has enough gold in its reserves to pull this off?" Rothstein asked.

The man paused and scanned the spartan office condescending-ly. When his eyes returned to Rothstein, his gaze was steady and his reply was curt, "Quite."

"So what's next?"

"When the time is right, my government will issue a press release announcing China's gold reserves have increased to 10,000 metric tons," he replied.

"Ten thousand tons?" Rothstein sounded both surprised and

impressed. "That's more than five times the amount you had in your vaults the last time you made a public statement seven years ago. And 2,000 tons ahead of where you were scheduled to be at this point." He paused. "How in the hell did you accumulate so much gold so fast?"

"As I told you, your commodity trading network in the U.S. exceeded our expectations. That, and the positions we have taken in gold mines around the world have also outperformed our original projections," the man replied smugly.

Taking note of his surprise, the man asked, "Is everything okay, Mr. Rothstein? This is a positive development, is it not?" He offered another forced smile. "Not having second thoughts are we?"

Rothstein's eyes flashed with anger. He was a dangerous man in his own right and he didn't appreciate his resolve being questioned, especially by some faggot Chinaman. "I *never* have second thoughts," he answered firmly.

"Good," the man said as if that were the end of it. But before he moved on, he asked with genuine curiosity, "So what are you going to do when the...what is the expression...oh yes, when the *cat is out of the bag*. Aren't you afraid you'll be a pariah in your own country?"

Rothstein glared back at the fastidious waif of a man. "It'll be familiar territory." He cocked his head slightly to the side and said, "But I'm counting on the fact my role in all of this will never become public."

"Of course," the man said, "so no doubts, then?" He searched for one last assurance.

"None," Rothstein replied tersely. "This country is going to pay for what it did to me," he said as he rapped his finger loudly on the tabletop, "whatever it takes." Then he eased back in his chair and said more calmly, "In the end, it's a win-win for me. I become one of the wealthiest men in the world and I destroy the country that tried to destroy me."

His answer appeared to reassure the man. The visitor returned to discussing the next phase of the plan. "As I was saying earlier, when we announce our increased gold reserves position, we will also announce we are willing to open our vaults to an international audit by the World Bank. But our caveat will be that other countries allow their gold reserves to be audited as well—starting, of course, with the United States."

"I can guarantee you that demand will get some butts squirming in their seats in Washington," Rothstein replied and smiled at the thought.

"Speaking of guarantees," the man said, "are you sure your government does not have the 8,000 tons of gold reserves they claim they do?" He uncrossed his thin legs and leaned forward deliberately. "Because if they do, our plans will be severely compromised." He paused before adding, "And I needn't remind you—that would be disastrous for *all* of us."

A large vein in Rothstein's neck bulged angrily, but he maintained his cool and let the veiled threat pass. "My people have run and rerun the numbers," he answered evenly. "You have nothing to worry about. The 8,000-ton figure the U.S. claims is complete bullshit."

He continued, "The official word from the Treasury for not allowing a physical audit of their vaults is they don't want to give credence to gold as money. But the reality is, after years of 'paper gold' transactions they don't have enough gold to back all of their investment obligations. I know for a fact the amount of gold subject to paper contracts is one hundred times the amount of physical gold backing those contracts."

The man understood Rothstein was referring to the common practice by holders of gold to loan, lease, and swap the same physical gold through Exchange Traded Funds. Basically electronically loaning or leasing the same cache of physical gold over and over again.

The system worked as long as nobody demanded to take possession of the physical gold they had purchased on paper. If everyone were to actually ask for their gold at the same time, there wouldn't be enough to go around—not by a long shot.

"Besides," Rothstein concluded, "I have the personal assurance from a highly placed and trusted contact at the Federal Reserve Bank of New York. The current U.S. gold reserves at both the New York depository as well as the vault at Fort Knox are precariously low."

"Excellent," the man from China replied. "Now there is one last thing," he said, changing gears. "We need someone with the credibility and preferably the political clout to apply public pressure on your government to open their vaults to an audit. It's one thing for the Chinese government to make the demand. It will be considerably more effective for someone inside your own political establishment to plant the seed of doubt; to create a public outrage about your government's refusal to allow an audit of their gold reserves."

Rothstein answered quickly, "I've done a lot of thinking since we first spoke about this. I believe I have just the guy for the job. His name is Carl Lynch and he's the current Libertarian candidate for president, running in the upcoming election. I think I can get him to turn up the heat on the gold audit issue for us."

"I'm familiar with the man. How do you propose enlisting his help?"

"That won't be hard. He's been privately courting most of the financial titans of Wall Street for funds to support his run for the presidency. And that includes me."

"You've arranged a meeting with him?"

"I have. As a matter of fact, he's coming to my home this evening. I plan to pledge a considerable amount of money to pad his war chest. But of course, my pledge will come with some strings attached." Rothstein smiled. "In exchange for my generous financial support, I'll make sure Lynch promises to start making a lot of noise about the U.S. government's gold reserves, or lack thereof."

13

Present Day

New York, NY

Kate had just finished leading her final yoga class of the day. Two nights a week she conducted evening sessions for clients who couldn't make her early morning classes. The studio had cleared out fifteen minutes earlier and she was ready to head home. Before turning out the lights and locking the door, she glanced up at the oversized clock on the far wall. It was after ten o'clock. Her day had started at six in the morning so it was no wonder she was beat. Luckily her studio was only a few blocks from her apartment in the West Village. She was looking forward to going home and collapsing into bed.

Slam. She was thrown against the front door of the studio.

She had just slipped the key from the lock and was about to turn to leave when someone attacked her from behind. She was so startled she couldn't talk, let alone move. By the time she realized what was happening, it was too late. She attempted to scream but a strong hand clamped down across her mouth. A muffled shout was all that emerged. Nobody was in close enough proximity to hear her muted calls for help anyway.

Kate was athletic and strong for her stature, but the man who held her in his grasp had her outsized by at least six inches and a hundred pounds. But it wasn't the man's size that made her knees buckle. It was his voice.

"Shut up," he said in a low, rumbling voice that sounded like a downshifting eighteen-wheeler.

It was a heavily accented growl. Her first thought was Eastern European, or maybe Russian. With her head pinned against the door, however, she had no way of turning around and getting a good look at his face. She strained to get a glimpse of him in the glass. But it was no use. His image was distorted like a grotesque reflection in a carnival mirror. Her first instinct was to fight, but she quickly realized it was fruitless. He was too strong.

She could feel his hot breath on the back of her neck. It made the hairs on her arms stand on end. After what seemed like an eternity, he finally spoke again. He leaned in very close to her ear and said just four words.

"Curiosity...killed...the...cat."

He said the words slowly to make sure Kate understood him through his heavily accented English. She did. But before she could react, the man jerked her head back and slammed it violently against the door frame. She crumpled to the ground.

By the time she regained her wits and struggled to her feet, the man had disappeared from sight. The force of the blow hadn't knocked her unconscious, but it had dazed her. Feeling nauseous, she leaned against the door frame and slid back down to a seated position. She put a hand to her forehead and felt blood oozing through her fingers. She fished a towel from her gym bag and applied pressure to stem the bleeding. A nasty welt had already begun to form.

As the initial shock of the attack wore off, her body began to shake uncontrollably. It had all happened so fast. She sat there on the cool pavement, her arms wrapped around her knees pressed up against her chest. For some reason she didn't cry. She was scared, of course. But her prevailing emotion was anger. That bastard's awful words, "curiosity killed the cat," kept repeating over and over inside her head. She knew what they meant the moment he uttered them.

It was a warning. Someone was telling her to stop pursuing Adam's death—and the conspiracy he had uncovered.

Standing on shaky legs, she gathered herself and made her way home.

She was still lightheaded as she climbed the stairs to her fourth-floor apartment. Her nerves were still on edge and she had no desire to be alone in a darkened apartment. She flipped on the foyer lights and caught a glimpse of herself in the mirror by the front door. She gasped. A startlingly pale face stared back at her. The cut on her head had stopped bleeding but a purplish egg-sized bump remained. She slipped off her shoes and padded over to the kitchen sink to wash her face. In a stunned trance, she filled a baggie full of ice, zipped it shut, and placed it gingerly to her forehead. She filled a tall glass with water and gulped it down.

"Mac," she called out softly for her cat. She felt the need to cuddle with something warm and loving. "Mac," she called out again as she walked down the hallway. She stuck her head in the bathroom but he wasn't there. He must be asleep on her bed, she thought. She flicked on the bedroom light...and screamed.

Mac was lying at the foot of the bed. His eyes were open and his tongue hung awkwardly out of the side of his mouth. She rushed over and picked him up. The Bengal cat's head lolled lifelessly to one side. His neck had been broken.

"No!" she screamed in anguish.

For the first time that horrible evening, she broke down and cried. As she sat there cradling Mac in her arms, sobbing uncontrollably, she remembered the awful words spoken by her attacker.

Curiosity killed the cat.

Matt picked up on the third ring. He had fallen asleep on the couch watching a ball game on television.

"They killed Mac," Kate shrieked into the phone through her sobs.

It took him a few minutes to piece together the gist of what had happened. His first concern was for Kate's safety. Those fears were allayed when she told him she had gone to a girlfriend's apartment.

After a few minutes, she regained her composure. Through sniffles she said, "Jesus, Matt, what have I gotten myself into? Who are these people?"

"I don't know. Do you have any idea how they got into your apartment?"

"No, it was locked as usual when I came home. They must have picked the dead bolt somehow."

"Listen, Kate, maybe we need to take a step back and reevaluate this whole thing based on what happened tonight. I mean…"

"No, Matt," she cut him off mid-sentence. "They murdered my brother, they mugged me, and now they've killed my cat. I will not let them get away with this," she said bitterly. "I won't."

"But, Kate, they know where you live."

"Promise me, Matt; promise me," she implored him, "you'll help me find these men. I couldn't live with myself if I gave in to their threats now. They need to pay for what they've done."

He could hear the resolve in her voice and knew she had made up her mind. He couldn't help but be impressed with her courage. And the truth was he was glad. He didn't want to give up either. In fact, he wanted to find these men now more than ever.

"I promise," he said emphatically.

14

Present Day
Washington, D.C.

For a history buff like Matt, a visit to Washington, D.C., was always a thrill, especially in the springtime. The month of May in the nation's capital offered a welcome, albeit brief, window of pleasant weather, coming on the heels of winter's bluster and before the onset of summer's cloying humidity.

He had always felt the best way to tour the city was on foot. Only then could you appreciate how much it had to offer. Its history was palpable, its museums were free, and its eclectic mix of restaurants second to none.

But he wasn't going to be a tourist on this particular trip. He had come to see a man he vowed never to see again.

He sat on an outdoor wooden bench on the western edge of the grassy National Mall with an unobstructed view of the Washington Monument. It wasn't by chance he chose a location for the meeting that was adjacent to the monument dedicated to the country's first president.

Buzz Penberthy and he had once been close friends. More like father and son, as Buzz was thirty years his senior. In a very short period of time, Buzz had filled a void in Matt's life, a void that had existed for years after the premature death of his father. Matt had no explanation for it. He and Buzz had simply clicked. He had made many friends in his lifetime, been involved in a number of relationships over the years, and even been married once. But no one seemed to understand him the way Buzz had. For first time in a long time Matt had someone to confide in and counsel him—as a father might do.

But that was before Buzz betrayed him.

At the time, Matt knew Buzz only as the president general of the Society of the Cincinnati, a patriotic organization founded by George Washington that had been in existence since just after the American Revolution.

He knew nothing of his secret double life.

Matt was so lost in his thoughts that he didn't see Buzz approaching until he was nearly standing in front of him.

"It's good to see you, Matt," Buzz said with a broad smile and an outstretched hand.

As Matt shook Buzz's hand, he noted his face appeared a bit more drawn than he remembered and his eyes looked fatigued. Even so, his one-time mentor was as trim as ever and his neatly cropped silver-gray hair shimmered in the bright morning sunlight.

Matt didn't say it, but seeing his old friend again made him realize how much he missed him. But the resentment he still harbored returned like a bitter aftertaste. He managed an awkward, "Thanks for coming," before motioning for Buzz to sit next to him on the bench.

Matt waited for an older couple taking an early morning stroll to pass out of earshot before beginning. "I'm going to ask you a question, Buzz, and I need you to answer truthfully," he said seriously.

"Of course," Buzz nodded.

"Is the Ring playing me again?"

It was the first time Matt had used the name of the secret organization that had manipulated him since Buzz had first revealed it to him. It sounded ridiculous to say the name out loud, almost as if he was referring to a shadow cartel straight out of a James Bond movie.

"No," came Buzz's quick reply. "What's going on, Matt, what happened?"

Matt studied Buzz's face for any indication he was lying. But his response seemed genuine. There had been no hesitation and the concern on his face appeared real.

He took a moment to collect his thoughts, then went on to tell Buzz everything. He started with the alleged conspiracy Adam Hampton discovered, along with Kate's suspicions that her brother was murdered. He went on to reveal the existence of the map of Geronimo's Gold, the numerous international gold repatriation requests, the Skull and Bones society's connection to the robbery of Geronimo's grave, and finally Kate's brutal assault.

Buzz's brow furrowed at the mention of Kate's attack, but he remained silent, deep in thought.

Matt looked hard at him once more. "I'm going to ask you again. Is the Ring involved in any of this?"

"I swear to you, Matt. This is the first I've heard of any kind of financial conspiracy."

After a final stare down, Matt breathed easier. Satisfied that Buzz was telling the truth, he switched gears. "Then I'm going to need your help." It was more of a demand than a request.

Buzz leaned back against the bench. He looked cautiously around. "My help or the Ring's help?"

"Either, both, whatever it takes to help me get to the bottom of this," he said. "When Kate was attacked I realized I was in way over my head. I can't do this alone."

"My offer still stands, Matt."

The last time the two men spoke was right after Buzz had revealed that the Ring was a secret organization embedded deep inside the Society of the Cincinnati. He had asked Matt to join their selective group even though he knew in his heart the betrayal Matt rightfully felt was still too fresh in his mind to even consider the offer. Still, he had tried to convince him that the covertly operated organization, known to its select members as the Ring, was a noble and necessary check against the usurpations of power within the U.S. government—perhaps even more so now than when George Washington and his original handpicked group of patriots began their operations just after the revolution.

Buzz didn't blame Matt for his anger. He had after all manipulated him—as he had done countless times before with others. In the past, he had always felt justified in his actions because he knew it was for the good of the country. This time, however, he felt guilty. Matt was the son he never had, and he missed him dearly. He hoped there was still a chance he might come around.

"I thought you might say that," Matt replied. "Look, Buzz, I believe your heart is in the right place, I just can't reconcile your methods."

Buzz nodded in understanding.

"Does that mean you won't help?" Matt asked hesitantly.

"Not only will I help," Buzz promised with a smile, "but you'll have the full resources of the Ring at your disposal." He was only too glad to have the opportunity to join forces with his protégé one more time.

For the first time in a long time, Matt returned the smile. "Thanks."

Buzz waved him off and then dived right in. "Tell me more about Adam Hampton," he said, wasting little time. The eyes that looked so fatigued just moments earlier had reclaimed their familiar shimmer.

15

Present Day

Washington, D.C.

The Society of the Cincinnati's national headquarters was located in the Dupont Circle neighborhood of D.C. It was housed in a spectacular Florentine villa-style mansion that was built just after the turn of the twentieth century. The nonprofit organization's stated purpose was to promote knowledge and appreciation of the achievement of American independence, and to preserve the memory of the patriotic sacrifices that made American liberty a reality. To become a member of the society, one's roots had to be traced back to an officer who had served in George Washington's Continental Army.

Evidently, the society had been named after Lucius Quinctius Cincinnatus, a farmer who had once served as Roman Consul. As the story went, an enemy invasion in 458 BC had necessitated the Senate to call Cincinnatus back to Rome, upon which he was given near-absolute authority. After vanquishing the enemy, however, Cincinnatus immediately resigned his authority and returned power back to the Senate. The founders of the society admired Cincinnatus and felt he embodied the mission of an organization like theirs—committed to preserving the ideals that had paved the way for the world's latest representative democracy, America.

Matt was the last to arrive at the second-floor office of Buzz Penberthy. Sitting with Buzz around the small conference table in the president general's office were Director James Fox and Kate Hampton. Matt immediately walked over to Kate and wrapped his arms around her in a warm embrace. A moment later, he pulled back so he could examine her black-and-blue forehead.

"Buzz called it my war wound," she said with a smile. "Pretty sexy, huh?"

He was glad to hear she could make light of the terrible events from just a couple of days earlier. "You can hardly tell it's there. I mean you hardly notice that big bruise across the middle of your forehead," he joked. She smacked him playfully on the shoulder.

He released her. "Seriously, it could have been a lot worse. I'm just happy you're alright."

"Thanks," she said. It suddenly struck her that she was reluctant to leave Matt's embrace. She felt safer by his side.

Buzz noticed the interchange. He cleared his throat. "Okay, Matt, where do you want to begin?"

Matt and Kate quickly took their seats around the conference table.

"I think it's time we confronted James Sinclair. That son of a bitch is guilty as hell," Matt said, wasting little time in sharing how he felt. "Barry Walker told us it was Sinclair who told him not to pursue Adam's inquiries into the conspiracy. *And* Sinclair's grandfather led the raid on Geronimo's grave, presumably to look for clues to the whereabouts to Geronimo's Gold."

Buzz, who was used to reigning in his impulsive, action-oriented friend, said, "Hang on a second, Matt. As much as I'd like to get my hands on Sinclair, too, we just don't have enough proof. As he told you, Walker likes his job too much to rat out his boss. And without more compelling evidence, Grandpa Sinclair's theft of Geronimo's grave, as it stands right now, is nothing more than a stupid fraternity prank."

"I'm telling you, Buzz, Sinclair is up to his ass in this conspiracy," Matt countered.

"He may be, but we need more evidence to make a case against him," Buzz insisted.

Fox turned to Kate and asked, "May we take a look at that map?"

Kate pulled out the old map of New Mexico her brother had with him the night he was killed. She placed it on the table. An involuntary shiver made its way down her spine. She was tired of carrying around the grim reminder of his violent death.

"Fascinating," Fox said, scanning the somewhat crude illustration. "I'd say it's from the early 1900s. New Mexico is still referred to here as a territory, so it predates 1912 when it became the forty-seventh state. My guess would be 1903 or 1904." In addition to being the executive director of the society reporting directly to Buzz, Fox was also a member of the Ring.

"What about Geronimo's Gold?" Matt asked. "Were you able to come up with anything on that?"

"After Buzz briefed me on your conversation with him, I did a little research on Geronimo," Fox answered. "Evidently, he was born in New Mexico near the headwaters of the Gila River in the Mogollon Mountains."

He reached into a manila folder before continuing, "I printed off a current map of New Mexico so I could compare it to the one Kate found. I went ahead and circled the area here"—he pointed to a spot on the map—"where Geronimo was born."

Matt flipped Fox's map around so he could compare it with the earlier version. "It looks like he was born in the general vicinity of where Adam's map claims Geronimo's Gold to be."

"Looks like it," Fox agreed, "so at least we know Geronimo spent some time in that area."

"What about the gold reference?" Kate asked.

"Unfortunately I didn't come up with anything that connected Geronimo to gold," Fox replied.

Kate looked despondent.

They all sat silently staring at the two maps lying side by side on the wooden tabletop. Finally, Buzz changed the subject. "Is it even possible there is any gold in those mountains?"

Fox answered immediately, "Oh yes, there is most certainly gold in those mountains."

His definitive statement got everyone's attention.

"How can you be so sure?" Kate asked, perking up a bit.

"Gold, silver, and copper for that matter, have been found throughout that part of the country for more than five centuries. Precious metals were first discovered by the Spanish conquistadores in the early 1500s. Additional discoveries by Spanish missionaries followed, and eventually droves of American prospectors came looking to strike it rich."

"Yeah, well, I've got an old navy buddy who lives in Tucson," Buzz piped in. "He's been prospecting in those hills for years and has never found a thing. Keeps him out of the house, though, which keeps his wife happy. And that's a good thing because she's as mean as a snake and outweighs him by at least fifty pounds," he winked in Kate's direction.

"The other reason," Fox continued, ignoring his boss's off-topic comment, "is because the latest U.S. Geological Survey states"—he pulled an official-looking report from his briefcase—"only half the gold that exists in this country has ever been found. And one of the highest potential areas for future discoveries is in the Southwest. In fact, New Mexico lies in one of the designated hot spots for undiscovered gold."

"Sounds like there really is gold out there," Kate said, her eyes wide with excitement.

"I would say so, yes," Fox concluded.

"But we're still no closer to figuring out how Geronimo's Gold is related to the conspiracy my brother uncovered?" Kate said soberly.

"I'm afraid not," Fox said.

"That's the least of our problems," Buzz said. "Even if Geronimo's Gold does exist, it lies smack dab in the middle of a national park, according to the present-day map."

"It looks that way," Fox concurred. "Geronimo's birthplace and the circle representing the location of Geronimo's Gold on the older map appear to both lie within the boundaries of the Gila National Forest."

Matt was silent, deep in thought. He eyed the two maps lying side by side on the table.

Buzz filled the void. "Back to Kate's question. How do we know if any of this is related to the financial conspiracy Adam uncovered? Or if Geronimo's Gold is even real?"

Matt looked up. "Adam was brilliant, Buzz. If he was carrying that map around in his jacket pocket on the night he was killed, it wasn't by coincidence. He believed Geronimo's Gold was real and that it was somehow connected to the present-day conspiracy."

Matt was so firm in his conviction that Buzz held up his hands as if in surrender. "Okay," he relented. "But the Gila National Forest covers almost three million acres of land—very rugged and remote land." Then he offered as an aside, "I took a trip out there twenty years ago with my wife. It's beautiful, but enormous. Even if Geronimo had discovered a deposit of gold out there, it would be next to impossible to find."

"Then we need to figure out a way to narrow our search," Matt replied undaunted.

16

Present Day

Washington, D.C.

Fox changed gears. "You have no idea where he may have gotten this?" he asked Kate, gesturing to the map. "He never mentioned it in any of your conversations with him?"

Kate sighed in frustration. "I'm sure," she said. "My brother had never even been to New Mexico. So I have no idea what he was doing with this map or where he could have possibly gotten it."

Fox picked it up so he could examine it more closely.

"It had to have come from James Sinclair," Matt filled the void in the conversation. "He's the only one we can connect back to Geronimo." He remained fixated on the current CEO of Morton Sinclair as their primary suspect.

"Well, Sinclair wouldn't have just handed it over to my brother," Kate reasoned. Then with a look of panic, she added, "You don't think Adam stole it from him, do you?"

"It's possible," Matt offered.

"Now this is interesting," Fox spoke up. He had been looking at the old map with an oversized reading microscope. After finding nothing on the front, he turned the map over. "Something was written back here at one time, toward the bottom of the page."

He leaned in to take a closer look, intently focused on a bottom corner of the map. He voiced what he observed: "Yes, there was definitely some writing here. But it's been erased."

"Can you make out what it said?" Buzz asked.

"Not with this level of magnification. It's too faint to read," Fox said, and finally tore his eyes away from the map. "But if we take it down to the clean room, I bet we could," he stated brightly.

"The clean room?" Kate asked, perplexed.

"It's a small lab we have attached to our manuscript department," Buzz explained. "It comes pretty well-equipped with some sophisticated technology. We use it to help preserve and stabilize our rare book collection and other important historical documents."

"There's a device called an ESDA which stands for Electrostatic Detection Apparatus," Fox explained proudly. "It's a specialized piece of equipment that allows us to recover writing by examining the indentations or depressions left behind on the paper."

"Yeah, and when we get done with that," Buzz quipped, pushing back from the table, "I'll show you our collection of exploding pens."

Even Matt cracked a smile. He had to admit he missed his old friend's wisecracking sense of humor.

Fifteen minutes later they sat in the lab watching Director Fox manipulate the document onto the Electrostatic Detection Apparatus. It was a piece of machinery about the size of a small copier. Fox had already placed the old map in a humidity chamber for a few minutes before placing it onto the machine. He stretched a thin sheet of polyester film over the document and smoothed it flat.

Like a doctor explaining a procedure to first-year residents, Fox began, "The top surface of the film must be electrostatically charged. So I'm using this handheld device. It contains a high-tension corona wire to produce an evenly distributed charge in the air above the surface of the film."

Fox waved the handheld unit back and forth over the surface of the film that now covered the reverse side of the old map of New Mexico. He carried on his one-way dialogue. "Once the charge has been passed to the surface," he said, "I can sprinkle this negatively charged printer toner on top of the film." He carefully poured the fine black powder onto the surface. "If successful, the indented impression from the erased words will appear as writing on the film."

Matt came around to the other side of the metal worktable so that he could look directly over Fox's shoulder. Apparently satisfied the procedure was a success, Fox took a step back so Matt could see. "Take a look for yourself," said Fox, beaming.

"What does it say?" Kate asked, barely able to contain her excitement.

"There's a name and a date," Matt replied. "It says *H. Benson,* and the date is *April 1905.*"

At the mention of the name, Matt thought he detected a spark of recognition in Buzz's eyes. He looked at Buzz quizzically. "Do you know who H. Benson is?" he asked.

Buzz answered in the affirmative, "I believe I do. H. Benson has to stand for Henry Benson."

"Who's he?" Matt asked. He had never heard the name before.

"Henry Benson was a good friend of President Theodore Roosevelt. Roosevelt appointed him to be the first chief of the newly created United States Forest Service," Buzz answered.

"When was the U.S. Forest Service created?" Kate asked.

"Right after Roosevelt was elected to his second term in office. His inauguration was in March, 1905, so the date fits," he said. "Back then, inaugurations were in March not in January as they are now," he clarified.

"How the hell do you know all this?" Matt asked in astonishment.

"Come on, Teddy Roosevelt is the best president of all time. That and he was also an honorary member of the Society of the Cincinnati," Buzz admitted with a wry smile. "So I've done my homework on his presidency."

A thought suddenly occurred to Kate. "You said Benson was appointed chief of the Forest Service, right?" she asked.

Buzz nodded.

"And we've determined the place my brother circled on the 1905 map of the territory of New Mexico was located in what is now the Gila National Forest, correct?"

They all nodded.

She paused for a minute to think. Then she pointed a finger at Director Fox and demanded, "When was the Gila National Forest created?"

"I don't know, but I can find out." Fox opened his laptop and quickly connected to the Internet. Less than a minute later, he had his answer.

He read aloud from the U.S. Forest Service's website, "The Gila was first established as a Forest *Reserve* in 1899." He looked up at Kate who seemed a bit crestfallen that the dates didn't match up. He continued, "*But*, by special proclamation—Proclamation 582 to be exact—signed by President Roosevelt himself, the Gila Forest Reserve was expanded by more than 200,000 acres in July 1905." He paused briefly and looked at Kate impressed. "You think there's a connection, don't you?"

"There has to be," she said, her heart pounding. "Is there a map on the website that shows where the Gila Forest was expanded?"

Fox scrolled down the page. "There is," he said, smiling. He turned his laptop so she could see the screen.

"What the hell are you two talking about?" Matt said, looking confused.

"Don't you see," Kate said excitedly, "the expanded territory authorized by Roosevelt is exactly the same area circled on my brother's map."

Catching on at last, Matt said, "But that would mean..."

She finished the sentence for him, "That would mean Roosevelt knew about Geronimo's Gold. And he purposely expanded the Gila National Forest to hide it."

The room went silent as everyone absorbed Kate's hypothesis. It was too much of a coincidence not to be true.

"But why...I mean how the hell did the president of the United States find out about Geronimo's Gold?" Matt asked.

No one had an answer to that question. Then, out of nowhere, Buzz blurted out, "I'm an idiot."

"Tell me something I don't know," Matt cracked.

Buzz smacked his forehead with his palm, then ran a hand through the stubble of his closely shaven steel-gray hair. He had worn it in a crew cut since his enlistment in the navy fifty years earlier.

"What's the matter, Buzz?" Kate asked, ignoring Matt's sarcasm.

"Roosevelt's inauguration," Buzz exclaimed, "Geronimo was there."

"Wait a minute," Matt said, indignant, "I thought Fox said he was being held as a prisoner of war at Fort Sill in Oklahoma?"

"He was, but there was an old black-and-white photo I came across when I was brushing up on my Roosevelt history. It was a remarkable picture of five or six Indian chiefs riding in full regalia in Roosevelt's inaugural parade," Buzz said. He struggled to recall the picture. "I'm almost positive Geronimo was one of them." He looked over to Fox for help. "Can you search around on that thing again"—pointing to the laptop—"and see what you can find out?"

Fox reached for his laptop.

"Okay," he said a minute later, "you were right, boss. Geronimo did ride on horseback with five other famous Indian chiefs in Roosevelt's inaugural parade on March 4, 1905." He beamed.

"Why?" Matt asked.

"According to this article," Fox answered, "Roosevelt invited the six Indian warriors to his inauguration to prove to the American people that Indians were being appropriately *Americanized* and were no longer a threat." He paused. "And apparently he also wanted to put on a good show."

"Sounds like TR," Buzz interjected.

"I'll be damned." Matt shook his head in amazement.

"Wait," Fox said, "here's the best part. It says here Geronimo had a private audience with the president later in the week at the White House. Nobody knew what the two men discussed but apparently Geronimo emerged from the meeting in an *agitated state.*"

"Well, young lady," Buzz said and winked at Kate, "I think we just discovered how President Roosevelt found out about Geronimo's Gold."

Matt got up and began pacing around the room. "Alright, so let's recap," he said. His mind was racing to reconcile the latest facts. "In March 1905 Geronimo told the president about the gold he found. A month later, Roosevelt created the National Forest Service and named his trusted friend Henry Benson to be its first chief. And finally, in July he expanded the Gila National Forest by an additional 200,000 acres."

"That about sums it up, counselor," Buzz quipped.

"Son of a bitch, Kate was right. Roosevelt was trying to keep Geronimo's Gold hidden," Matt said excitedly. Then he added, "What I don't understand is what was so threatening about the gold that the president of the United States expanded a national park to keep it a secret?"

"And not to beat a dead horse, but how the hell is it connected to the present-day conspiracy?" Buzz asked.

The room fell silent until Kate added somberly, "And why would someone kill my brother to prevent him from finding it?"

17

June 1905

Oyster Bay, Long Island, NY

The shingle-style, Queen Anne home known as Sagamore Hill was completed in 1884. In the summer of 1905, it was also known as President Theodore Roosevelt's Summer White House. Located about twenty-five miles east of Manhattan on the North Shore of Long Island, the twenty-three-room rambling Victorian home stood atop a small bluff that overlooked forest, farmland, and a tidal salt marsh. It was Roosevelt's favorite place on earth.

From late June until mid-September the president ran the country from his study on the first floor. A phone had been installed a couple of years earlier so he no longer had to ride his horse into town to take important calls at the local drugstore. And if senators, businessmen, or foreign dignitaries wanted an audience with the president of the United States during the summer months, they had to take the train out to Oyster Bay.

When visitors got to Sagamore Hill, their meetings with Roosevelt were oftentimes cut short so he could rollick outside with his five younger children from his second marriage. This was his playground. Whether he was exploring, boating, picnicking, hiking, or running obstacle courses, the president never tired. And when he wasn't romping with his children, he was pitching in with summer-haying, tree-chopping, and a host of other physically demanding chores that were required to maintain the one-hundred-fifty-five-acre property and working farm.

Roosevelt was alone in his library study when a member of his executive staff escorted in his afternoon guest. The president removed his ever-present pince-nez glasses from the bridge of his nose and bounded out of his chair to greet him.

"W.H.," the president exclaimed in a somewhat high-pitched voice that didn't quite match the barrel-chested, thick-necked bear of a man. Jack, the president's beloved smooth-haired Manchester terrier, tore out from under Roosevelt's desk, startled by the sudden burst of energy from his master.

"Mr. President," W.H. Sinclair replied, extending a bony hand, "it's good to see you again, sir."

Roosevelt grinned broadly, brandishing his famous and formidable teeth. He squeezed Sinclair's hand while at the same time pulling him back toward the door he had just entered. "Come, W.H., I must show you my new room," Roosevelt practically squealed with delight. Sinclair, who was ten years older and forty pounds lighter than Roosevelt, had little choice but to follow him, lest his shoulder be pulled from its socket.

At a pace that for most men would be considered a jog, the president stomped his way into the latest addition to his Sagamore Hill home—a chamber dubbed simply the North Room. But there was nothing simple about it. It was an impressive thirty-by-forty, two-story room with walls and ceilings paneled in rich mahogany and assorted exotic woods. But it was the animal trophies that were designed to catch the eye of visitors. Stuffed buffalo, elk, and bear heads adorned the walls, all bagged by the president himself. There were also paintings and sculptures of a multitude of wildlife as well as a number of animal skins strewn across the floorboards. The overall intended effect, as per

Roosevelt's wishes, was to bring the outdoors in.

Perhaps the favorite keepsake of all, however, for Roosevelt was the saber and cavalry hat from his time as the leader of the Rough Riders during the Spanish-American War. They decorated an elk head on a far wall.

"Magnificent, isn't it?" Roosevelt beamed. "Now then, W.H., please sit so we can discuss the matter at hand." He motioned for Sinclair to join him at a round, oversized game table in the center of the room.

"Something has come up for which I'd appreciate your counsel," Roosevelt began.

W.H. Sinclair was a wealthy industrialist who had made his fortune in the railroads. Like the president, Sinclair had overcome much in his life and achieved great success. They had lived only a few blocks from one another in Manhattan as children. Both had been sickly, weak-sighted, and frail. Whereas Roosevelt had chosen a political path to fame and success, Sinclair had chosen business. And he had surpassed even his own expectations. He presently owned four railroad companies and had a net worth approaching one hundred million dollars.

Even though Roosevelt was a progressive reformer and often found himself at odds with wealthy industrialists, he was also a pragmatist. Like any politician he relied on campaign financing from rich friends and acquaintances. And Sinclair, the railroad baron, had been one of the biggest donors to Roosevelt's 1904 presidential reelection campaign. In return, Sinclair fully expected to secure certain favors and political appointments of men aligned with his business interests.

While they didn't see eye to eye on everything, Roosevelt respected Sinclair's work ethic, drive, and most of all, his knowledge as it related to financial matters. Over the years, Roosevelt had not hesitated to consult with him on a number of financial and economic questions. Sinclair was also no neophyte when it came to politics, which is why Roosevelt had beckoned him to Sagamore Hill that day.

Roosevelt began by telling Sinclair about his serendipitous White House meeting with Geronimo earlier that spring. He went on to reveal to him the secret of Geronimo's Gold and the claim by the one-time U.S. government nemesis that the deposit was of an enormous size.

"Fascinating," Sinclair responded, twisting one end of his gray walrus mustache with his thumb and index finger.

"And potentially disastrous for the new gold standard," Roosevelt replied gruffly.

Roosevelt's comment pertained to the Gold Standard Act signed into law by his predecessor President William McKinley just five years earlier. The new act had established gold as the only standard for redeeming paper money. The passage of the act had ended a bitter, decade-long political debate over the relative value of gold and silver— and which of the two precious metals should be preferred over the other in the U.S. monetary system.

"Ah, I see," said Sinclair, nodding, "you're afraid the discovery of a gold deposit of this size would allow the 'silverists' to reopen the gold standard debate."

"Exactly, and the last thing I need right now is the distraction of another blasted 'Cross of Gold' speech," Roosevelt scoffed.

Roosevelt was referring to an impassioned speech at the 1896 Democratic National Convention by then presidential nominee William Jennings Bryan. Leading up to that speech, in the 1880s and 1890s, crop prices had decreased, creating great hardship for farmers. Pro-silver advocates and populists had argued for an increase in the money supply through the reintroduction of silver, which was more plentiful than gold, to make it easier for farmers to gain access to capital.

East Coast bankers, who represented the wealthy elite and wanted to protect against inflation, favored the gold standard. Tying the money supply to silver made the bankers very nervous because silver was being discovered much more often than gold. Constant infusions of silver into the market would only cause inflationary pressure, they argued—as the money supply would have to be expanded to keep pace with new silver discoveries. And inflation was a very bad thing for bankers because it meant the value of their outstanding loans was reduced. They preferred the gold standard because gold was much less plentiful and thus considered more valuable.

Running on a pro-gold standard platform, McKinley eventually defeated Bryan, clearing the way for the passage of the Gold Standard Act. But Bryan had created quite a stir with his rousing speech.

"I agree," Sinclair said. "Our party argued vociferously for the gold standard because we believed in the scarcity of gold. If a discovery on the scale of this so-called Geronimo's Gold deposit were to become public, it would cause price levels to become very unstable—and perhaps even throw our economy into another recession. That's exactly what happened after the gold discoveries in California in the 1850s."

"Well, I'll be goddamned if I'm going to let that happen on my watch," Roosevelt replied as he slammed his fist down on the game table. Cribbage pegs inside a carved ivory elephant tusk became dislodged from their holes and scattered onto the floor. "That is exactly why I sent my new chief of the U.S. Forest Service down to New Mexico to find Geronimo's Gold. As a matter of fact, he's there as we speak."

"And what will he do when he finds it?"

"He's going to record its exact location and report directly back to me. Then we'll need to devise a plan to keep it hidden," Roosevelt replied.

A look of alarm suddenly crossed Sinclair's face. "How many other people know about Geronimo's Gold?" he asked anxiously.

Seeing the railroad baron's concern, Roosevelt said, "Calm down, W.H., nobody else knows about this but you, me, and Henry Benson."

"Good, you must keep it that way," Sinclair replied.

"I fully intend to," Roosevelt declared.

An hour later, the two men had still not moved from the table. Sinclair sat staring at the map of the territory of New Mexico that Roosevelt had laid out in front of them. Subsequent to his meeting with Geronimo, Roosevelt had circled the location where the old Indian told him the gold was located. Sinclair noticed that according to Geronimo the gold was located just outside of the current boundaries of the Gila Forest Reserve. A simple but elegant solution suddenly occurred to him.

"Why not just expand the boundaries of the Gila Forest Reserve to include the spot where the gold is believed to be deposited?" Sinclair suggested.

It took Roosevelt only a moment to absorb the idea.

"That's brilliant!" he boomed excitedly. "It will ensure the site remains free of development and settlement, which will prevent anyone from discovering the gold deposit."

"Can you do it unilaterally?" Sinclair asked.

"Believe me; I can make it happen," Roosevelt said confidently. "I'll issue a special proclamation. And once I've expanded the boundaries, I'll transfer oversight of the Gila Forest Reserve to Henry Benson." It was only two months earlier that Roosevelt had created the U.S. Forest Service and appointed Henry Benson as the agency's first chief.

"And then what?" Sinclair asked.

"Then I'll order him to make sure nobody ever gets within spitting distance of that gold," Roosevelt replied with a sly smile, "assuming, of course, it's there at all."

18

Present Day
Washington, D.C.

Matt still couldn't get over the fact that Geronimo had once had a private meeting with Theodore Roosevelt. It was one of those odd historical concurrences that never ceased to amaze him. He was sure, outside of a few historians, nobody would ever guess the fierce Indian warrior, who had once been the most wanted man in the country, had been an invited guest in the White House. And he was equally certain even the most well-informed historians had no idea the two men had discussed a secret cache of gold.

Matt, Buzz, and Kate had just returned from lunch. Director Fox stayed behind to catch up on some paperwork. Their discovery of the meeting between Geronimo and Roosevelt had made for a productive morning. They were all convinced it was during this private meeting in the White House that Roosevelt had found out about Geronimo's Gold. It was simply too coincidental that the Gila National Forest was expanded shortly afterward. At least they now knew where the map Adam discovered had originated. And that Geronimo's Gold was real, or at least Roosevelt believed it to be. And that was progress.

But this revelation had only led to more questions. Not the least of which was where the hell had Adam gotten the map? Matt could hear Becker's words ringing in his head: "If you can connect enough loose ends it eventually leads you to the truth." Matt hoped that would be the case this time.

When they got back to Buzz's office, there was an urgent message waiting for them to rejoin Director Fox in the clean room. They hurried down to the basement level of Anderson House and into the small lab attached to the society's manuscript department. Director Fox was retrieving some documents from the printer when they walked in.

"Come in, come in," he said excitedly. "I had an idea while you were out to lunch so I came back down here to follow up on it."

"What is it, James?" Kate asked.

"I just printed off the results of the eraser test I ran so you could see for yourself. I already ran it once but I wanted to double-check," he said.

"Eraser test?" Matt said, baffled.

Fox explained, "Sorry. You see, after you left I got to thinking about why the name and date had been erased from the back of the map. Obviously I couldn't answer that question, but it did lead me to another question—when was it erased. And that one I could answer."

"Go on," Buzz prodded.

"I know from past experience with documents here at the society, erasers leave behind detectable amounts of eraser material in the paper. I did a little research online and found out older erasers, like the kind used during Roosevelt's time, were made mostly from natural rubber," he explained. "But modern erasers are made mostly from either a synthetic rubber compound or from vinyl."

"So you tested the rubber residue from the back of the map to find out if the writing had been erased recently or back in Roosevelt's day," Buzz remarked, impressed. "Damn, and to think my biggest accomplishment in the last two hours was to substitute a house salad for fries," he joked.

"So what did you find out?" Kate asked anxiously.

"Here," Fox said, handing her the printed pages, "see for yourself."

Kate scanned the computer printout. "I'm not sure what I'm looking for here, James," she said. "What is styrene-butadiene rubber?"

"That's the chemical that makes up the most common form of modern synthetic rubber," he answered.

"So it was erased recently," Matt stated.

"It was, and based on the thickness and color of the residue, I'd say *very* recently," Fox replied.

"Wow," Kate said, "you're brilliant, James. I would have never thought of that. But why would someone want to erase Henry Benson's name from the back of the map?" Kate asked the group.

Matt had been thinking along those same lines. And he believed he had the answer. "Someone was trying to cover their tracks. Benson's name was erased to protect the source of the map, or to prevent someone else from finding the source of the map," he posited.

Fox smiled. "That's exactly what I thought."

"Wait a minute," Kate interrupted, "you're implying Adam was hiding the identity of the person who gave him the map. But I assume Henry Benson has been dead for a long time by now."

"That's true, he died in 1952 to be exact," Fox confirmed.

Now it was Matt's turn to smile, because it was clear Fox had already done his homework on Henry Benson. "But Mr. Benson had children and most likely grandchildren, too, right James?"

"Alright you two geniuses," Buzz spoke up, "would one of you care to dumb it down a little so an old warhorse like me can follow?"

"Matt is right on the money," Fox answered his boss. "Henry Benson has a granddaughter living in Virginia. My guess is she ended up with her grandfather's personal papers—one of which was the map. Somehow Adam must have found out about its existence and paid her a visit."

"That's quite a leap, don't you think?" Buzz countered.

"Maybe, but it would sure explain a lot," Fox said.

"I don't think it's a leap. I think that's exactly what happened," Matt said, satisfied they had solved the mystery of where Adam had obtained the map. Another loose end had been tracked down.

"You said she lives in Virginia?" Kate asked.

"Yes, not more than an hour from here," Fox replied.

"If this is where your brother got the map, then maybe she's got more information she can share with us," Matt said hopefully.

"You think she'll talk to us?" Kate asked.

"Only one way to find out," Matt said.

"I'm guessing there's a road trip in my future," Buzz mumbled as they filed out the door.

19

Present Day

New York, NY

Built in 1929 by the grandfather of Jacqueline Kennedy Onassis, 740 Park Avenue was considered the most luxurious residential building in New York City. An Art Deco–style structure, the seventeen-story building was home to some of the most powerful financiers in the country. The last apartment that came on the market a few years back sold for a reported seventy million dollars. In the 1930s the building was home to John D. Rockefeller Jr., son of the one-time richest man in America. And for the last thirty years it had been home to Samuel Rothstein, a man who hoped to one day match Rockefeller's acclaim as the ultimate capitalist of his era.

Rothstein had purchased his triplex back in the late 1980s when prices were only a fraction of what they were now. It was one of the few assets he was able to hang on to during his notorious stint in prison. Nonetheless, he still received condescending glares from some of the older blue-blood residents. They believed his presence tarnished their carefully guarded personas as members of New York's reputable elite. But his neighbors' petty snubs meant nothing to Rothstein. In fact, he relished rubbing their noses in his lifestyle. Far from behaving in an understated manner, Rothstein threw lavish parties with exclusive guest lists that included the latest trending names in Manhattan—from beautiful starlets to professional athletes to power brokers. Tonight, however, the guest list had just one name on it—Carl Lynch.

Lynch was a veteran of the political arena, holding elected office both on the state level and as a member of the U.S. Senate, representing the state of Texas. He had won his senate seat running as a Republican. Since that time, however, he had switched his allegiance to the Libertarian Party, for whom he had run once already for president of the United States. Even though his bid was unsuccessful, he gained widespread fame for his meteoric style and controversial views.

He was a fiery orator who battled regularly with Democrats and Republicans, and a favorite of the press because of his willingness to grant interviews and dole out incendiary quotes. For better or worse, he had become the face of the Libertarian Party. And once again he had announced he would be running for the highest office in the land in the next presidential election.

The two men sat sipping their twenty-year-old Scotch whiskies in the pine-paneled library of Rothstein's cavernous twenty-thousand-square-foot, thirty-two-room apartment. The pine boards lining the library had been repurposed from a nineteenth century barn in upstate New York. It was all part of an eight-million-dollar redecorating effort his third wife, a well-known Manhattan socialite, had recently undertaken. It had included, among other excessive perks, the installation of his-and-her saunas, custom-made marble flooring flown in from Italy, and even a special servants' quarters. By most people's standards the cost of the overhaul would have been considered a fortune. For Rothstein it was pocket change. But he had his eye on more—a lot more—which accounted for Carl Lynch's presence that evening.

"So, Mr. Lynch, let me cut to the chase. I like you and I agree with most of your views, so I'm prepared to offer my substantial financial backing to your campaign for president," Rothstein said tantalizingly.

"That's what I was hoping to hear, Sam," Lynch enthused. "And please, call me Carl. If I'm going to fleece you for a few million dollars, at least we should be on a first-name basis." He threw the presumptuous figure out as a test balloon. Lynch was a veteran of soliciting high-wealth donors for contributions so he knew how to play the game. Aim high in hopes of settling on a figure you can live with.

"A few million, huh, is that all you're after?" Rothstein countered sardonically. He, too, was no stranger to negotiations.

Lynch held his hands up. "Now that's just me talking before thinking," he backpedaled good-naturedly. "I'm from Texas, remember. We think big down there." He smiled greedily and countered, "What figure did you have in mind?"

Rothstein swirled the whisky around in his glass. He took a sip, appearing in no hurry to answer. He set his glass down slowly on the glass of the designer coffee table.

"What if I told you I'd be willing to donate ten million to your campaign?" Rothstein offered tantalizingly.

Lynch raised his eyebrows in surprise. "I'd say thank you," he replied quickly, "and then I'd walk my skinny ass right out the door before you told me all the conditions attached to that kind of money."

Lynch was no dummy. He knew Rothstein had something in mind. He assumed it had to be related to a change in financial regulatory policy that Rothstein's company could somehow exploit and no doubt profit handsomely from as a result. So he added, "I'm one hundred percent committed to reducing if not eliminating government interference in the financial markets. So if that's what you're after, consider it done."

Rothstein replied, "I look forward to that day, believe me." He paused for a moment. "But I'm after something a little more... sweeping than that."

"I'm listening," Lynch answered warily.

Rothstein knew he needed to tread very carefully over the next few minutes so as not to raise any suspicions. He began with a statement he knew would be received favorably by the Libertarian candidate, "It's my belief the gold standard is the only way for the U.S. to return to fiscal responsibility. Only when we require our government to have enough physical gold to back increases in the money supply will we be able to reign in the deficit spending that continues to stifle growth in this country."

"I couldn't agree more, Sam," Lynch replied eagerly. "It's what I've been saying for years. Most of my fellow legislators as well as the current administration believe the solution to all of our problems is to simply print more money. But all that's doing is mortgaging our future by running up larger and larger deficits and increasing the national debt. A return to the gold standard is the only way to provide long-term economic stability and growth, prevent inflation, and reduce the size of our bloated government. Besides, if you look historically, our economy has performed best under a gold standard."

Rothstein's statement had elicited exactly the impassioned reaction by Lynch he had intended. Now it was time to set the bait. He continued, "It's true you and others have been arguing for the gold standard for years. The problem is nobody is listening. The American public doesn't give a shit."

Lynch sat up straighter in his chair, ready to defend himself against Rothstein's affront. But before he could speak, Rothstein held up a hand and said, "We need to find a way to make them care, Carl." He paused before adding intriguingly, "I think I've got a way to get that done. And at the same time give your campaign a tremendous amount of media exposure."

The muscles in Lynch's face relaxed. A smile even played at the corners of his mouth. "As the saying goes, 'you had me at hello,' Sam."

Rothstein knew Lynch had taken the bait. Like any politician, the allure of the spotlight was a powerful enticement. "I'm sure you've heard the conspiracy rumors that there is no gold left in Fort Knox?" Rothstein began.

"Of course I've heard them. I've even made a few inquiries myself and gotten stonewalled. Which makes me think there may be some truth to those rumors," Lynch answered.

"I think so, too. In fact, I've got a highly placed source who says the government is lying about how much gold we've really got in reserve. He wouldn't tell me how much is in there, but don't you think the American public has a right to know?"

"You're damn right I do," Lynch answered quickly.

"As you said, we just can't keep printing more dollars; the balloon is going to eventually burst."

"So what's your solution? The one that would make the American public care about this situation," Lynch asked. He inched toward the edge of his seat and added, "And the one that would give my campaign all that exposure you mentioned." The desire in Lynch's eyes was unmistakable.

Rothstein had let him swim with the hook in his mouth long enough. It was time to reel him in.

"The only way to get our government to begin to act responsibly again as it relates to fiscal matters is to call them out on their gold reserve lie—*publicly*. At least it would be a start. And that is where you come in. I want you to use your access to the press to demand an official audit of the vault at Fort Knox."

"To what end? How will that make them adopt a return to the

gold standard?" Lynch asked.

"It won't, at least right away. But a sensational claim such as 'there's no gold left in Fort Knox' coming from a man running for president will sure as hell make the political talk show circuit. It will create a springboard for your real message."

"Real message?"

"Yes," Rothstein said emphatically. "Once you've put the gold debate front and center, you can begin introducing America to your three-part plan for reintroducing the gold standard as the basis for the international monetary system."

Lynch looked confused. "Uh, what three-part plan?"

"Don't worry about that. My people will help you develop one. The point is, the plan will pave the way for a return to the gold standard within four years," Rothstein said enthusiastically. "But in the near term, you'll have created an enormous public platform to gain exposure for your campaign. You'll be seen as the *only* candidate with a plan to limit our government's irresponsible practice of printing money at will; the *only* candidate with a plan to reduce our deficits; the *only* candidate leading the charge to a return to fiscal responsibility."

"The Fort Knox conspiracy thing is pretty brilliant," Lynch said, thinking aloud. "It's an attention-grabber. I'd get some headlines and the American public's attention, for sure."

Rothstein nodded but remained silent. He wanted to give Lynch some room to mull his offer over.

After a few moments, Lynch asked, "So what's in it for you?"

Rothstein had anticipated the question and had a prepared answer. "Lower deficits, lower inflation rates, and a reduced risk of recession are all good things for someone in my business," Rothstein lied through a forced smile. He wasn't about to reveal his seditious arrangement with the Chinese to Lynch now—nor would he ever.

Lynch wouldn't realize until it was too late that he had been used as a pawn in a scheme that would only benefit two parties, China and Sam Rothstein.

A week later, Rothstein was at home settling in to watch *Fox News Sunday*. He didn't normally watch the Sunday morning news programs, but today was different. Carl Lynch was scheduled to be a special guest. Rothstein walked into his study carrying a steaming-hot cappuccino. He grabbed the remote control and turned on his one-hundred-twenty-inch flat-screen television. He tuned in just in time to hear Lynch launch into an impassioned case for there being no gold in Fort Knox. The Libertarian candidate appeared to be hitting all the right notes. Rothstein had feared Lynch might come across as a conspiracy nut, but these fears were quickly alleviated. His arguments were lucid and convincing.

Lynch cited the fact the government hadn't allowed an audit of Fort Knox in more than a half-century. He claimed that since that time they had sold off most of the gold bars they once had stockpiled—including the gold being held for other nations. Why else was it going to take them eight years to fulfill Switzerland's repatriation request? he posited.

The panel ate it up. They asked him why it was important the United States have gold reserves in the first place. Lynch explained the world had once been on the gold standard and during that time each country was required to have enough gold in reserve to back their currency. Since the gold standard was abolished in 1971, the Fed had printed copious amounts of new money—causing the national debt to more than double in that time frame. Printing more greenbacks, Lynch argued, was the Fed's answer to everything, but in reality it was nothing more than an irresponsible stopgap that was eventually going to catch up to us. The massive expansion of the money supply, he concluded, had put the country at risk of significant inflation, and deeper, longer recessions in the future. This final point led into candidate Lynch's big announcement.

With a dramatic flourish, he revealed that one of the major pillars of his campaign was going to be a proposal to repeal the Federal Reserve Act and restore the gold standard. He adroitly went on to list all the benefits of such a proposal—low inflation, reduced deficits, reduced debt, stronger economic growth, and so on. But, he asserted, in order to return to the gold standard, the United States had to have enough gold in reserve to back the dollar—thus the need for an audit of Fort Knox.

One of the panelists asked what would happen if they performed the audit and there actually wasn't any gold left in Fort Knox. Lynch answered that at least the American people would finally know the truth. And if that were the case, he would make it his personal mission to replenish the country's gold reserves as quickly as possible.

As Rothstein turned the television off, he had to chuckle. The fool Lynch had no idea by that time it would be too late for the United States to replenish their reserves of gold.

20

Present Day
Leesburg, Virginia

The town of Leesburg changed hands so many times during the Civil War the locals lost count. Both the Union and Confederate armies had traversed the area during the Maryland and Gettysburg campaigns. The town was even occupied by Robert E. Lee for a time. And for the last seventy-five years it had been home to Charlotte Benson, granddaughter of Henry Benson, the first chief of the U.S. Forest Service.

Even at the age of seventy-five, Lottie, as she was known to her friends, was a handsome woman. Her high cheekbones, soft blue eyes, and gray hair swept high into a stylish updo gave her an almost regal bearing. But Lottie's disposition was far from queenly. In fact, she was as salt-of-the-earth as they came. She had been considered quite beautiful as a teenager and had more than her share of suitors. But she had grown up a tomboy, the son her father never had. Given the choice back then, she usually chose camping or fishing over getting dressed up for the local dance hall.

Today, she lived on a beautiful tract of land abutting the Potomac River about fifty miles northwest of Washington, D.C. She had married the love of her life at the age of twenty-one. But after a few short years of marriage, and before she had the chance to have any children, her husband became one of the first casualties of the Vietnam War. His death devastated her and she never married again. She had been involved in a few relationships over the years, but could never rekindle the same passion she shared with her husband. But that hadn't prevented her from living a full and productive life. Like her grandfather before her, she loved the outdoors and had been involved in local conservation efforts for years. She was well-known and very well liked in the community.

It was early afternoon and Lottie was sitting in her small but comfortable stone cottage in the woods when the doorbell rang. She was expecting visitors from the Society of the Cincinnati who had called her the day before. They wanted to ask her some questions about her grandfather. She was only too happy to pass along her remembrances of him. She had done so on many occasions, granting interviews to various reporters and authors over the years. She prepared iced tea and insisted they sit in her sunroom overlooking the back woods. As if on cue, a doe and three fawns scampered past the picture window just as they sat down.

After introductions were made and pleasantries exchanged, Matt gave Kate a quick nod. She cleared her throat, "Lottie," she began. Lottie had insisted they call her by her nickname. "I think my brother might have come to visit you a while back. His name was Adam Hampton." She waited.

Lottie cocked her head to one side. "I have lots of visitors, dear. Was he doing research about my grandfather's job as chief of the Forest Service?" she said.

"In a way, yes, but he wasn't an author," she said. She reached into her bag and pulled out the old map of New Mexico. "Did you by any chance give him this?" She held it up for Lottie to see.

Matt noticed a glimmer of recognition pass over Lottie's face.

But an instant later it was replaced with a look of suspicion. "Where did you get that?" she asked hesitantly, placing her glass of iced tea on the table beside her.

Kate's nerves got the best of her. "Lottie, my brother is dead," she blurted out. "He was struck and killed by a subway train."

Lottie put a hand to her mouth in shock.

Kate continued, "The police sent me personal items he was carrying with him that night. And this map was in his suit pocket." Tears welled up in Kate's eyes. She thought enough time had passed that she could keep her emotions in check. But the thought she could be sitting in the same room Adam had been sitting in just a few months earlier had brought back the jarring reality of his loss.

"Oh, you poor girl, that's awful," Lottie gasped, "I'm so sorry."

Matt reached over and squeezed Kate's hand. Then he looked back at Lottie. "Adam *did* come here to see you, didn't he?" he asked quietly.

"Yes," she admitted, "and he was such a nice young man, too. But so serious for someone his age."

"Can I ask what you mean by that?" Matt asked.

"Well, there was a real sense of purpose about him. He seemed to think finding that gold was *very* important, but not for the reasons you might think," she replied.

Buzz jumped in and asked, "You mean he already knew about Geronimo's Gold when he came to see you?"

"Oh yes. But he didn't seem like one of those greedy treasure hunters," she said with a look of disdain. "In fact, the only reason I gave him granddaddy's map was because I believed what he told me."

"What did he tell you?" Kate asked, suddenly wanting to hear everything they had talked about. She found herself wondering what Adam had been wearing that day; if Lottie had fixed him iced tea; if he had been sitting in the same chair she now occupied. As if the answers to these questions could somehow bring a piece of him back to her.

Lottie could see the pain on Kate's face. She knew what losing a loved one felt like. She replied empathetically, "He said his reasons for needing to find Geronimo's Gold were a...what was the expression he used...oh yes, a matter of 'national security' he called it."

Buzz and Matt exchanged a puzzled look.

Lottie caught the exchange and added, "I wasn't quite sure what he meant by that either, and frankly, I didn't want to know. He seemed nervous. You might even say scared. But he was also very earnest and that made me trust him."

"Did Adam know you had the map?" Buzz asked.

"Oh heavens, no, how could he? I was the only person on earth who knew about it. But the minute your brother inquired about Geronimo's Gold I knew exactly what he was talking about. I came across that map years ago," she said as she pointed at the old map of New Mexico lying on the table. "It was in my grandfather's dusty old files. I had always wondered what Geronimo's Gold meant. But as time passed I forgot all about it."

The room fell silent. Buzz took a sip of his iced tea. Kate stared at the sun filtering through the foliage outside, lost in her own thoughts. Matt decided it was time to find out what exactly Lottie knew. He was desperate to find out if she could provide any insight as to the whereabouts of Geronimo's Gold.

"Lottie, we have a theory we'd like to share with you," he began.

He told her the story of Geronimo's visit to the White House and how it coincided with her grandfather's appointment as the first chief of the newly created U.S. Forest Service. He then shared their belief that it was at this meeting Geronimo told President Roosevelt about the secret gold deposit he had discovered in the mountains of Southwest New Mexico, and that Roosevelt shortly thereafter expanded the Gila National Forest in order to hide it.

"So you see, Lottie, if our hypothesis is correct, your grandfather knew about Roosevelt's cover-up," Matt concluded. "And we think the fact he possessed this map proves it."

"Perhaps they just wanted to protect the land," Lottie said defensively. "From my understanding, gold mining is a dirty business. The land is literally stripped bare to get to the gold," she said with a look of disgust. "My grandfather devoted his life to the cause of conservation, so I wouldn't be surprised in the least if he were in favor of expanding the Gila National Forest to prevent it from being overrun by men and machinery," she said defiantly.

Buzz and Matt exchanged glances again. They both knew Roosevelt's reasons for covering up Geronimo's Gold were tied to something more than simple conservation. But they also knew accusing Lottie's grandfather would get them nowhere.

"Perhaps you're right," Buzz allowed before changing the subject. "Did you get to spend much time with your grandfather?" he asked in a more conversational tone.

The lighter touch seemed to work as Lottie's demeanor changed instantly. "Oh yes, as a little girl we'd go for long walks in the woods—right out here, as a matter of fact"—she pointed outside—"and he'd tell me all sorts of wonderful stories."

"Sounds a lot like my grandfather," Buzz said. "Only he'd take me flying. He was a barnstormer back in the '20s. He had amazing stories about his time in the flying circus as a stunt pilot. They'd travel from town to town performing midair tricks—barrel rolls, wing-walking, loop-the-loops, the whole nine yards." Buzz chuckled. "They'd pay a local farmer to use his field as a runway and charge the townspeople admission."

"He sounds wonderful," Lottie beamed.

"He was; he's the reason I joined the navy and became a pilot myself," Buzz answered wistfully.

"I wish I had the chance to spend more time with Granddad,"

Lottie said. "I was only twelve when he died. But he had been stricken with Alzheimer's for a number of years prior to his death."

"And he never mentioned Geronimo's Gold?" Buzz took one more opportunity to probe.

Lottie looked down and shook her head from side to side.

Buzz turned to Matt with a look that implied they probably weren't going to get any more information from Lottie. Especially since her grandfather's mind had been compromised at the end.

"Well, we've taken enough of your time," Buzz said. He stood up to leave. Matt stood up, too.

Kate, who had been staring out the window in a daze for some time, didn't make a move to leave. Instead she said, "We weren't totally honest with you, Lottie. You were right about Adam, he was scared." A look of grim determination had replaced the sadness in her eyes. "And it turned out he had reason to be."

"I'm not sure what you mean, dear," Lottie replied in confusion.

"My brother was *murdered*, Lottie. He was pushed in front of that subway train," Kate stated bluntly. She made no attempt to sugarcoat what she firmly believed to be the truth.

Matt and Buzz stood frozen in place, mouths agape, waiting to see how Lottie would react.

"Oh dear Lord!" Lottie exclaimed, her face turning a shade paler. "And you think my grandfather's map had something to do with your brother's murder?" She was horrified at the thought she might have unknowingly contributed to Adam's death by giving him the map.

"No, Lottie," Kate said reassuringly, "Adam had uncovered a conspiracy and he was attempting to expose the men behind it. The map you gave him was just another lead he was pursuing. But we do think Geronimo's Gold could be the key to this whole thing. So we came here today hoping you might be able to tell us something about it, even the smallest anecdote your grandfather might have shared with you." Kate's tone was desperate, almost pleading. She looked completely wrung out.

"What kind of person would do such a thing to another human being?" Lottie said quietly. She was thinking about the ruthless manner in which Adam had been murdered.

"We don't know," Matt said, "but we're trying our best to find out."

"You poor thing," Lottie said as she walked over and wrapped Kate in a maternal embrace.

A moment later, she backed away from Kate as another thought entered her mind. "If these people killed once then they'll kill again if they think someone else is getting too close, right?" Without waiting for an answer she turned and looked out the window, scouting the tree line. "And all of this over some silly story about Geronimo's Gold? It's so absurd."

She stood staring out the window mulling over what to do. Then all at once, she made up her mind. "I refuse to put anyone else in danger," she said resolutely. "I think it's time you folks were on your way."

"Lottie," Matt said reassuringly, "you can't put us in any more danger than we're already in." He pleaded, "Please, help us. The only way Adam's killers will be brought to justice is if we can find them. Nobody else is going to do it."

"What about the police?" she croaked.

"The police think Adam committed suicide. They're not going to investigate a murder if they don't think a crime has been committed."

Lottie walked to an overstuffed chair and sat down heavily. The room fell silent. Everyone held their breath waiting to see what she would do next.

Seconds stretched to minutes. Still nobody moved or spoke. The room was still except for a wicker ceiling fan that clicked rhythmically as it stirred the warm sunroom air above their heads. A grandfather clock, unnoticed until then, tick-tocked loudly in the corner.

Finally, Lottie looked up at Buzz and cleared her throat to say, "You asked me earlier if my grandfather ever mentioned Geronimo's Gold."

Buzz nodded.

"Well...the truth is...he did."

She had their full attention now.

As she spoke, her soft blue eyes shone with renewed intensity. "I'm going to tell you something I've never told anyone else in my life."

She took a sip of iced tea to wet her mouth. "After he was stricken with Alzheimer's, granddaddy didn't even recognize me," she said very quietly. "But I'd sit with him anyway, just to keep him company." Her mind raced back to a time more than sixty years earlier. "I never wanted to talk about it because he was such a proud man. I didn't want to diminish his legacy."

She paused yet again. They waited patiently. "It's funny how you remember some things," she said with a wan smile.

"He'd sometimes ramble on incoherently," she finally revealed.

"He had this riddle he'd repeat over and over again, in a childlike, sing-song voice," Lottie said before mimicking her grandfather, *"Don't dwell on Geronimo's Gold. It's under the nose of the Indian I'm told."*

She repeated the rhyme, *"Don't dwell on Geronimo's Gold. It's under the nose of the Indian I'm told."*

When they left Lottie's gracious home, Matt, Buzz, and Kate had no idea they were being watched by a man hidden in the woods with high-powered binoculars and a long-range directional listening device. He had heard every word that had been spoken. The minute they got in their car and pulled out of Lottie's driveway, the man reported the meeting he had just witnessed to his boss in New York City.

21

June 1905

Somewhere in the Gila Forest Reserve

By the time he stepped off the steam-powered passenger train in Silver City, New Mexico, Henry Benson had been traveling for more than a week. Silver City had been founded as a mining town in 1870 shortly after the discovery of silver ore deposits nearby. The Atchison, Topeka & Santa Fe Railway had extended standard gauge rail service to the town in 1886 after a smelter had been constructed there. Like most boomtowns around the turn of the century, Silver City had had its share of violence. In the mid 1870s, the soon-to-be-notorious criminal Billy the Kid had even roamed its streets for a time. It was here, in fact, he had his very first run-in with the law, being arrested twice for theft. Over the next few years, Billy would purportedly go on to murder more than a dozen men.

Henry Benson's cross-country trip from the nation's capital was made slightly longer due to a planned stop along the way. He had diverted from his route two states earlier so he could pay a visit to a man being held as a prisoner of war at Fort Sill, Oklahoma. He had come to see Geronimo to personally deliver a message from the president. Benson told Geronimo that Roosevelt was seriously considering his offer but before he could agree to it, he needed to verify the gold's existence. Benson disclosed he had been sent to New Mexico on behalf of the president to do just that. Geronimo was delighted. He sprang to his feet and quickly offered to accompany Benson back to his homeland. He insisted he could show him the exact location of the gold deposit.

Roosevelt and Benson had anticipated such a response—but they had no intention of allowing Geronimo to leave his confinement at Fort Sill. So Benson lied. He told Geronimo if he went back to his native land he'd very likely find a rope awaiting him; that there were still a great many people in the territory spoiling for a chance to kill him. Geronimo brushed aside these concerns insisting he was not afraid, but Benson stood firm. The elderly Chiricahua warrior would not be allowed to make the trip.

Benson insisted, however, that Geronimo provide him specific details as to the location of the gold. That way, he could find it and verify its existence for the president. Only then, he maintained, would Geronimo be given his freedom and be allowed to return to the mountains of New Mexico. Geronimo suspected it was a trap but he had nothing with which to bargain. And he was desperate not to live out his final years as a captive at Fort Sill. After much deliberation, he finally shared critical details regarding the location of Geronimo's Gold with Henry Benson, chief of the U.S. Forest Service. He had no idea it would be the last time he would ever speak to Benson or Roosevelt again.

The violent crime rate had abated considerably by the time Benson arrived in Silver City. Even so, the rugged western town was quite a contrast to what the East Coast, Yale-educated man was accustomed. The brand-new Palace Hotel was the only establishment in town that offered modern conveniences such as closets, bathrooms, and electric lights. After checking in, Benson took advantage of another modern amenity the hotel provided—a telegraph. He wired President Roosevelt he had arrived safely and had secured the necessary information from Geronimo. All was going according to plan. A guide who knew the Mogollon Mountains well was waiting for him. They would be leaving the following morning on horseback into the rugged backcountry of Geronimo's youth. The guide knew nothing about the gold; only that Benson was there to survey land for the government. Once there, however, Benson would dismiss the guide so he could search for the gold alone. He was an experienced outdoorsman and was confident he could find his way back to Silver City once the mission was accomplished.

After a day and a half of painstaking travel on horseback, the two men reached the area believed to be near where Geronimo had spent his childhood. Along the way they passed ancient cliff dwellings that had become popular after being discovered only a couple of decades earlier. The cliffs contained the ruins of interlinked cave dwellings built in alcoves by the ancient Mogollon peoples near the end of the thirteenth century. They were in an area surrounded by steep-sided bluffs and deep ravines. It wasn't long after sighting the cliffs that Benson dismissed his guide. Based on the information Geronimo had supplied him, he knew he was within no more than a half-day's ride of his ultimate destination.

Benson spent the next two days searching in earnest for Geronimo's Gold. After doubling back for yet a third time he was beginning to wonder if the information the old Indian had given him was correct. Geronimo was in his eighties by then and Benson questioned if his memory might not have become clouded. Or perhaps the shrewd schemer was up to his old tricks once more. The terrain was so rugged and the forest so dense, at times Benson became disoriented and found himself traversing the same terrain he had covered just hours earlier.

Then disaster struck. A snake spooked his horse and threw Benson from the saddle. He gave chase through the dense forest of ponderosa pine for more than a mile, but it was useless. His steed was nowhere to be found. He began to panic because he knew if he ever hoped to get back alive he had to find his horse. His rifle and supplies were strapped to her back. Without them he would be easy pickings for cougar, bobcat, or black bear that all roamed the area. Plus, it got very cold at night due to elevations that topped out at ten thousand feet. So after a brief rest, Benson resumed the search for his mount.

Hours later, exhausted, he found himself back at the fork in the river he had searched the day before. He bent down and put his lips to the icy waters. He drank thirstily. Suddenly, he felt, then heard another presence directly behind him. He had hiked and hunted enough to know the difference between an animal and a human sound. And the thing that had made that sound wasn't human. He slowly lifted his head, terrified a black bear had come to drink from the same river.

To his surprise however, he saw it was his horse. She was happily munching on a tuft of tall grass not more than twenty yards behind him. His saddle was still strapped to her back and he could see, amazingly, all his gear was intact. He was so happy he rolled over onto his back and burst into a fit of laughter. It was only then he realized just how exhausted he was after expending so much energy chasing after his horse. But his joyous relief was quickly replaced with the reality that if he didn't find Geronimo's Gold soon he would have to abort the mission.

With this depressing thought in mind, he pushed himself up onto one elbow. That's when he looked up and noticed something in the rocky cliff he hadn't noticed the first time he passed through the area. Perhaps it was the angle of the late-day sun or his prone vantage point that caused him to see the surrounding terrain differently. Either way, what he spotted was exactly as Geronimo had described.

A renewed energy coursed through muscles that had ached with fatigue just moments before. He scrambled to his feet and began running. His eyes never leaving the spot he knew with absolute certainty would lead him to Geronimo's Gold.

Upon his return to Silver City, Benson immediately sent a telegram to President Roosevelt in which he shared the exact location of his find. Roosevelt couldn't have been more relieved. But he soon realized, based on Benson's information, he would have to expand the boundaries of the Gila Forest Reserve even more than he and W.H. Sinclair had initially calculated.

And that's exactly what he did.

Less than a month later, on July 21, 1905, Proclamation 582 entitled "Enlargement of the Gila Forest Reserve, New Mexico" was issued.

It stated in part, 'Now, Therefore, I, Theodore Roosevelt, President of the United States, by virtue of the power in me vested by the aforesaid acts of Congress, do hereby make known and proclaim that the Gila River Forest Reserve, in the Territory of New Mexico, established by proclamation of March second, eighteen hundred and ninety-nine, is hereby so changed and enlarged.'

The net result of the proclamation was that the Gila Forest Reserve was expanded by more than 200,000 acres. It was more than enough to encompass the location and surrounding area that was home to Geronimo's Gold.

An ominous warning toward the end of the proclamation stated: "Warning is hereby expressly given to all persons not to make settlement upon the lands reserved by this proclamation."

22

Present Day

Ruidoso, New Mexico

Matt once again found himself sitting in the copilot seat of "Air Buzz." That was the nickname he had given to retired navy commander Buzz Penberthy's 1965 Piper Comanche six-seater airplane. This was just the latest in a long line of impromptu flights the two men had taken together over the past few years. If Buzz offered a frequent flier program Matt would have earned platinum status by now. Their destination this time was the tiny resort town of Ruidoso, New Mexico.

The idea for the trip had been hatched two days before on the car ride back from Lottie Benson's cottage in the Virginia woods. Though they had confirmed that the one-hundred-year-old New Mexico map had come from Lottie's grandfather, Henry Benson, that fact hadn't put them any closer to determining the specific location of Geronimo's Gold. The only additional clue Lottie had supplied them with was the nonsensical riddle her grandfather had recited aloud in his Alzheimer's-induced fog.

They had discussed that even if they narrowed their search to the section of the Gila expanded by Roosevelt, via Proclamation

582, it still comprised hundreds of square miles. It would take years to cover that much territory. They were convinced now more than ever Geronimo's Gold was real and was buried out there somewhere. But they also knew they'd never find it unless they could come up with a way to narrow the scope of their search. That's when Matt came up with the idea of contacting Geronimo's descendants.

At the time he made the suggestion, he had no idea if Geronimo had any children let alone grandchildren. But he reasoned that if there were living descendants of the infamous warrior then perhaps they had information about Geronimo's Gold. When they got back to the Society of the Cincinnati headquarters in D.C. that afternoon, Matt immediately did some research online. It didn't take him long to find the name of a man who was the undisputed great-grandson of the famous Chiricahua warrior.

He lived near the reservation of the Mescalero Apaches in the high country town of Ruidoso, which claimed to be home to the southernmost ski resort in America. While the town only had ten thousand permanent inhabitants, thousands of tourists flocked to the slopes of the twelve-thousand-foot-high Sierra Blanca mountain each year to ski and snowboard. Gambling was another big draw. The Inn of the Mountain Gods Resort and Casino located on the Mescalero Indian Reservation was just a short drive from the slopes.

Buzz and Matt agreed this was not a conversation they wanted to have over the phone, so they decided to fly out to meet Geronimo's great-grandson in person. They claimed they wanted to interview him about an article they were writing about his famous ancestor. They would eventually tell him the truth, but they would do that face-to-face. Kate had an art show back in Manhattan, so she stayed behind.

The two men had been flying in silence for the better part of an hour when Matt suddenly blurted out, "So who recruited you?"

The unexpected sound of Matt's voice through the communications headset startled Buzz. "Jesus, son," he said, grabbing at his heart, "you don't want to do that to the guy flying the plane."

"I'm serious, Buzz, how long have you been a member of the Ring?" Matt pressed.

The initial anger Matt had felt upon first learning that the Ring had manipulated him had turned increasingly into an intense curiosity. At first he hadn't wanted to believe Buzz when he told him the Ring had played an integral role in preserving American democracy countless times over the past two centuries. His own experience, however, was more consistent with Buzz's claim. Matt had seen firsthand how they had prevented a corrupt politician from ascending to the presidency and thwarted an attempt to overthrow the U.S. government. Now he wanted to know how Buzz had gotten involved with the secretive organization.

The retired navy commander scanned the horizon in front of them for a moment before responding. "To answer your first question, the man who recruited me was an admiral in the U.S. Navy. I met him after my tours in Nam. He got me my first job in D.C. and we became good friends. It wasn't long after that he recruited me to join the cause. Christ, that would be close to forty years ago now."

"Why did you decide to join?"

Buzz chuckled. "I was outranked. When an admiral asks you to do something, you do it," he joked. "The truth is I was reluctant at first, just like you. But as I began to understand the motivation behind the Ring's unorthodox methods, I started to come around."

"Just like that?"

"No, not quite. You have to remember, it was an unsettled time back then. We had just come out of the 1960s, one of the most tumultuous times in American history. Political assassinations, the Vietnam War, the country was coming apart at the seams."

"Something must have pushed you over the edge, though. What

was the tipping point?"

Buzz understood Matt was wrestling with the same decision he himself had made forty years earlier. He decided to share a secret—one that very few people had ever heard.

He began, "The admiral I mentioned, the man who recruited me, told me a story that helped me come to the conclusion that sometimes the means justify the end, especially when the cause is a noble one."

He flicked a few switches up and down in succession and turned a few knobs on the plane's instrument panel before continuing. "You've no doubt heard the many conspiracy theories surrounding John F. Kennedy's assassination, right?"

"Of course, everything from the Mob, the Russians, the CIA, even invaders from outer space," Matt replied cynically.

"Sometimes the conspiracy theories aren't too far off," Buzz allowed.

"You're not going to tell me aliens knocked off our country's thirty-fifth president, are you?" Matt replied in jest.

"No, but the Russians did," Buzz stated matter-of-factly. "The conspiracy theorists were right about one thing: Oswald didn't act alone. He was enlisted by the Kremlin to kill Kennedy."

Matt sat in stunned silence. "How can you be so sure of that?"

"Believe me, Matt, when I tell you, the Ring was sure. The evidence they uncovered was indisputable—so much so it forced them to take extreme action."

"What do you mean?"

"I mean they had Oswald killed."

"What? But Jack Ruby killed Oswald." Matt turned fully toward Buzz, or at least as much as the cramped cockpit would allow.

Buzz said simply, "Yes he did."

Matt processed this information for a moment before replying, "The Ring put him up to it or manipulated him into doing it, didn't they?" He wiped a bead of sweat from his brow. "Shit, I remember reading the transcripts from the case against Ruby back in college. He kept insisting that the true facts would never be known because the people who put him in the position to do what he did would never let it happen. Everyone always assumed he was talking about the CIA, but you're telling me it was the Ring?"

Buzz nodded.

"Now before you judge the Ring for using Ruby to kill Oswald you need to understand why. If word ever got out that the Russians had been behind the assassination, we would have had World War III on our hands. Tensions were at their apex in 1963. We had just come off the Cuban Bay of Pigs standoff and trigger fingers on both sides were twitching. Only it wasn't rifles pointed at one other, it was nuclear warheads."

"Jesus."

"Even he couldn't have helped at the time," Buzz quipped. "The Ring ran every scenario of the world finding out that the Russians had killed our Camelot president. And they all ended in nuclear annihilation."

"So you had Oswald taken out."

"The right call given the circumstances, wouldn't you agree?"

Matt's head was swimming. He wasn't ready to agree with Buzz but he also couldn't disagree.

Buzz knew Matt well enough to read his thoughts. "Like I said, if the cause is noble, the end justifies the means. That's the conclusion I came to anyway. You'll have to make up your own mind."

He paused before adding, "When you do, the decision you've been wrestling with will have been made."

23

Present Day

Ruidoso, New Mexico

After touching down at Sierra Blanca Regional Airport located just fifteen miles northeast of town they walked toward the front door of the tiny terminal. A man approached them as they exited the building. He was built lean and sinewy like a bull rider. As he got closer, Matt noticed his penetrating hazel eyes and thinning dark hair. If Matt had to guess, he'd put him in his late fifties.

"Kenny Morgan," the man said amiably with an outstretched hand. "Are you Matt?"

"That's me," Matt said shaking his hand, "and this is Buzz."

Buzz insisted on buying Kenny dinner and he readily accepted. He told the men he knew just the place. A few minutes later, they pulled up in front of a run-down sprawling shack on the outskirts of town. The sign out front read The Wooden Indian. Matt glanced at Buzz skeptically. He was hoping Buzz had remembered his pack of Tums, because it looked like the food in this joint wasn't going down without a fight.

As they walked through the front door, however, their opinion of the place turned a hundred eighty degrees. The decor was one-third roadside Indian trading post, and two-thirds funky eatery. There must have been two dozen, six-foot tall wooden cigar store Indians scattered throughout the restaurant. Matt was very familiar with this type of advertisement figure. They were used by tobacconists beginning in the late eighteenth century and they were still being produced today. He had sold one or two in his shop over the years, but none were as nice, or as old, as these. They were exquisitely hand carved. Some even still had their colorful original paint, which was rare since they were most probably more than a hundred years old.

Kenny saw the look on Matt's face and smiled. "Pretty cool, huh?"

"Incredible," Matt answered. He stepped forward to take a closer look at one. He marveled at the artistry that went into the carved feathers atop the figure's head. "But also a little risky, especially around here," he said, referring to the location of the Mescalero Reservation nearby. "Don't the local Native Americans take offense?"

"They probably would, if the place wasn't owned by an Apache," Kenny said and smiled slyly.

"This is your place?" Matt turned around in surprise.

Kenny nodded, grinning at the irony.

"Kenny," Buzz said, chuckling, "I like your style. Let me buy you a beer."

The men found three unoccupied stools at the corner of the horseshoe-shaped bar and sat down. Kenny called one of his staff over and instructed him to bring them an order of sage-rubbed bison ribs. The appetizer was a house favorite because it was slow-cooked in the oven and finished off on the grill with a blueberry barbecue sauce. He also ordered some fry bread stuffed with shredded chicken. Kenny's mother had taught him how to flash fry dough in oil so it would be light and fluffy, not greasy. Over the years he modified the recipe by stuffing it with chicken.

As the men devoured the surprisingly sophisticated cuisine, Kenny asked how he could help them. Buzz pointed a half-eaten barbecue rib in Matt's direction and said with a wink, "Why don't you start."

Matt knew the only reason Buzz had deferred the question was so he could watch Matt squirm when he had to tell Kenny about their white lie—that they were not there to interview him for a book about Geronimo. He shook his head in amused defeat. He pointed at Buzz's lip and said, "You've got sauce on your face, wiseass."

He then turned to Kenny and explained the real reason for their visit. For some reason the man struck him as somebody he could trust. So he made an on-the-spot decision to tell him about the murder of Adam Hampton and their visit with Lottie Benson. Kenny listened to Matt's lengthy explanation without comment.

When Matt finally finished, Kenny took a long pull on his bottle of beer. "I'm not going lie, that's not what I expected to hear," he said. "I've had people come to talk to me about my great-grandfather before, but nobody's ever asked me about Geronimo's Gold."

"Wait," Matt said surprised, "you mean you've heard of it?"

Kenny looked at Matt coolly. "I didn't say that," he noted.

Buzz took a swig of beer and joined in. "No, you didn't," he replied, peering over the rim of his beer mug at Matt. Buzz thought it best to slow down so they could establish a little more rapport with their host, so he adroitly changed gears. "How many descendants of Geronimo are there, anyway?"

"A lot less than there are people who claim to be," Kenny said in disgust. "There's some debate about exactly how many wives Geronimo had or how many kids he fathered. So naturally, there are lots of pretenders out there claiming some connection to him. But they're just trying to take advantage of his famous name to make some easy money."

"Anything for a buck, I guess, right?" Buzz commiserated. Something caught his eye. "I see you like to hunt." He pointed with his beer to a slew of animal trophies mounted on the wall above the bar. "I'm assuming those are yours?"

"Yup," Kenny said. "Before he passed away, my father and I used to hunt all the time. My dad was old-school though. We only used crossbows, never rifles. He insisted it was much more challenging that way."

"Not sure that elk would agree," Buzz said with a smile.

"I noticed a donation box on the way in," Matt said, changing the subject. "Something about an after-school program?"

"Yeah," Kenny's face lit up as he explained, "it's something I started a few years back. We built a recreation center to give the kids something to do after school. We offer club sports, art programs, and other stuff. It keeps them off the streets and away from drugs and alcohol—at least some of them." He shook his head sadly. "The truth is we've helped a lot of kids stay clean but no matter how hard we try, some always slip through our hands."

Matt reached into his back pocket and pulled out his wallet. He slipped five twenty dollar bills out and laid them down on the bar. "We'd like to contribute to the cause. Consider this our way of saying thanks for seeing us today."

"Every dollar helps," Kenny said appreciatively. "So, guys, what is it you really came here to ask me today?"

Buzz looked at Matt and nodded. It was time.

Matt waved the bartender over and ordered three more Budweisers. Then he said, "After our meeting with Lottie Benson we became more convinced than ever Geronimo's Gold was real."

The bartender returned with their round of beers. Matt waited for him to leave before continuing, "The problem is we don't have enough clues to narrow down our search. You know better than we do that the Gila National Forest is enormous. Even taking into account Proclamation 582, we're still talking about hundreds of miles of rugged wilderness."

"So what do you want from me?"

"Come on, Kenny," Buzz said. He decided it was time to cut to the chase. "It was obvious when Matt mentioned Geronimo's Gold that it wasn't the first time you'd heard about it. We came here to see if you might share what you know to help us find it."

Kenny didn't answer right away. He looked back and forth between Matt and Buzz, studying their faces. Finally, he said, "Even if I did know something, why would I share it with you? So you can go and pillage my great-grandfather's cache of gold?"

They had come this far, so Matt shared the rest of the story with him. He told him about the conspiracy Adam had uncovered. And that it was their belief somehow the conspiracy involved Geronimo's Gold. He told Kenny he wasn't in this for the money, but rather he was doing it to avenge the death of his friend. At the mention of Adam Hampton's name, Matt had gotten emotional. Never one to show his emotions, he turned away embarrassed.

Kenny could see Matt's sincerity. "I'm sorry for the loss of your friend," he said. "But you've got to understand, my great-grandfather's name has been misrepresented for years and my people haven't exactly been treated fairly by the white man." Kenny's normally genial face hardened as generations of deep-seated anger bubbled to the surface.

His eyes narrowed. "How do I know you guys are who you say you are and not just a couple of treasure hunters looking to take even more of my people's possessions?"

"You don't," Buzz said evenly. "And I don't blame you one bit for being cautious. Hell, I'd have thrown our asses out of here already if I were in your shoes." He ran a calloused hand through his bristly gray hair. "But I will tell you this, Kenny. Everything we've said today is the absolute truth. We may sound crazy and we probably are, but I promise we're not bullshitting you."

Kenny's eyes never left Buzz's. After a few moments of tension, he appeared to reach a decision. "Fair enough," he said. "Hell, it's probably just a legend anyway."

Then his look softened slightly. "You were right, I have heard of Geronimo's Gold."

He took another sip of beer before saying, "My mother used to tell me stories of a magical cave of gold in the Mogollon Mountains that my great-grandfather found when he was just a boy. She said the cave literally glowed because there was so much gold inside. Gold veins the size of pack mules, she'd say." He smiled skeptically.

"According to her, Geronimo only spoke of it toward the very end of his life—and mostly after he had been drinking," he added dubiously. "We just always assumed it was something he made up, so we passed it off as Indian folklore. You have to understand, there were lots of stories about my great-grandfather—that he had supernatural powers, bullets couldn't kill him, stuff like that. I guess I always assumed the cave of gold was just another story...until you guys came along and started asking about it."

"Thanks for telling us the truth, Kenny," Buzz said.

"One truth deserves another," Kenny replied matter-of-factly.

"So there's nothing specific you can remember?" Matt asked, desperately hoping there was something that could help them.

"I'm afraid not," he said.

"Damn," Matt and Buzz said in unison.

Kenny looked intently at them and a thought occurred to him, "If you guys are thinking about going out there to track down Geronimo's Gold, I'd like to come with you," he said. "My father used to take me out to the Gila all the time. He called it the history lesson I never got in school." He smiled sadly at the memory of his deceased father. "We'd go out for weeks at a time, hiking and camping in the same mountains and valleys where Geronimo once roamed."

He continued, "The cave has to be in the vicinity of where Geronimo was born, because according to the story, he found it when he was just a boy. And nobody knows that land better than me, I can promise you that."

Buzz and Matt exchanged glances, but remained silent.

"You'll have a much better chance of finding what you're looking for with me than without me," Kenny added truthfully. "So what do you say?"

On their flight back to D.C., Buzz banked the plane to the west and flew a hundred and fifty nautical miles off their charted course. He wanted to see what they'd be up against if they decided to search for Geronimo's Gold.

As they flew over the Gila National Forest, they were simultaneously awestruck and terrified. Spread out in front of them as far as they could see was an endless sea of green. The only thing disrupting the emerald horizon was massive mountain peaks that punched through the clouds on their seemingly endless ascent.

As he steered the plane back to their original easterly direction, Buzz breathed heavily into his headset. He glanced at Matt sitting beside him and uttered just two words.

They were the same two words Matt was thinking at that exact moment: "We're fucked."

24

Present Day

Silver City, New Mexico

The sprawling two-story structure that took up an entire city block dated back to the turn of the twentieth century. After being neglected for years, the Palace Hotel had fallen into a severe state of disrepair. It was only after a painstaking restoration by its current owners that the historic building had been restored it to its former landmark prominence. The grand old hotel could at long last once again be called the showpiece of Silver City.

A pair of black-and-white King Charles spaniels sniffed curiously at Buzz's and Matt's feet as the two men checked in. Faded black-and-white photographs of a somber looking couple hung on the wall behind the registration desk tucked into the rear of a small but tidy lobby. Matt assumed them to be the original proprietors of the Palace. Their fixed-in-time gazes seemed to scrutinize the men as the day clerk handed over their room keys. Exhaustion registered in the faces captured in the grainy images. Matt had the absurd impulse to remove the gilt-framed photos from the wall and lay them face down on the floor—so as to relieve the poor souls from their never-ending vigil.

A high-pitched sneeze from one of the spaniels snapped Matt back to reality. He looked down and saw the dogs had lost interest in the new visitors. They had returned to their shared bed at the base of the purple-colored, lushly carpeted main staircase. The stairs led one flight up to where eighteen period guest rooms ran around the perimeter of the rectangular-shaped building. Drowsiness had apparently trumped the pups' curiosity. Their interlocking bodies soon formed a perfect circle and they were asleep in seconds. Matt wondered how many times a day they repeated this routine.

The men had arrived in Silver City by way of Tucson International Airport. Their westbound flight had been followed by a three-hour eastbound drive on I-10 into the rugged mountains of southwest New Mexico. Kate Hampton had accompanied the men on their trip out West. She had already checked in and made her way upstairs to her room to grab a quick afternoon nap.

"I'm thirsty," Buzz announced. "Why don't we see if we can find a saloon in this one-horse town?"

Silver City was as advertised—a small, eclectic mountain town with a thriving artist community. The residents were equally divided between aging hippies and college-aged students. The campus of Western New Mexico University sat on the outskirts of town. Young or old, however, the inhabitants had two things in common: a preference for an alternative lifestyle far away from the conformity and crowds of urban America, and a love for the outdoors. Silver City offered both. Positioned at an elevation of over six thousand feet, the town served as the unofficial base camp for the Gila National Forest. For campers, hikers, bikers, and outdoor adventurers looking to explore hundreds of miles of wilderness, the southernmost boundary of the Gila was located just a few miles north of the city limits.

It didn't take the men long to find what they were seeking. The sign outside the local watering hole read Little Toad Creek Brewery. As they stepped inside, it appeared to be a no frills but popular operation. The staff was friendly, the bar was stocked, and the location was convenient—right in the center of downtown, just a block from the hotel. The men found a wooden high-top table in the center of the main bar area.

As they sat down on their stools, Buzz commented, "I read in a tourist brochure in the hotel lobby that Billy the Kid once lived in this town."

"Oh yeah?" Matt replied absently as he scanned the beer menu.

"Yup, in fact a guy named Harvey Whitehill was the first lawman ever to arrest him. Right here on the streets of Silver City."

"All I know is young Billy died at the wrong end of a gun before he was twenty-one," Matt looked up and said. "What ever happened to Whitehill?"

"Evidently, the fair sheriff passed away peacefully twenty years later. In fact, he's buried in the Masonic cemetery somewhere nearby."

A roller-skating waitress named Chloe arrived to take their drink order. Matt couldn't help but notice that none of the other staff were wearing skates. But that didn't seem to bother Chloe in the least. Apparently nobody had ever questioned her choice of footwear, so neither did Matt. As she took their orders, she leaned over so her ample cleavage was on full display. She paused an extra minute to flirt with Matt, coyly twisting a lock of her blue-dyed hair between her thumb and forefinger.

Once she moved on, Matt changed the subject. "So this gold-panning friend of yours; is he really a geologist?" Matt was referring to Buzz's old navy buddy, Hal Billings. Buzz had invited Hal to join them on their search for Geronimo's Gold.

"Of course he's a geologist."

"I thought you said he was a weekend prospector," Matt added doubtfully, "and the only reason he panned for gold was to steer clear of his ornery wife."

"Hey"—Buzz held up his hands in innocence—"I never claimed she was horny," he deadpanned.

"I said ornery, not horny, smart ass," Matt said, trying to suppress a smile.

"I'm serious. Do you trust this guy to tell the difference between gold and pyrite if we actually find something out there?" He was referring to a mineral commonly mistaken for gold.

"Relax, Matt. After Hal's stint in the service, Uncle Sam paid for his education. I swear on a stack of Bibles, he's got a geology degree from the University of Arizona."

"But didn't you also tell me he just retired after twenty-five years from the Parks and Recreation department in Tucson?"

"Yes...that's true," Buzz admitted evasively, avoiding Matt's eyes. "Okay, so technically speaking he didn't parlay his degree into a career in the geosciences." He took a contrite sip of beer.

Matt raised his eyebrows in skepticism.

"But," Buzz added defensively, "I'll bet you he's logged more hours in the field than most professional geologists. Besides," he challenged, "you're the one who wanted someone we could trust to keep his mouth shut if we happen to find Geronimo's Gold."

Matt held his hands up in defeat. "You're right, I guess this falls into the category of beggars can't be choosers." Matt drained the last of his beer. "Where the hell is he anyway? Shouldn't he be here by now?"

"He's probably checking into the hotel as we speak. By the way, don't be put off by the way he looks," Buzz added nonchalantly.

"What's that supposed to mean?" Matt asked, afraid to hear the answer.

"You'll see," Buzz replied with a sly grin.

"Oh great." Matt shook his head disapprovingly.

Buzz moved on. "You do realize this is a wild goose chase,

right?" he said. "I mean, we don't exactly have an 'X marks the spot' treasure map. Our map has a circle on it that encompasses thousands of acres of pure wilderness. Not to be a Pessimistic Patty, but the chances of us finding anything out there are pretty slim."

"I know," Matt admitted, "but we have to try. We owe it to Adam—at least I do." The truth was he had been thinking the same thing as Buzz. Their search for Geronimo's Gold would probably prove futile.

"Hey," Buzz said encouragingly, "maybe Kenny Morgan will be our ace in the hole. He's Geronimo's great-grandson, right? Maybe being back out in the mountains of his ancestors will trigger a memory—a forgotten story his father shared with him that could provide a clue to the whereabouts of the gold."

"Maybe," Matt replied without much conviction. "Speaking of Kenny, I hope he made it up to the Cliff Dwellings today."

"I'm sure he did," Buzz said, "but cell service is pretty spotty up in mountains, so we probably won't know until we get up there ourselves tomorrow morning."

The plan called for Kenny to arrange horses and camping gear for their expedition into the remote Gila backcountry. Kenny and his father had rented from a place called the Gila Hot Springs Ranch on many occasions in the past. Operated by the Campbell family since 1940, the ranch was located just four miles south of the famous seven-hundred-fifty-foot-high Gila Cliff Dwellings National Monument.

A professional guide from the ranch normally accompanied clients on pack trips into the heart of the Gila Wilderness, but Matt had insisted on keeping the reason behind their trip a secret. Kenny was an old friend of the Campbells' and someone they trusted. So when he said he would be personally guiding the expedition they didn't hesitate to supply him with all the gear and provisions he required. They were confident in his abilities, because there were only a handful of people who knew the Gila better than Kenny Morgan.

Buzz suddenly sprang from his seat.

He rushed to the front door and out onto the sidewalk. Matt turned around to see where he had gone in such a hurry. He spotted Buzz waving and calling to someone down the street. A minute later he returned with a man in tow. Matt knew in an instant it had to be Hal Billings.

Dressed in a crushable fedora hat and leather bomber jacket, Billings looked like the president of the Indiana Jones fan club. He even had the khaki pants and matching rumpled safari-style shirt. About the only thing missing from the ensemble was a leather bull-whip.

As Matt stood up to greet Buzz's old war buddy, he noticed a long gray ponytail protruding out from underneath the back of the fedora and snaking down to the center of Hal's back, and a gold earring in his left ear. Matt caught Buzz's eye and raised one eyebrow as if to say, "This is our expert?" Buzz took the opportunity to conveniently look the other way.

25

Present Day

Pinos Altos, New Mexico

It looked like one of those classic Old West ghost towns, only smaller. With little more than a hundred and fifty residents, it could barely be called a town at all. A more accurate description might be an occupied hamlet. Sitting astride the continental divide, Pinos Altos was founded in 1860 after gold was discovered in a nearby creek. Only a smattering of rustic log cabins and adobe structures remained. They lined the narrow thoroughfare that comprised the main street—remnants of the heady days when thousands flocked to the mountains of New Mexico to stake their claim.

It wasn't much to look at now but the quasi-ghost town was rife with history. It didn't take a vivid imagination to conjure up images of brawling miners, parlor girls in rhinestone bustiers waiting tables, and Apache Indian raids—all of which had occurred within the confines of the tiny settlement back in the 1860s and 1870s. One of the few original structures still standing was the Buckhorn Saloon. The building had been refurbished a number of times over the years. But remarkably it retained its original mirrored Brunswick mahogany bar—more than one hundred and fifty years after it was first installed.

The latest in a long line of gold seekers had just ridden into town. These hopeful prospectors had not arrived on the backs of horses, but rather in the air-conditioned comfort of a Chevy rental car. Pinos Altos, Spanish for "tall pines" was located only six miles north of Silver City. It was a breathtaking drive that snaked its way up the side of a mountain. The sun had just begun to dip over the horizon, and the views from the car windows were spectacular as the vehicle climbed more than a thousand feet in elevation.

After parking the car in a dirt lot out front, Matt, Buzz, Kate, and Hal Billings walked across the rustic, western-style front porch of the Buckhorn Saloon. As they approached the entrance they heard live music coming from inside. The first thing they noticed after entering through the thick wooden front door was a woman in a red felt dress and matching silk stockings. She was lying on a small wooden platform above the bar in seductive repose. She had a challenging, seen-it-all look on her face that said, "What's the matter, honey? Ain't you ever seen a sportin' woman?"

Matt did a double take before realizing the mysterious courtesan was a life-size mannequin. But the concubine theme didn't end there. A preponderance of oversized oil paintings hung on the walls of the dimly lit nineteenth-century saloon. They depicted an assortment of "soiled doves," as prostitutes were called back then, in various states of undress.

"My kind of place," Buzz commented to no one in particular.

A table of people in the cramped barroom emptied and Kate quickly nabbed it. They had a few minutes to kill before their reservation was ready in the adjacent dining room, so they decided to grab a drink. Matt veered in the opposite direction toward the restroom. The beers from his earlier visit to the brewery in Silver City had caught up with him.

Coming to the Buckhorn Saloon had been Hal Billings's idea.

Friends back home in Tucson assured him they wouldn't enjoy a tastier steak or a more authentic atmosphere. So far it hadn't disappointed. The building itself was comprised of eighteen-inch-thick adobe walls supported by hand-hewn timbers. The decor inside belied the saloon's somewhat dilapidated exterior. Period fixtures such as converted gaslights, salvaged from other Pinos Altos buildings, and an 1897 potbellied stove helped the place remain true to its late nineteenth-century roots. A terrific three-piece band played country and bluegrass at the far end of the bar. And a lively crowd gave the place a great energy.

On his way back from the restroom Matt paused to take a closer look at the magnificent original back bar. It appeared to be very old and quite solidly built.

"Impressive, isn't it?" a voice next to him said.

Matt turned. A man sat at the corner of the bar. He was overdressed for the surroundings, in an expensively tailored business suit and tie. Two unshaven men in jeans and flannel shirts with matching "Vietnam Veteran" baseball caps sat in stark contrast on the barstools next to him. The two veterans were in an animated discussion over a proposed local tax ordinance while downing tankards of beers. The man in the suit seemed oddly out of place, like a shiny penny in a handful of soiled change.

"Yes, it is," Matt replied politely. "This is quite a place." He knew his friends were waiting for him so he politely excused himself.

"I'm told it was handcrafted in Iowa," the man continued. "Apparently it was so big and heavy it had to be freighted here in pieces. It came over the mountains by wagon train."

Matt turned back around. "Wow," he said, impressed. Given the man's knowledge of the saloon and his choice of attire, he asked, "Do you own this place?" It seemed like a logical conclusion.

The man chuckled and replied, "No, I'm just passing through, as they say." He extended his hand. "My name is James." Matt shook the man's outstretched hand. Just as Matt was about to introduce himself, the man added, "James Sinclair, to be more specific."

Matt froze at the mention of the Sinclair surname. His eyes went wide with surprise. He quickly released the man's hand and looked furtively to his left and right, not sure what to expect.

Sinclair noticed Matt's anxiousness. He assured him, "There's no one else here but me. Actually, that's not true," he quickly acknowledged, "my driver is outside, but he's harmless."

"What the hell are you doing here?" Matt said angrily. "How did you even know we were here, you son of a bitch?" He demanded. It took every bit of control he could muster not to slug the guy. After all, this was the man responsible for Adam's death and Kate's mugging. And now he was sitting there calmly chatting Matt up like they were old friends.

Reading Matt's mind, Sinclair insisted, "I didn't do the things you think I did, Matt."

"Bullshit," Matt fired back rapidly.

"I understand your anger, but it's misguided." Sinclair pointed to an empty stool. "If you'll just sit down for a minute, I think you'll realize I'm not your enemy."

Matt didn't make a move for the stool. "What do you want?" he said guardedly.

Sinclair calmly removed his eyeglasses and wiped them down with a bar napkin. He was handsome in a statesmanlike way. His steel-gray hair had turned graciously white at the temples. And he had a strong chin and penetrating blue eyes. Some might have even mistaken him for a nightly news broadcaster. But Matt knew the truth. The stranger sitting before him was the corrupt CEO of Morton Sinclair. When Sinclair removed his glasses, Matt could see crow's feet around the man's eyes and deep creases on his forehead. They were the only hints of age in an otherwise well-preserved face. Still, if he had to guess, Matt would put him somewhere in his early seventies.

"I want the same things you do," Sinclair answered evenly. "I want to catch the men behind the conspiracy. And I want to bring them to justice for murdering Adam."

He looked Matt squarely in the eye as he spoke. "And as for how I knew you were out here... let's just say I've been keeping tabs on you, ever since you and Miss Hampton paid a visit to Barry Walker at my firm." He cleared his throat and continued, "I apologize for having you followed, but there's a lot at stake here. Of course, you already know that."

Matt was caught off guard by Sinclair's honest admission. Even so, he remained on high alert.

"Why the hell would I trust a word you say?"

Sinclair considered the question for a moment before revealing, "Because I'm the one who told Adam to go see Lottie Benson."

The response was not what Matt had expected. His anger morphed into confusion. A slew of questions ran through his head at once: *How did Sinclair know Lottie Benson? How did he know Lottie Benson had the map? Was Adam working with Sinclair?*

Matt looked over and spotted Buzz eyeing him from the table across the room. He saw the concern on his face. Even though Buzz hadn't heard the exchange, Matt could tell he had witnessed it. He started to get up, but Matt quickly shook his head from side to side. Buzz sat back down, but his eyes remained fixed on the two men. As always, Matt took comfort in knowing the ex-navy man had his back.

Before reaching down and dragging the empty barstool toward him, Matt hesitated for one final moment. Then he took a deep breath and sat down cautiously on the cushioned calfskin leather seat. The bartender came over and Matt ordered a longneck Budweiser. He had the feeling he was going to need it.

"Okay, Mr. Sinclair," he said, "you've got my attention. Start talking."

"It's a bit of a long story," Sinclair began. "It's hard to know where to begin."

Matt was in no mood for games. "Why don't you start by telling me about your grandfather," he offered, "the famous Preston Sinclair and his merry band of tomb raiders?" Matt decided to put Sinclair immediately on the spot. He sat back and waited for his response, ready to pounce on any lie.

"Ah, the famous Fort Sill 'crook,'" he smiled thinly. "I see you've done your homework."

"They were after more than Geronimo's skull, weren't they?" Matt continued to press.

"Indeed," Sinclair confirmed. "I'm impressed, Matt. What else have you figured out?"

"We're pretty sure Geronimo told Roosevelt about his gold discovery during their private meeting after the inaugural parade. It's the only time they were alone together. But I can't figure how your grandfather found out about it." Matt admitted.

"He found out about it from his father, my great-grandfather, W.H. Sinclair. You see," he explained, "W.H. was a wealthy industrialist who made his fortune in the railroads. Even though they didn't see eye to eye on everything, over the years W.H. became a sort of informal adviser to President Roosevelt. He was someone the president turned to for advice on what he considered to be financial matters of a more *sensitive* nature."

James Sinclair took a small sip of the Scotch on the rocks he had been nursing since he arrived. He continued, "One day, Roosevelt invited W.H. out to his summer house at Sagamore Hill. It was right after TR was reelected president for a second term. That's when he told my great-grandfather about his meeting with Geronimo at the White House."

"And eventually W.H. told his son Preston about Geronimo's Gold," Matt filled in the blanks. "And when young Preston was fortuitously assigned to Fort Sill, he and his Skull and Bones society buddies decided to take advantage of their luck and rob Geronimo's grave. No doubt to see if they could find a clue to help them find the gold."

"You're mostly right," Sinclair interjected, "except that my grandfather was the only one who knew about Geronimo's Gold. He never told his fellow Bonesmen about it. The other boys were just in it for the thrill of the crook."

"So all Preston found was Geronimo's skull and some rotting bones? He didn't find anything inside the grave that would lead him to the gold?" Matt asked.

"I'm afraid not."

Matt took a long pull on his bottle of beer. After placing it back down on the bar, he asked, "So why did Roosevelt consider Geronimo's Gold to be a *sensitive* financial matter, as you called it? Why did he feel the need to hide the gold?"

"What makes you think he hid it?"

"Because he expanded the Gila National Forest by two hundred thousand acres so nobody would find it," Matt replied. He eyed Sinclair evenly before adding with undisguised agitation, "But you already knew that, so stop screwing with me and tell me what Roosevelt and your great-grandfather discussed at Sagamore Hill." Matt didn't like being toyed with and he wanted answers.

"I'm sorry," Sinclair held up his hands, "I'm just impressed at how you were able to deduce all of this. The papers don't lie, Matt, you're as good as advertised." Sinclair was referring to the notoriety Matt had obtained over the past few years both for uncovering a conspiracy to overthrow the U.S. government, and separately, unearthing a seditious surrender letter written by George Washington during the American Revolution.

Sinclair went on to share the full story. He told Matt about his great-grandfather's meeting with President Theodore Roosevelt. About how Roosevelt was worried the effect a gold find of such magnitude would have on the newly created Gold Standard Act—the one President McKinley had signed into law in 1900. He told Matt one of the reasons for returning to the gold standard was because gold was more scarce than silver. He explained that at the end of the nineteenth century, silver was being discovered everywhere and as a result was becoming much more commonplace than gold. And this didn't sit well with the men in control of the money, namely the East Coast bankers, because every time a new silver deposit was discovered, it exerted inflationary pressure on the economy. And inflation of any kind reduced the value of the bankers' outstanding loans.

Sinclair went on to say the last thing president Roosevelt could afford was a shock to the nascent gold standard system. So when Geronimo told him about the gold, the president became deathly afraid that if a discovery of this magnitude became public it could throw the U.S. economy into a recession.

"So he believed Geronimo's gold discovery was that substantial?" Matt interrupted.

"He didn't just believe it. He knew it."

"How could he know that?"

"Because he sent his new chief of the Forest Service, Henry Benson, to New Mexico to confirm it," Sinclair revealed.

"Are you telling me Henry Benson actually found Geronimo's Gold?"

Benson smiled knowingly. "Yes, he did. President Roosevelt divulged as much to my great-grandfather."

"Holy shit," Matt said. Even though he had hoped it was true,

Matt was still shocked to find out Geronimo's Gold was real and not just a circle on a map. Another thought popped into his head. "That's why you sent Adam to see Lottie Benson. You knew about the map."

"No, I didn't know about the map. I just thought Mrs. Benson might have knowledge that could be useful...considering her grandfather's involvement in the cover-up," Sinclair added.

Matt processed this new information for a moment before asking, "So Geronimo's Gold deposit was really big enough to disrupt the U.S. economy?"

"According to Benson, Geronimo's Gold was the mother of all mother lodes. He told Roosevelt it would dwarf the deposit that started the California gold rush." Benson paused before commenting, "So you can see why the president wished to keep it a secret."

"Pretty ballsy to hide it inside a national park, that's for sure," Matt said in amazement.

"Yes, and it worked. Because Geronimo's Gold has been sitting undisturbed for more than a hundred years."

26

Present Day

Pinos Altos, New Mexico

Even though Matt believed everything Sinclair had told him thus far was the truth, he still didn't trust him. The Sinclair family tree had deep roots in both the scheme to cover up Geronimo's Gold and the subsequent raid on his grave. And the investment firm that bore the family name was at the center of the modern-day financial conspiracy. Matt remained convinced James Sinclair was involved in this thing up to his ass. Now all he had to do was figure out how to nail him.

"You said earlier that you're not my enemy. I think it's time you proved it," Matt demanded, locking eyes with Sinclair. "Tell me what you know about the conspiracy Adam Hampton uncovered."

"You mean you haven't figured it out yet?" Sinclair said, surprised. "Come on, Matt, you're a smart guy, what do you think it involves?" Sinclair knew he was playing with fire by stringing Matt along. But he was also curious to see just how much he had deduced.

Matt's eyes flashed with anger. He wanted straight answers not games. But unless he planned on beating the information out of him, which had already crossed his mind once, he had no choice but to play along. "The fraud involves the gold market," he answered. "Barry Walker admitted as much when we spoke to him in your offices in New York."

"The conspiracy most definitely involves gold," Sinclair allowed, "but how?"

Matt's face reddened. More games. He was reconsidering his decision not to take the pompous blue blood out back and pummel him. Sinclair took notice and held up his hands apologetically. "I'm sorry, I'm just curious to see how much you've sorted out," he said, "because if *you* haven't been able to put it all together, then I doubt anyone has."

"I don't know, damn it. But I get the feeling the conspiracy is bigger than just a simple gold fraud. I have no proof, but my gut tells me all these countries suddenly clamoring to get their gold back from the U.S. are involved in this thing somehow."

Sinclair could tell Matt was losing his patience. It was time to come clean. He leaned back in his chair, took a deep breath, and said, "You're instincts are correct, Matt. It is bigger than a simple gold fraud. Do you remember the names Nelson and William Hunt?"

Matt looked down at the bar, his brow furrowed as he struggled to remember. *Why did those names sound familiar?*

Then it came to him. "The Hunt brothers," he said snapping his fingers.

Sinclair nodded.

"Nelson and William Hunt," Matt continued. "The famous Texas billionaire brothers who tried to corner the silver market back in 1979," Matt said, recalling the story.

"Indeed," Sinclair said, impressed, "at one stage they held the rights to more than half of the world's deliverable silver. They gained sufficient control of the world's silver supply, which enabled them to manipulate the price. They had effectively cornered the silver market—an audacious feat to say the least."

"But as I recall, the government stepped in and shut them down. It cost the Hunt family billions," Matt said. "But why did you bring them up…"

Then he sat up straighter in his stool as the answer suddenly became clear to him. "Holy shit, you're trying to tell me someone is attempting to corner the gold market," he declared a little more loudly than intended.

The two older Vietnam veterans at the bar turned their heads, but they lost interest just as quickly and returned to their beers.

"Of course. It all adds up," Matt said in a more muted voice. "But they'll never get away with it. When the government finds out about it, all the traders involved will be thrown in jail."

For the first time since their conversation began, Sinclair appeared worried. He leaned forward and said in a confidential tone, "It will be too late by then."

"What do you mean, too late?" Matt said, frustration returning to his tone. "Look, Sinclair, I've had enough of your riddles and half answers. Tell me what you know. *Who* is trying to corner the gold market?" He added accusingly, "For all I know, it's you. How do I know you didn't come all the way out here just to protect your firm's interests and your own corrupt ass? You sure as hell would stand to make a lot of money if you were in on the gold fix."

"I'm not trying to corner the gold market," Sinclair answered flatly.

"Then who is?" Matt demanded.

Sinclair's demeanor changed noticeably. Matt detected paranoia, perhaps even fear. The CEO scanned the room. The dinner crowd had begun arriving and the bar was filling up. But the music was loud enough so their conversation could continue in relative privacy.

"Listen to me," Sinclair began in a hushed tone. "You have to understand. This is bigger than you think. The people behind this conspiracy have unlimited resources," he said with a sense of urgency, "and we both know they'll kill anyone standing in their way." It was an unmistakable reference to Adam Hampton.

"I don't scare easily, Mr. Sinclair. Go on," Matt insisted.

Sinclair drained the last of his Scotch. He put his glass down on the bar and scrutinized Matt. "Listen, son, I've been cagey with you thus far because I needed to make sure I could trust you—that you were prepared to handle the truth. Because if I tell you what I know, then there's no turning back for you. The only other person who knows what I know is dead," he said ominously. "I want your help, Matt, but I've got to know you're ready to do what's necessary to stop the conspiracy before it's too late."

"Look, you said yourself this isn't the first time somebody's tried to corner a commodity market," Matt responded. "There will always be crooked traders out there trying to beat the system. But these guys murdered my friend, so you're damn right I'll do what's necessary to put these guys behind bars."

"No, Matt," Sinclair said, shaking his head gravely. "This is way bigger than just some crooked traders. Cornering the gold market is merely a strategy in a much *larger* plan. It isn't their ultimate objective."

Matt froze. He cocked his head in confusion. "What larger plan? Who the hell is masterminding this thing?"

Sinclair's eyes darted left and right. His calm disposition had long since disappeared. Finally, he leaned in very close to Matt and whispered, "China."

Matt jerked back as if someone had thrown a glass of water in his face. "China?" he said, bewildered. "What do the Chinese have to do with this?"

"Look, Matt, you're the best option I've got, so I'm going to tell you everything I know. Then you'll have to decide for yourself what you do with that information, okay?"

Matt nodded for him to continue. But the truth was Sinclair's erratic and paranoid behavior had begun to rattle him.

Sinclair eyed Matt intensely for a moment before he began, "China's ultimate objective is to move the international monetary system off of the U.S. dollar and replace it with a Chinese world reserve currency, the renminbi."

Matt stared at him dumbfounded.

"But in order to do that they need to start a war," Sinclair continued.

"A war?" Matt asked.

"Yes, a *financial* war that will shake the international community's confidence in the U.S. dollar."

"To what end?"

"So the world will be forced to return to the gold standard."

"The gold standard? Why would that be a good thing for China?"

Sinclair sat back and thought about how best to lay it out. "To answer that question," he said, "you have to understand where China is coming from. You see, the Chinese are sick and tired of playing second fiddle to the United States. They're frustrated that the U.S. Treasury's solution to the American debt problem is to simply keep on printing money, because this only drags down the value of the billions in U.S. Treasury bills China already owns. The Chinese want more control. They want to be the world's greatest superpower, but they recognize they can only achieve that goal if they have the world's dominant currency."

"So how does cornering the gold market help destabilize the U.S. dollar and make the renminbi the world's currency?" Matt asked.

"The Chinese know that they can gain a huge advantage by backing their currency with a precious metal. So over the past few years they have been slowly and stealthily buying up the world's supply of gold. Once they have amassed enough of the precious metal to allow them to back their currency with gold, they will attempt to launch a new global monetary system, not based on the U.S. dollar but based on the gold standard."

Matt was beginning to grasp the enormity of what Sinclair was suggesting. He posited, "So the winner in a financial war like this, when the gold standard is reestablished, is the nation with the most gold. They would effectively have the most influence in the international monetary system because they would have the most gold to back their currency."

"Exactly," Sinclair said emphatically. "There is a certain level of confidence when your currency is backed by gold. Governments don't like to admit it, but it's true. The fact is countries with the least amount of gold won't be included in any gold revaluation discussion. And any country with an insufficient cache of gold will be at a tremendous disadvantage in international trade—which unfortunately will include the United States. Going forward, the dollar will be just another currency."

"So China's real objective is to control the global financial markets by making the renminbi the currency of choice for all international trade," Matt reasoned. "That's why they are trying to corner the gold market."

"Not trying to, Matt. They already have," Sinclair stated direly. "Make no mistake, China is now the nation with the most gold in its vaults...by a long shot."

"But they did it illegally; it's financial terrorism, for chrissakes," Matt spat out angrily.

"That may be true, but I'm afraid it's also irrelevant at this point. They've got the gold," Sinclair said, "and we don't."

"You think China really has that much gold?" Matt said.

Sinclair had begun to perspire in the crowded bar. He loosened the Windsor knot in his tie a bit. "I do," he said.

He continued, "It's all part of China's overall plan to reduce the world's faith in the U.S. dollar by proving it has no backing in a hard asset like gold. The impact of a return to the gold standard on the value of the dollar cannot be underestimated. It would be catastrophic. And in the end, the Chinese will be economically untouchable."

Remembering the repatriation requests that had been in the news lately, Matt said, "Oh my god, all these other countries that have asked for their gold to be returned to them from U.S. vaults. They're all part of the conspiracy, aren't they?"

"You noticed that too, huh?" Sinclair shook his head in disgust. "To answer your question, yes, I believe China is orchestrating these suspiciously timed repatriation efforts. There's no way those countries would have ever made those requests on their own. It's also no coincidence the countries involved are all cozy trading partners with China."

"How are you so sure China has more gold than we do? Are you telling me you believe the conspiracy rumors that our gold reserves have been depleted to the point where there is actually no gold left in Fort Knox?" Matt asked.

"Our vaults may not be empty, but I think they're probably close. But it doesn't matter what I think. All that matters is that China believes it. It's why they set out to corner the gold market in the first place. They believed we were vulnerable due to our depleted gold stocks, and they want to back the U.S., and the rest of the world for that matter, into a corner."

The two men sat quietly, each lost in their own thoughts. Matt downed the last of his beer. He couldn't believe what he had just heard. Even though he had been initially convinced that Sinclair and his ancestors were corrupt, his gut now indicated James Sinclair had told him the truth. And Matt had learned to trust his instincts over the years. They had helped him become a top bond trader, convinced him to relocate to Savannah and start a successful antiques business, and gotten him out of more than a few pinches in his life. Admittedly, there were a few misses over the years, too—including an impulsive marriage to the wrong woman—but for the most part his gut had served him well. Everything Sinclair had shared with him that evening rang too true to be a fabrication.

And it also jibed with Adam's last words to his sister, Kate. Matt recalled that Adam warned Kate of a massive financial conspiracy. Matt knew now Adam had chosen his words carefully. He hadn't just said he had uncovered a fraud or a scheme, but rather a financial conspiracy big enough to cripple the economy. Cornering the gold market was corrupt and brazen, but by itself it wouldn't cripple the U.S. economy. Devaluing the dollar, however, and removing it from its vaunted place as the world's currency surely would.

Matt looked at Sinclair and asked solemnly, "So what happens to the average Joe on the street if the Chinese are successful?"

"Now *that* is the real question," Sinclair replied professorially. "And I'm afraid the answer isn't very pretty." He paused and shook his head at the smiling patrons having a good time in the festive bar atmosphere. "The people in here are like the proverbial frog in the pot of water who doesn't realize until it's too late that he's about to be boiled alive," he said bitterly. His eyes narrowed in anger. "A return to the gold standard would be hyperinflationary for the dollar. The entire American way of life"—he snapped his fingers—"would be gone just like that."

He explained, "Under a new gold standard the dollar will be devalued against gold. The implication of these changes on the average American would be disastrous. Our consumption-led way of life would be impossible to afford, because everything we consume would become dramatically more expensive overnight. In short, all hell would break loose. When you destroy a currency, everything else goes along with it. Hyperinflation would wipe out savings accounts, retirement funds, college funds, annuities, and so on. Bank failures, staggering unemployment, food lines, riots, you name it, will threaten the way of life we take for granted."

He ran a quivering hand through his gray hair. He finished with one final ominous thought, "I don't believe it's an exaggeration to say this conspiracy will shake the very foundation of America."

"Jesus," Matt muttered darkly.

He felt as if he had just taken a punch to the stomach.

27

Present Day

Pinos Altos, New Mexico

Matt ordered another Budweiser for himself and a Scotch on the rocks for Sinclair.

Even though some color had begun to return to the wealthy CEO's face, he still remained a shade paler than when Matt had first sat down. "I thought you could use another one," Matt said.

"Thanks, I'm not much of a drinker, but tonight I think a second is in order."

"You know," Matt said, changing the topic, "when Kate and I met with Barry Walker at your Wall Street offices, he told us it was you who ordered him to back off the conspiracy investigation."

"What?" Sinclair responded in genuine surprise. "I can assure you I had no such conversation with Mr. Walker." He paused. "But it does raise an interesting question. How did Walker know about the conspiracy at all?"

"I told him," Matt admitted. "I lied and said Adam told Kate he had gone to Walker about his discovery of the conspiracy. I needed to see if the guy was holding out on us. So I threatened him and told him if he didn't tell us what he knew then I'd take it up the ladder—to you."

"And what did he say? Did he admit he knew about the attempt to corner the gold market?"

"Not exactly, no. He got very nervous and finally acknowledged that Adam told him he had discovered anomalies in some of the firm's trades. Gold trades to be specific. But he never said anything about an attempt to corner the market."

"He's lying. I know for a fact Adam never told anyone but me about the anomalies or his suspicions of a larger conspiracy," Sinclair declared indignantly. "You've got to believe me."

Matt held up his hand, "I believe you, James." It was the first time he had used Sinclair's first name all night and it didn't go unnoticed.

"That means a lot to me, Matt," he said appreciatively. "More than you can know. Ever since Adam's death, I've been alone with the knowledge of this conspiracy and it's been eating me up inside." He looked genuinely pained. For the first time Matt felt sympathy for the man.

"Barry Walker is a sleaze-ball," Matt scoffed. "I knew it the minute I met him. I knew he was lying through his teeth but I couldn't prove it."

"You realize his admission of being aware of the conspiracy can only mean one thing," Sinclair posited.

"Yeah, I know," Matt replied angrily, "he's in on it."

Matt's mind raced with dozens of conflicting thoughts and questions. He was reminded of the time his laptop vibrated violently right before the hard drive crashed. He massaged his temples in an attempt to avoid a similar fate.

Sinclair could see the stress on Matt's face. "Believe me, I understand this is a lot to take in."

Matt smiled humorlessly. "Yeah, you think?"

They had covered a lot of ground, but there was one topic they hadn't breached. "So what does Geronimo's Gold have to do with the conspiracy?" Matt asked. "I mean, why did Adam think it was so important to find?"

"Ah yes, Geronimo's Gold," Sinclair said wistfully. He took a sip of Scotch. "It all started with an offhanded comment Adam made when we were speaking late one evening. We were discussing the fact that it was most likely true U.S. gold reserves were far lower than our government was admitting."

Sinclair paused with a far-off look in his blue eyes before finishing the thought. "Adam joked that only the discovery of the 'mother of all mother lodes' could restore the world's confidence in the U.S.'s ability to back the dollar with physical gold."

"The mother of all mother lodes," Matt said. "Aren't those the same words..."

Sinclair cut him off. "Yes, the exact words Henry Benson used to describe Geronimo's Gold deposit," he said with a sardonic smile. "That's what prompted me to let Adam in on my family's secret."

"Wait, Adam really thought finding Geronimo's Gold could make a difference?"

"I don't think Adam believed finding Geronimo's Gold, by itself, was the answer to all of our problems. But he thought it would help, yes."

"How?"

"Remember, the only purpose for gold in the current international monetary system is *confidence*. Gold reserves are viewed as a hedge against a currency crisis. So it's not too much of a stretch to think a discovery of an enormous gold deposit on U.S. soil would go a long way to restoring the world's confidence in the U.S.'s ability to back their dollar with physical gold. Of course, it would have to be a massive discovery to do that."

"The mother of all mother lodes," Matt repeated aloud.

"Exactly. At first I only shared the story of Geronimo's Gold with Adam as an ironic anecdote. But the minute he heard about it, he insisted on pursuing it."

"Sounds like Adam."

Sinclair smiled and said, "Sounds like someone else, too." He nodded at their surroundings as if to remind Matt he was about to pursue the same treasure.

"Good point," Matt admitted.

"Anyway, since he was so insistent, I offered up Lottie Benson as a potential lead. I had read an article somewhere along the way that Henry Benson's granddaughter was still alive. I thought maybe she'd have some useful information."

"Unbelievable," Matt exclaimed blankly, "so Adam went to Virginia and asked Lottie about Geronimo's Gold. And she gave him her grandfather's map of the New Mexico territory."

Sinclair saw the sadness on Matt's face. He said, "Adam was a courageous and extremely intelligent young man, Matt. I can see why you two were such good friends. I'm very sorry for what happened to him. It's something for which I will always feel partly responsible."

Matt shook his head. "Don't blame yourself, James. Adam knew he was treading in dangerous waters. He would have kept going no matter what you said to him."

"Thanks for saying that, but unfortunately my firm is involved in this conspiracy, so Adam's blood is on my hands, too." He hung his head remorsefully. "You don't know this, Matt, but Adam was on his way to see me the night he was killed."

Matt couldn't hide his surprise.

"He called me at home a little after eleven o'clock that evening. He told me he had something big to tell me. He had somehow figured out who was orchestrating everything. His exact words were 'I've found the smoking gun.' Unfortunately, that's the last time I spoke to him."

"Do you have any idea what or who the smoking gun was?" Matt asked.

"None whatsoever."

Matt knew he would never be able to relieve Sinclair of the burden he felt for Adam's death, so he let it pass. James Sinclair would carry guilt for a murder he didn't commit for the rest of his life regardless of whether Matt tried to convince him otherwise. There was little else to say, so Matt got up from the bar to rejoin his friends.

Without looking up, Sinclair reached out and grabbed Matt's forearm. "Wait," he said. His eyes were moist and his face was drawn. "I'm going to tell you something only a handful of people have ever known about. And all of them are long-since dead, except me."

Matt's pulse began to quicken. He sat back down.

"My family has done some things over the years for which I am not proud. I can't right them all, but I can right this one." He looked at Matt with a renewed intensity. "I left out a critical detail earlier when I told you about my grandfather Preston's raid on Geronimo's tomb."

He continued, "After Preston and his Bonesmen pals stole Geronimo's skull, Preston wasn't finished. He had heard a rumor from some local Apaches that some of Geronimo's personal effects were still being stored in an old warehouse on the base. Remember, Geronimo had been dead for less than a decade at that point. So Preston broke in to the storage facility to see if it was true. He hoped to find a clue that might lead him to Geronimo's Gold."

"And?" Matt said, his face flushed with excitement.

Sinclair slowly reached a hand into his suit coat pocket. He took out an object and unrolled it from a piece of white cloth. Matt immediately noticed a stag handle protruding from a leather sheath.

"This was Geronimo's Sheffield bowie knife made by the famous English knife maker, George Wostenholm." He held it out for Matt to see. "If you look closely, you'll see a design has been etched into the silver decorative hardware adorning the leather sheath."

Matt leaned in for a closer inspection.

The etching showed what looked like a turtle with water spurting out of its mouth. Just below the image of the turtle were two intersecting lines forming a squiggly V shape. And at the center of the two intersecting lines was a tiny gold flake.

"This is remarkable," Matt said, astonished.

Sinclair continued, "My grandfather believed this was a map and the gold nugget represented the spot where Geronimo's Gold could be found. I believed it, too. Unfortunately, we were never able to make heads or tails of the drawing, so the map was useless to us."

"But these squiggly lines must depict the intersection of two rivers," Matt spoke excitedly as he examined the depiction. "And the turtle must represent the name of a river or some other landmark in the Gila National Forest," he deduced.

"That's what I thought, too. But believe me, I've searched every map from the late nineteenth century and early twentieth century ever produced. There isn't a single reference to a turtle anywhere. Nothing named after a turtle, nothing shaped like a turtle, nothing."

He pointed a finger toward the mountains that lay in the black, moonless night just outside the bar's large picture window. "And as far as the intersecting rivers are concerned, do you know how many rivers and streams intersect in the thousands of miles of wilderness out there?"

Matt thought he had been handed a breakthrough clue only to find out it was another dead end. The disappointment was crushing. "If you can't make heads or tails of this," he said in frustration, "what makes you think I can?"

"I wasn't thinking about you," Sinclair said as he eyed Matt contritely. "I thought Geronimo's great-grandson might be able to make some sense of it." He added, "It never even crossed my mind to contact Geronimo's descendants. Hell, I didn't even know he had any. That was a brilliant idea, Matt."

"But how did you..." Matt began to ask with a slightly bewildered look.

"I know Kenny Morgan will be serving as your guide in the Gila," he admitted. "Don't ask me how I know. It doesn't really matter at this point. Just please, show him the knife."

Matt was torn between being hopeful and pissed off by the shrewd CEO's seemingly endless knowledge of his comings and goings. He shook his head in resigned exasperation. "Okay," he relented, "I'll show it to Kenny tomorrow. Maybe it will trigger something."

"And one more thing, Matt."

"What's that?"

"Whether you find Geronimo's Gold or not, I don't ever want to see that again," he pointed to the stolen artifact lying on top of the stately mahogany bar. "That knife belongs to Mr. Morgan's family, not mine."

Sinclair got up slowly, like a man with the weight of the world on his shoulders.

Matt felt numb as he watched the silver-haired CEO exit through the front door of the old saloon.

28

Present Day

Silver City, New Mexico

The light from a solitary streetlamp cast an eerie glow inside the otherwise darkened room. Two stories below a car sped by. Elongated shadows cast by the passing headlights tracked across the ten-foot-high ceilings of the historic hotel. In a fit of restlessness, Matt tossed aside his top sheet and comforter. He lay on top of the antique four-poster bed staring at the ceiling in nothing but his boxers. His mind was stuck in a continual loop replaying the conversation with James Sinclair earlier in the evening. It was well past midnight, but Matt was too wired to sleep.

The discovery someone was trying to corner the gold market was bad enough. But the revelation that kept him awake was the larger conspiracy Sinclair had disclosed. Matt was no financial novice, but even he wrestled with the magnitude and audacity of China's plan to collapse the world's confidence in the dollar. The implications of the Chinese renminbi replacing the U.S. dollar as the world's currency were far-reaching. Matt understood Sinclair was not exaggerating when he warned that runaway inflation caused by a return to the gold standard would be catastrophic to the American economy—a direct result of the depleted state of America's gold reserves. Not one to give up hope, Matt was determined to do everything in his power to prevent such a disaster from occurring. He wasn't sure how, but he trusted Adam's instincts that finding Geronimo's Gold was a good place to start.

He knew Sinclair was telling the truth when he said Adam believed finding Geronimo's Gold might prevent the Chinese from achieving their goal. At least it might buy the U.S. time to come up with a more encompassing plan to stop them. Matt reached over and picked up Geronimo's bowie knife from the bedside table. *Would the etchings on the sheath mean anything at all to Kenny Morgan? Would they provide the final clues to help them find the gold?* He took a deep breath and exhaled slowly, hoping to relax his frayed nerves. He returned the knife to the bedside table and rolled over in an attempt at sleep once again.

A moment later a soft knock on his hotel room door broke the silence. When Matt reached the door, however, it was quiet again. He was about to chalk it up to his imagination when it came again, another soft knock. He gripped the antique glass knob and slowly opened the door.

Peering tentatively into the hallway, he saw Kate silhouetted by the dim light of a vintage bronze wall sconce. She was wearing an oversized New York Giants football T-shirt that barely covered her thighs. Her feet were bare and soft pink nail polish adorned her manicured toenails. As Matt's eyes adjusted to the light, his mild surprise turned to concern. Kate's eyes were red and her face was blotchy. She had been crying.

"Sorry," she said hesitantly, "but I couldn't sleep." She paused, trembling slightly. "I just keep thinking if Sinclair hadn't told Adam about that map than maybe he'd still be alive." A fresh tear leaked down her cheek.

Matt stepped forward and wrapped her in a comforting

embrace. "Shh," he said softly, "with or without that map, Adam wasn't going to give up until he had exposed the conspiracy and the men behind it. We both know that."

Kate's head rested on Matt's chest. "I just wish he hadn't been so damn stubborn," she said sniffling.

"Come on," Matt said. He ushered her inside his room so they wouldn't disturb the other guests. He softly closed the door and switched on the light of a standing lamp.

All at once Kate felt awkward standing half-naked in Matt's hotel room. Her face flushed. "I'm sorry for bothering you, Matt. I just needed someone to talk to...but I should probably leave." She turned to go.

"Kate," Matt said as he stepped in front of her. "It's okay, I was wide awake anyway." He smiled genuinely. He sensed there was something more she wanted to say. "Tell me what's on your mind."

"Do you believe in God?" she unexpectedly blurted out.

The question took Matt off guard. He had grown up attending the large stone Catholic church in his hometown. His mother never let the family miss a Sunday. As an adult, however, he had grown disenfranchised with the dogmatic nature of Catholicism. He often found himself at odds with the Church's point of view, especially on social issues, so much so that he hadn't attended services in more than a decade. Not coincidentally, the date coincided with the time of his divorce, another thing the Church did not view favorably. He harbored a considerable amount of guilt about his nonattendance, but his absence didn't mean he had lost his faith. The fact was he did believe in a Higher Power. He just preferred the definition of that Higher Power be more open to individual interpretation.

"I do," he said truthfully. "What about you?"

"I used to, but now...I don't know." She paused before continuing. "I just can't understand how a loving God would let something so horrible happen to my brother. He was one of the good ones, you know. With so many bad people in the world, why did He choose for Adam to die?"

Matt could see the pain on Kate's face. He knew he had no good answer for her. But then some familiar words popped into his head. "My mother used to tell me we're not meant to understand everything that happens," he said, "that faith is the evidence of things not seen."

He continued, "I don't know what God, or the Universe, or whatever you want to call the thing that connects us all, has planned for us. But I have faith Adam's death will not be in vain. I don't believe God would let that happen." He smiled reassuringly. "And neither will I."

She remembered the first time she had met him almost twenty years earlier; he had smiled at her the exact same way. It was an easy smile, one filled with kindness but also filled with an unshakable confidence. A combination she had always found incredibly appealing. Even though she had been only fifteen at the time, and Matt was her older brother's college roommate, she had been instantly smitten. And she found herself no less attracted to him now.

Her eyes shifted momentarily down to his bare chest. She suddenly yearned for him to wrap his arms around her again. His touch had been comforting, but there was something more to it than that. She knew she had been experiencing a roller coaster of emotions these past few weeks and she was probably vulnerable. But there was no denying the attraction she felt for him—that was real. She was well aware it had been part of the reason she had come to his room that evening—perhaps a large part.

Her eyes met his and she smiled. "Thanks for being here, Matt. There's no way I could have done any of this without you," she said. "I mean, look at me, I'm a mess." She laughed self-deprecatingly. "Imagine how I'd be if you weren't around to hold my hand." A pause, then she said, "But I am sorry I dragged you into all this."

Matt reached over and tucked a loose piece of hair behind Kate's ear. "Right now, I'm exactly where I'm supposed to be," he said. His blue eyes shone with a different kind of intensity.

"Matt," she said shyly, "I need to tell you a secret." She hesitated for a moment. "When I was younger I used to...well, I used to...fantasize about you."

Matt's eyebrows raised and he smiled wickedly. "Why Kate, I never knew you had such a naughty mind."

She slapped him playfully on the arm. "Not those kind of thoughts." She giggled. "Well not only those kinds of thoughts," she admitted. "I used to fantasize that you'd come find me and we'd..." She stopped.

"We'd what?" Matt prodded.

"Oh, you know how teenage girls are," she said hesitantly. "We'd ride off into the sunset or something. And live happily ever after." She looked away, feeling silly for sharing her adolescent secrets with him.

Matt took a step closer. "Sunsets are overrated," he said softly. "Sunrises are much more interesting." He leaned in and pressed his lips to hers.

She stood on her tiptoes and kissed him back. Her kiss had a longing that even she had not anticipated. Sexual tension crackled between them like an electrical current. Her body pressed against his. Her nipples hardened instantly beneath the thin cotton jersey. She ran her fingers across Matt's broad shoulders and down his back. Her pulse quickened.

Then just as suddenly, she broke free from their embrace. She took a tentative step back, but her eyes never left his. Matt looked momentarily confused.

Finally, she said with a coy smile, "I'm not a teenager anymore."

With crisscrossed hands, she took hold of the bottom of her shirt. Slowly she slipped it over her head, revealing her full breasts and a firm abdomen. Without hesitating, she wriggled out of her panties and tossed them aside.

Matt stared at the woman standing naked in front of him. "No, you're not," he said. He glanced down at the discarded T-shirt on the floor. "I didn't like that shirt anyway," he said with a smile, kicking it further away. "I'm a Patriots fan."

She giggled and reached behind her to switch off the light.

He stepped forward and scooped her up in his arms. Her body felt warm against his bare chest. She wrapped her arms around his neck and kissed him deeply. He walked over to the bed and laid her down so he was astride her. She slipped her fingers inside the waistband of his boxers and removed them with an urgent tug.

She had waited for this moment for a long time and there was no holding back—from either of them. Kate, especially, had a boundless energy. Every time Matt thought he couldn't go any longer, she would find a new way to arouse him. And they would make love again. Somewhere along the way, he made a silent vow to take up yoga. Utterly exhausted, in the early morning hours they finally drifted off into a deep, sated sleep.

It was just after sunrise.

29

Two Weeks Earlier

New York, NY

His cell phone began to ring.

It was early on a Sunday morning but Sam Rothstein recognized the number, so he answered. It was a brief but extremely unsettling conversation. After hanging up he knew he would have to resolve this particular problem himself. He decided to call in an old favor.

He looked up a private number he hadn't called in years and punched it into his cell phone.

"Victor, it's Sam Rothstein," he said.

"It's been a long time, my old friend," was the reply. "You've done well for yourself."

"As have you," Rothstein answered. "Thanks to me," he added as a reminder.

Rothstein had met Victor Oleg in prison. Victor was the son of a highly placed Russian mafia Don. During his incarceration, Rothstein had offered Victor's father investing advice and their relationship continued for a time after prison. Eventually the two men had gone their separate ways. But not before Rothstein had made the Oleg family millions of dollars on their investments with him. In return, they had promised Rothstein if he should ever need anything, he only had to ask. They were indebted to him.

Based on a phone call he had received moments earlier, Rothstein made the quick decision that now was the time to call in that chit. "I need a favor," he said, getting right to the purpose of his call.

"Name it, my friend," the Russian replied without hesitation.

"There's a woman, her name is Kate Hampton," Rothstein began.

30

Present Day

Gila National Forest, New Mexico

The drive from Silver City to the Gila Hot Springs Ranch took a little less than two hours. It was only forty miles, but the route traversed some of the highest elevations and most remote geography in the state. The scenery was breathtaking as they motored up and down the peaks and valleys of the southern edge of the Rocky Mountains. The spectacular landscape had been created some twenty-five million years earlier when the entire area had been an active volcanic province.

Along the way, Matt said a silent prayer that the brakes in their rental car had been recently serviced. If they hadn't, they'd sure as hell need to be at the end of this roller coaster ride. He was glad he was the driver and not a passenger. It kept his mind occupied as they drove around switchback after terrifying switchback. At times, the mountain road narrowed so severely he had to maneuver all the way over to the edge of the pavement so that oncoming vehicles could pass. The car skidded and kicked up loose gravel on one particular hairpin turn. He spotted Kate in the rearview mirror looking anxious in the backseat. She had a firm grip on the armrest but smiled back at Matt bravely.

He shifted uncomfortably in his seat. That's when it occurred to him he was sore from the extended romp with Kate in his hotel room the night before. He shook his head, still marveling at the stamina of the beautiful creature sitting behind him. Sore or not, if Buzz and Hal weren't in the car with them, he might have pulled over and resumed where they had left off just a few hours earlier. She stirred something in him he couldn't seem to turn off. When he glanced again into the rearview mirror Kate batted her eyes and smiled devilishly as if reading his mind. Matt smiled in return but was brought abruptly back to reality when an oncoming truck forced him once again to the edge of the asphalt.

After arriving at the ranch, Buzz got down on his hands and knees and dramatically kissed the ground—like a fifteenth-century sailor might have done upon reaching the New World.

"Next time, I'm driving," he cracked.

Matt rolled his eyes. "Stick to flying," he countered.

They started up the path toward the reception building. "Looks like you've got a little hitch in your giddy-up, partner," Buzz said softly with a sly smirk.

"I have no idea what you're talking about," Matt replied picking up the pace.

"Mm-hmm." Buzz chuckled under his breath.

A shrill whistle stopped them in their tracks. They turned to see Kenny Morgan waving them over. He was across an open field standing in front of a large horse stable.

After introducing himself to Hal Billings and Kate, Kenny ushered them inside so that he could acquaint them all with their transportation for the next few days. Kenny had personally selected five horses and three pack mules for their trip into the Gila backcountry.

Matt had only ridden a horse twice in his life. The first time was at a childhood friend's sixth birthday party at a local farm in Massachusetts. His steed was tired and well past its prime. And his time in the saddle consisted of being led slowly around a pathetic dirt paddock by a bored-looking, chain-smoking worker. Still, it hadn't stopped Matt from pretending he was a famous gunslinger in the Old West.

The second time he had mounted a horse was with his ex-wife. It was on an ill-fated vacation to a dude ranch in Wyoming. Upon arriving, they had gone out for a romantic trail ride, but his city-raised wife complained the whole time. After a huge argument, they ended up cutting the vacation short and returning to their Manhattan apartment. It was another in a long line of omens that foretold of their inevitable divorce just a few years later.

"And that's your horse, Matt," Kenny said, pointing to a far stall. He had already introduced everyone else to their rides. "His name is Thunder." He smiled wryly.

Matt approached slowly. "How come Buzz gets a horse named Peanuts," he objected, "and I get a brute named Thunder?" He stared at the biggest, blackest stallion he had ever laid eyes on.

Kenny smiled. "I'm told he's not as tough as he looks."

"Yeah, right, let me talk to the last guy who rode him," Matt said cynically.

"May he rest in peace," Buzz interjected theatrically, touching his fingers to his forehead and across his chest in the sign of the cross. Everyone burst out laughing. Matt smiled weakly but continued to eye his horse warily. Just before he turned and walked away he could have sworn he saw Thunder wink at him.

An hour later, as they were readying to leave, Matt approached Kenny. Morgan was busy lashing the excursion's considerable provisions, including tents, food, propane canisters, bedrolls, and other sundries to the pack mules. Matt also noticed a high-tech crossbow and a few packages of carbon-shafted, 100-grain field point arrows, or bolts as they were called by hunters, tied to Morgan's horse.

"Planning on doing some big game hunting?" he asked, knowing the weapon affixed to Kenny's saddle wasn't for shooting squirrel.

"I never go into the Gila backcountry without my crossbow," Kenny replied. "Insurance policy," he said, "you never know what you might run into out there."

Matt hadn't even considered what types of wildlife they might encounter. And he decided it wouldn't do him any good to start now. But he found himself suddenly comforted to have Kenny, and his imposing crossbow, along for the ride.

He switched gears. "Hey, Kenny, do you have a minute? I want to show you something," he said. He reached into his backpack and removed the stag-handled Sheffield bowie knife and sheath given to him by James Sinclair the night before.

He went on to share the story of how the Sinclair family had come to possess one of Geronimo's most cherished possessions. Morgan's face darkened when Matt told him how the Yale Skull and Bones tomb raiders led by Preston Sinclair had dug up his great-grandfather's grave and made off with his skull. And how Preston had subsequently broken into a storage warehouse on the Fort Sill Army Base and stolen the knife.

Morgan grunted after Matt finished. "Bastards," he said.

"No argument here," Matt concurred. "But it might just give us the break we need."

"How's that?" Morgan looked hard at Matt, still disturbed by how his ancestor's remains had been mistreated.

Matt held up the sheath for Kenny to see. "Sinclair believes these decorative markings are actually a crude map," he said, pointing to the silver etchings on the outside of the sheath. "A map to Geronimo's Gold. And I think so, too," he added.

Morgan took hold of the weapon. He slipped the knife out of

its sheath and turned it over almost reverently in his hands. He felt the weight of the blade and carefully tested its fineness with the tip of his fingernail. He found it still remarkably sharp after all these years.

Matt watched in silence. It was obvious the knife had made an enormous impression on Kenny. Just at that moment a cloud passed in front of the sun. Matt had seen pictures of Geronimo in articles he had found online. But it wasn't until just then that he noted the remarkable resemblance between Morgan and his great-grandfather. The jawline, the creases in the forehead, the firmly set mouth as he inspected the bowie knife, all belonged to Kenny. But they were also the features of perhaps the most feared Indian warrior in American history—Geronimo.

A shiver ran down Matt's spine. "So what do you think," he said as he recovered, "do those symbols mean anything to you?"

Morgan continued to examine the finely carved symbols.

Matt filled the void. "There seems to be a turtle with water spurting from his mouth. The problem is Sinclair says there is no turtle associated with any river, lake, or any other landmark for that matter, in the entire Gila National Forest."

Still, Morgan said nothing.

"Those intersecting lines have got to be rivers," Matt said, forging ahead, "but there are scores of rivers and tributaries out there." He pointed over his shoulder in the direction of their intended destination. "So it doesn't give us much to go on."

After more silence, Matt said more firmly, "We were kind of hoping these symbols might mean something to you. Kenny?"

At long last, Morgan looked up. His jaw muscles relaxed slightly and a hint of a smile played at the corners of his mouth.

"I know this place," he said definitively.

After a half day in the saddle everyone was exhausted and sore. They had left Gila Hot Springs Ranch just after one o'clock in the afternoon and traveled close to fifteen miles into the heart of the Gila National Forest. Kenny was out front leading the pack of hardworking mules. The rest of the group plodded along behind him. They had ridden through a diverse landscape of vistas and valleys, staying as close to the river as possible to avoid traversing the more arduous mountainous terrain.

They had just emerged from a dense thicket of forest onto a natural clearing. It abutted a crystal-clear tributary of the Middle Fork of the Gila River. They had crossed and recrossed the Middle Fork many times already as they headed in a northwesterly direction toward their ultimate destination—the site of Geronimo's Gold. It was approaching six o'clock in the evening and Morgan suggested they make camp for the night. After dismounting, Buzz and Kate led the horses down to the river to drink. Matt, Hal, and Kenny set about staking out tents and unpacking food and other provisions for the evening.

After dinner, Matt took a walk around the perimeter of camp. He stopped to marvel at the beauty of the lush meadow provided them by Mother Nature. It was filled with more wildflowers than he had ever seen in one place before in his life. The palette of colors was breathtaking. An intoxicating fragrance of wild mint filled the air. The horses, silhouetted by the setting sun, munched on tufts of sweetgrass by a stand of willows lining the water's edge. A steep and rocky cliff rose majestically in the distance.

Kate walked up beside him and slid her arm around his waist. "Beautiful, isn't it?" she said.

Matt smiled and breathed in deeply. He leaned over and kissed her gently on the lips. "It's perfect."

The sun dipped behind the towering one-hundred-fifty-foot ponderosa pines across the river. The two lovers stood arm in arm as a mountain breeze freshened out of the north. It signaled a cool evening ahead.

"Come on," Kate said, with a shiver, "Hal's gathered enough dead branches and logs to keep us warm all night." She took Matt's hand and pulled him back toward camp.

As darkness overtook daylight, the intrepid adventurers sat around a roaring campfire. They sipped whisky and gazed at the starlit sky. Matt joked, "Alright, Kenny, are you going to tell us where we're going or is Buzz going to have to beat it out of you?"

"Not me, I'm a lover not a fighter," Buzz deadpanned.

Morgan chuckled. He reached down into the fire and fished out a small twig. He used it to light a cigarette and inhaled deeply. After blowing a stream of smoke into the cool night air, he finally revealed, "We're going to a place called Turtle Spring."

"Turtle Spring?" Matt repeated. "But Sinclair said he couldn't find any turtle references anywhere on any map," he said, confused.

"That's because only my people called it that," Morgan responded. "When the Chiricahua Apache were removed from these lands in the late 1800s the old names went with them," he explained. "When the white man came in, he put new names on *our* sacred landmarks."

"Sounds like the white man," Buzz interjected sourly. "So where is this Turtle Spring?"

"About thirty-five miles, give or take, from the Gila Hot Springs Ranch," Morgan answered. "Based on the ground we covered today, I'd say we've got another twenty miles to go. We should be there by tomorrow afternoon if we leave early in the morning."

"Why the name Turtle Spring?" Kate interjected.

Morgan smiled at the question. "The turtle is my people's symbol for protection. According to my mother, the place we're headed was where Geronimo hid when he was on the run from the U.S. Army back in the 1880s. The name came from the fact that water from the spring pooled into the shape of a turtle. Geronimo named it himself."

He paused, his mind racing back to his childhood. "My mother used to tell me Geronimo stories all the time. So when Matt showed me the etching of the turtle with water spurting from its mouth, I knew exactly what it was."

"What about the two squiggly lines that intersect beneath the symbol of the turtle?" Matt asked.

"That's easy. Turtle Spring is located just north of the spot where Canyon Creek joins up with the Middle Fork of the Gila River."

"So it shouldn't be that hard to find Geronimo's Gold, then," Kate said with naïve excitement. "According to the gold flake on the knife handle, the gold is somewhere between Turtle Spring and the junction of the two rivers."

"Not so fast, young lady," Hal Billings said. "My guess is there's plenty of territory out there between where the two rivers meet and the location of that spring." Billings had spent enough time in the field searching for gold and other precious minerals over the past thirty years to know nothing was easy when it came to prospecting. He turned to Morgan and asked, "Am I right?"

Morgan nodded. "You're correct Mr. Billings. It sounds like you've had some firsthand experience."

"Son, I've been prospecting longer than a whore's dream," he said with a raspy chuckle.

Matt looked at Buzz, perplexed.

Buzz shrugged and replied dryly, "Don't look at me. I gave up trying to make sense of him a long time ago."

"So how much territory does our search area cover exactly?" Kate asked, returning to her original query.

Kenny scratched his head while doing some mental calculations.

"I'd say it's about five miles from Turtle Spring to the intersection of Canyon Creek and the Middle Fork," he estimated.

"Five miles," Matt shouted. He sat up straighter. "That's a lot of ground to cover," he said, "especially when we don't know what we're looking for."

"Well, kids, it looks like it's going to be a helluva long day tomorrow," Buzz announced, "I suggest we get some shut-eye."

31

Present Day

Gila National Forest, New Mexico

"There it is," Kenny shouted out.

They had just rounded another bend in the river. Less than a half mile ahead the river branched off in two separate directions. "That's where the West Fork of the Gila intersects with Canyon Creek," he said excitedly.

"Thank the Lord," Hal Billings grumbled. "I'm sorer than a hooker on dollar night."

"Which branch is Canyon Creek?" Kate asked, ignoring Hal's crude comment.

The one on the right," Kenny replied. "And about five miles due north is Turtle Spring."

With renewed energy they quickened their pace. Ninety minutes later they arrived at the place Geronimo had used as a hiding place more than one hundred thirty years earlier. It took them some extra time to locate the spot where the natural spring bubbled out of the earth. While it lay only three hundred yards to the east of Canyon Creek, it had become overrun by a thicket of wild shrubs. Their search was further slowed as the spring no longer pooled into the shape of a turtle. It was much smaller than it had been in Geronimo's day and much less defined in shape.

After double-checking to make sure they were in the right place, they hiked back to the river to devise a plan to search for Geronimo's Gold. According to the readings Buzz had taken from a handheld GPS tracking device, their current position was exactly four and a half miles from where Canyon Creek merged with the West Fork of the Gila. If they were to take the etchings on the knife sheath at face value, then Geronimo's Gold lay somewhere along that stretch of land. They decided to split into teams so they could cover more ground. Matt and Kate would form a team, as would Buzz and Hal. Kenny would be by himself. But he knew the backcountry better than any of them and could probably cover more ground alone anyway.

They divided the river into three sections of a mile and a half each. They agreed to reconvene at the downstream fork in three hours, which would still leave plenty of time to set up camp for the night. Hal Billings instructed them to look for outcroppings of rock that could possibly contain a cave. They were to mark any promising spots on maps Buzz had hastily drawn up using the GPS coordinates he had taken as markers. Buzz handed out a pocket-size GPS device and a map to each team.

About an hour later, Matt and Kate were scouting the middle section of Canyon Creek. They had started out with high hopes. But it quickly became apparent that the search was going to be more time-consuming than they had anticipated. The entire length of the creek was lined with sloping cliffs and rocky outcroppings—many of which looked like they could hold hidden caves. It would take them weeks, not days to fully explore each one.

Kate marked yet another promising spot on her map. "That's the tenth one and we're not even halfway through our section of the river," she said, exasperated. "If the other two teams find as many as we have, we'll have more than sixty potential locations to explore."

Matt stretched his leg up on a large boulder and caught his breath. "I know, but we don't have any choice," he said, massaging his leg.

"Was that your knee?" Kate asked, after hearing a loud pop.

"Yeah, getting old sucks. And besides, you were a little rough with me last night," he kidded. He flashed his trademark crooked grin.

"I don't remember you complaining at the time," she shot back coyly. She stepped between his legs and wrapped her arms around his neck.

Sunlight splashed across her face and Matt smiled at her natural beauty. He pulled her close and kissed her deeply. She leaned her pelvis into his.

Matt winced. "Are you trying to kill me, woman?"

"Someone's out of practice, I see," she teased.

"Oh, really?" he said.

He moved so fast she had no time to react. She was over his right shoulder in an instant and he was off and running. Matt spotted a patch of grass and playfully tossed her to the ground. He pinned her down and began to tickle her mercilessly. "We'll see who's out of practice."

Kate laughed so hard she nearly passed out. But somehow she managed to squirm out from underneath him. Matt forgot he was dealing with a former professional athlete. She was strong and agile, and before he knew it she was straddling him and had both hands planted firmly on his chest. "So you like to play rough, huh, big boy?" She said, bright white teeth gleaming.

"Just be gentle with me," Matt quipped with feigned innocence.

Kate threw her head back and laughed.

As her head was tilted toward the sky, the sun dipped behind a rock formation across the river, directly in front of her. There was something about the shape of the cliff that caught her eye. She paused and looked more closely. Her laughter ended abruptly.

Noticing the strange look on Kate's face, Matt said, "Hey, are you alright?"

As the sun sank lower behind the rocks, the silhouette of the outcropping took on a more discernible shape. Her eyes narrowed. Suddenly it hit her.

It was the shape of a man's head.

But not just any man, it was an Indian's head—an Indian wearing a headdress. Something began to gnaw at the back of her mind. She continued to study the face of the Indian carved into the rocks over the millennia by Mother Nature. It had a sternly set brow, high cheekbones, and a rather prominent nose.

The nose.

Suddenly, words began scrolling through her mind. She could hear a woman's voice. It was Lottie Benson's voice and she was reciting a riddle.

"Kate?" Matt said, concerned.

She shaded her eyes and looked beneath the nose of the Indian. There was a small opening.

"Oh my god!" she yelled. She hopped off of Matt's lap and pointed toward the cliffs looming over the opposite bank. "There it is." She beamed with excitement.

Matt scrambled to his feet. He followed Kate's outstretched hand to where her index finger was pointing.

"Do you see the Indian's nose?" she said excitedly. "There's a cave right below it. Don't you see it? Geronimo's Gold is right where Henry Benson's riddle said it would be!" she shouted.

Matt was still trying to comprehend what Kate was telling him.

Then he spotted it. The Indian's roughly hewn face took shape right before his eyes. He scanned down from the Indian's forehead past the bridge of his nose. Finally, he spotted the opening to the cave. His jaw went slack. He couldn't believe it.

He recited Lottie's words aloud as if in a trance, *"Don't dwell on Geronimo's Gold. It's under the nose of the Indian I'm told."*

"Yes!" Kate shouted and jumped into Matt's arms. "Yes!"

Matt spun her around and they whooped and hollered like a couple of lunatics.

After making their discovery, Kate and Matt knew there wasn't enough daylight left to traverse the rocky slope and explore inside the cave. They would have to wait one more day.

It was a long, restless night. Everyone was filled with anticipation as to what they might discover the next day.

They arose early to hike the three miles back upstream to the spot on the map Matt had carefully marked with precise GPS coordinates. As they packed up their gear to leave they noticed Kenny Morgan was missing. This was not a particularly surprising development since they knew Kenny liked to get up before dawn to hunt. But thirty minutes later, when he still hadn't returned, Kate scrawled a quick note telling him they had set out to explore the cave. She left behind an extra map with exact coordinates so he could find them.

A short time later they stood at the base of the rock formation staring directly up at the granite nose of the Indian. The mouth of the cave was approximately fifty feet above them. The slope was steep so it wasn't going to be easy. But it was doable.

They set out without hesitation. When they reached the opening to the cave, they were out of breath but brimming with energy. Buzz paused to scan the riverbed below. There was still no sign of

Kenny.

Noticing the concern on Buzz's face, Kate said, "You don't think something happened to him do you?"

Buzz glanced quickly at Matt and Hal Billings, each of whom shared his unspoken concern. He looked back to Kate. "Nah," he said, "he's probably tracking a big buck or maybe even a bear. You know Kenny's been itching to use that crossbow ever since we came out here." He smiled reassuringly.

"Let's do this," Matt said, unable to wait a minute longer.

Everyone agreed it was time to see what secrets the cave held. They pulled headlamps from their backpacks and strapped them around their heads. They also donned waterproof rubber gloves to protect their hands.

Hal Billings had given them a quick tutorial. He told them there were many classifications of horizontal caves, ranging from first degree all the way through fifth degree—the hardest classification. The degree of difficulty was influenced by, among other things, the slope or pitch of the terrain, the presence of potholes, which would require roping techniques for vertical descents, and finally, the amount of water inside a cave. If parts of the cave were filled with water and swimming entered the equation, then the risk of injury would rise dramatically. They hoped the cave passage they were about to enter was more horizontal than vertical.

Hal checked the opening for scorpions, spiders, and poisonous snakes, because they would most likely be found near the entrance to the cave. He poked his head out of the small opening and grinned devilishly. "It's tighter than a skeeter's ass in a nosedive, but it's passable," he declared. He gave the all-clear sign. Matt followed him inside, followed by Kate. Buzz brought up the rear.

As they plodded carefully forward on uneven, rocky ground, Matt thought back to the unlikely series of clues that had brought them here. The discovery of Theodore Roosevelt's map of New

Mexico had started it all. The symbols etched onto the sheath of Geronimo's bowie knife pointed the way to Turtle Spring. And most remarkably of all, the afflicted ramblings of Lottie Benson's grandfather had helped pinpoint the exact location of the cave—beneath the Indian's nose. All in all, it had been an incredible journey. The only question that remained unanswered was whether Geronimo's Gold lay somewhere inside.

About fifty yards inside the darkened shaft, the cave split into three different tunnels. The team gathered in a circle to discuss which route looked most promising. After some debate, they chose the middle pathway for no other reason than it was the largest opening. For safety's sake they opted not to split up. They would explore the cave together.

Less than a half hour later, the middle path ended abruptly in a gaping pothole. Hal almost walked right into it. He was chattering on about rockfalls and not paying close enough attention to where he was going. If not for Matt's alertness and strong hands, Hal would have fallen headlong into the darkened abyss. Matt reached out and yanked him backward just in time. Breathlessly peering over the edge of the chasm they could hear the sound of rushing water some fifty meters below. Knowing he most likely would not have survived the fall, Hal clapped Matt on the back with a shaky hand and offered his thanks.

The middle path was a dead end. One down, two to go.

32

Present Day

Gila National Forest, New Mexico

They retraced their steps back to the spot where the cave had split into three tunnels. This time they chose the path on the left. Unlike the first route which ended in a deadly pothole, this one continued on in a gentle, sloping arc downward. And there was no rushing river, only the soporific sound of moisture dripping from the smooth, stone walls.

"This looks more promising," Billings said.

But the going was slow. Their path was obstructed every ten yards or so with rocks that had been forced out of the surrounding walls by moisture seeping through fissures over the centuries. Their pace was further slowed because the cramped and dark confines necessitated that they walk stooped over like Neanderthals.

The narrow passageway started to wear on Kate. She had always been slightly claustrophobic, but as they marched further into the subterranean cave she began to feel uncomfortably hemmed in. The light from their headlamps seemed to be no match for the darkness that surrounded them. With a sense of panic, she began to wonder how long their batteries would last. The stale air didn't ease her mind any either. She reached forward and grabbed Matt's hand.

"How deep do you think this tunnel goes?" She asked anxiously.

Matt could hear the uneasiness in her voice. He gave her hand a reassuring squeeze. "We haven't reached the center of the earth yet," he joked.

The reality was they had only traveled the length of three football fields. It just seemed like more. Even so, Matt had begun to wonder if this route would be a dead end as well. But he didn't let on. "Hang in there, Kate," he said optimistically. "It can't go on forever."

Still out front, Billings came to an abrupt halt.

"Look at that," he said, pointing up ahead. An eerie glow emanated from around the next bend in the tunnel. "Something seems to be catching the light from our headlamps and reflecting it back at us."

They picked up their pace to investigate the source of the strange glimmer. When they rounded the corner, the cramped tunnel opened into a wide chamber, about the size of a two-car garage. The light from their collective headlamps brightly illuminated the four walls surrounding them. The room was bathed in a soft yellow light—the color of gold.

"Jesus," Matt remarked in awe as he took in the golden walls surrounding them.

"It's beautiful," Kate said with a look of astonishment.

"I haven't seen this much gold since my last stay in a Vegas hotel room," Buzz cracked.

Billings stepped forward to examine the massive golden veins that crisscrossed the chamber's quartz-lined walls like a busy city road map.

"Tell me that stuff is real," Matt said expectantly.

"It certainly passes the eyeball test," Billings replied. He had his nose pressed right up against the nearest wall. He removed a magnifying glass from his shirt pocket. "It's got the right buttery yellow color."

"I didn't think gold could be found so close to the surface. I thought it had to be extracted," Buzz said.

"It is unusual," Billings' replied without turning around. "It's extremely rare, in fact, for this much gold to be visible in the ore. Most gold contained in quartz veins like this one is in tiny particles that aren't always easy to see." He paused. "But I'll tell you what, if this is real, this deposit is what miners refer to as a bonanza."

"So is it real?" Kate asked breathlessly.

"There's one way to find out," Billings said. He removed a small mining pick strapped to his belt. "There are many different types of rock that can be confused with gold—like silica, mica, and, of course, pyrite. These minerals can all have a goldish tint to them like the stuff in these walls," he explained. He labored to pry a fist-sized chunk of quartz from the wall.

"Don't lecture us, Hal, just tell us if the damn stuff is real," Buzz admonished his navy buddy.

"Hold your horses. I need to run a couple of simple tests to be sure," Billings said.

He rolled the golden colored chunk of quartz over in his hands. "It's heavy as sin, and that's a good sign," he said more to himself than the group. His hands were shaking with anticipation. In all his years of prospecting he had never seen anything like this. He chipped a small piece of golden-colored rock out of the quartz ore. He placed it on the floor of the cave.

"If it turns to dust then it's probably pyrite," he explained. "But if it flattens out, it very well could be gold." He smacked it with his hammer. The piece of rock flattened but didn't crumble. "That's another good sign."

Finally, he took out a small bottle and unscrewed the top. Inside was a rubber plunger. He squeezed out two drops of liquid onto the surface of the stone.

"What's that?" Matt asked.

"Muriatic acid," Billings replied. "If it's gold then nothing will happen. But if the surface starts to foam and the rock dissolves, then we're definitely dealing with fool's gold."

The chunk of golden quartz was illuminated by the four head-lamps perched on the heads of the interlopers. They held their collective breath as the liquid hit the surface. Nobody said a word. Thirty seconds passed and nothing happened.

Buzz spoke up. "How long does it take? Should there have been a reaction by now?"

Billings stood up slowly. He flipped his long gray ponytail over his shoulder. A broad grin replaced the serious expression on his face. "Well, I'll be dipped in shit and rolled in bread crumbs," he said. "This stuff here, my friends, is the real deal."

He paused and pointed at the walls surrounding them. "And judging by size of the veins in these walls, there's an *enormous* lode buried in this cave."

As they emerged from the cool, dark confines, it took their eyes a few minutes to adjust to the bright sunshine. After so much time underground, the warm summer sun was a welcome change. Amid high fives and shouts of excitement, they quickly shed their outer jackets and gloves.

Kate hugged Matt. "We did it. We actually found Geronimo's Gold."

"It's hard to believe," Matt said. Then he became more serious. "You could have given up, Kate. Especially after everything you've been through. But you didn't. Adam would have been proud of you."

"I'm proud of me, too," Kate said, smiling. "I'm proud of all of us." She leaned in and kissed Matt.

"Are you proud of me, too?" Buzz said leaning in with his lips in an exaggerated pucker.

Kate laughed. "Yes I am," she said. She gave him a peck on the cheek.

"What about me?" Billings whined.

Kate patted his cheek and joked, "I'm not quite ready for you yet, Mr. Billings."

Kate turned and walked back to retrieve her pack and prepare for the long trek out of the Gila. Stifling a chuckle, Matt winked at Billings and moved away to help Kate.

Billings pulled up short. He clutched his heart theatrically. "I'm crushed," he hammed.

"Come on, Romeo," Buzz turned in the other direction, "time to go."

A moment later, however Billings fell to the ground in a heap.

"Come on, Hal," Buzz said, pivoting around. "Enough kidding around."

As he turned, however, he saw Billings flat on his back with his eyes open wide in shocked surprise. One look at his face and Buzz knew Hal wasn't playing around this time. He didn't fully comprehend what was going on until he noticed his friend's chest.

The steel handle of a fierce-looking hunting knife protruded grotesquely from his rib cage, just below his heart.

33

Present Day

Gila National Forest, New Mexico

"What the hell?" Buzz stammered. He spun around to see where the knife came from.

Just then, a man emerged from behind an outcropping of rocks.

"Now that I've got your attention," he said in broken English. He pulled out a 9-millimeter handgun and pointed it directly at Buzz. "Nobody move."

Startled by the stranger's voice, Matt and Kate turned around. They had been packing up their gear and hadn't seen Billings fall.

"We meet again, my little curious cat," the man said smugly to Kate.

Kate recognized the Russian accent instantly. The voice finally had a face. His cold, gap-toothed smile sent a shudder through her body.

Ignoring the man's orders not to move, Buzz raced to his fallen friend's aid. He knelt down by his side. Billings's hands were clutching frantically at his shirt. Blood had begun to ooze out of the wound at the base of the knife handle. Buzz knew if he tried to remove the blade from Hal's chest, the bleeding would only worsen.

"Well, if that don't beat the Dutch," Billings quipped in stunned amazement. The reality of his dire situation had begun to set in.

"Easy now, partner, don't try to talk," Buzz said reassuringly. "We're going to get you out of here. I promise."

"Don't make promises you can't keep, Buzz," Billings spoke through clenched teeth. "We both know I've got a five-inch blade buried in my chest. And it feels like it punctured a few things on the way in." His voice was raspy. Blood began to trickle out of the side of his mouth.

He found Buzz's hand and squeezed it hard. "You make sure Cora's taken care of, you hear me," he said, referring to his wife of thirty years. "She put up with me all this time and she's tough as nails," he said, smiling through the tears welling in his eyes, "but she's going to need some help."

"Don't start talking like that, you old warhorse. I'm going to get you fixed up," Buzz said gamely, but the grim expression on his face gave him away.

"Shit." Billings grimaced through the pain. "We both know I'm dying." His breathing had become short and choppy. "Just promise me. Please, Buzz."

Buzz gripped his friend's hand tightly. He knew Hal was right. There was no way he was going to survive. He looked into the eyes of the man he had called a friend for so long. "I promise," he said firmly.

Billings nodded and tried to smile through the searing pain. A few moments later, his body jerked in spasm. Then he was gone.

Matt looked on in horror. It had all happened so fast.

He was still trying to process everything when the Russian spoke up. "It's a shame, yes. You celebrate historic gold find, but unfortunately nobody ever will know about it," he said in broken English.

"How did you find us?" Kate blurted out, struggling to comprehend his presence.

"I've been following you ever since our first date," he said with a cocky smile. "You don't think I broke into your apartment to kill cat, do you? That was just little message to scare you off. But in case it didn't, I place tiny GPS trackers in some of your things." He shrugged. "Inside that watch you're wearing is a tiny disc that tells me exactly where my little curious cat is at all times."

Kate looked down at her watch in horror. It suddenly dawned on her she was the reason they had been followed.

"I follow you out to Virginia and eavesdrop on your conversation with Mrs. Lottie Benson—very interesting lady. I follow you lots of places. You are very *curious cat*." He smiled evilly. "I admit, finding you here was not easy," he waved his beefy arm at their remote surroundings. "But I am strong and fit, trained by the best army in the world. The *Russian* army." He paused and glared at Buzz. "And I am paid very well," he said, "but, of course, only if I succeed." The evil smile appeared once again.

"Paid by who?" asked Matt.

"Tsk tsk," the Russian cautioned, wagging the gun in front of him, "we have no time for that."

Buzz stood up slowly and deliberately. There was revenge in his eyes. The Russian had seen that look before in other dangerous men. He was not going to take any chances. Without any warning, he raised his gun and fired. The force of the bullet's impact spun Buzz around and knocked him hard to the ground.

"No!" Matt screamed in desperation. Without thinking, he charged the Russian.

The man smiled knowingly. Matt's response was exactly what he had anticipated. He was impressed by Matt's grit but he also had a job to do. He leveled his gun one more time.

But before he could squeeze off another shot, the Russian inexplicably dropped to his knees. The gun slipped from his hands and fell harmlessly to the ground. He clawed desperately at his throat, but it was futile. A moment later he fell forward, landing face-first on the hard ground—dead.

It took a moment for Matt's brain to process what his eyes were telling him—there was an arrow protruding out of both sides of the Russian's neck. Unsure of where it had come from, Matt instinctively dropped to a knee and looked to his left. About forty yards away, he saw Kenny Morgan standing up from a crouched, shooter's position. He already had another bolt loaded in his crossbow. But the look on Matt's face told him it wouldn't be necessary.

They would later find out Kenny had discovered a fresh set of tracks along the section of Canyon Creek the day before. He had become immediately suspicious. He knew if the tracks had been made by a hiker or hunter, he would have seen or heard him. He was convinced this person, whoever it was, did not want to be seen. That's why Kenny had disappeared early from camp that morning. He had arisen before dawn in an attempt to find the man he believed was tracking them. The art of tracking game, and adversaries for that matter, had been passed down to him by his father, who had learned it from his father before him.

It took the better part of the morning, but Kenny had finally caught up with his prey. The man was dressed in camouflage and was good at keeping himself hidden from view. Kenny knew he was dealing with a professional and he'd have to be careful. Unfortunately, by the time he crested the ridge just west of the mouth of the cave, he was too late to save Hal Billings.

Matt gave a quick nod of thanks to Kenny and then hurried back to check on Buzz. His hands were shaking and his stomach was churning.

As he reached the spot where Buzz lay bleeding, he had an epiphany. He no longer saw the man who had betrayed his trust or the man who led a secret double life as a member of the Ring. The only thing he knew with an absolute certainty was that he couldn't lose him again. In that moment, he realized he had judged Buzz too harshly and any remaining hostility vanished. As soon as it did, he was able to see the person who had always been there—a man with principles and an unrelenting love for his country who had become a friend and a father figure to him. He silently prayed for a miracle as he knelt down beside him.

Kate was already tending to his wound.

"How is he?" Matt asked, fearing the worst.

Buzz's eyes fluttered open. Then, remarkably, he winked at Kate and said, "He's died and gone to heaven if this angel is any indication." His face was pale but his sense of humor was clearly intact.

Matt smiled tentatively. "Seriously, Buzz, how are you feeling?"

"I'm fine, son," he replied honestly. "I think the bullet went clean through my shoulder. I'll live to fight another day."

Buzz could see the relief on Matt's face. He was touched by his young friend's concern. He smiled through the pain. "That was damn stupid, by the way, you charging a man with a loaded gun," he mocked.

Matt fired back, "Yeah, well, I wasn't going to just stand there and let myself get shot like you did." He gave Buzz a crooked smile. "I figured the least I could do was give him a moving target."

"Wiseass," Buzz grumbled.

"Yeah, but you still love me like a son," Matt joked.

The smile disappeared from Buzz's face. "Yes, I do."

Matt was caught off guard by Buzz's sentiment. He reached down and squeezed his hand. "You scared the shit out of me," Matt said, his voice catching in his throat.

Kate looked on with tears in her eyes. She had never seen Matt look so vulnerable.

"Come on," Buzz said, "help an old man up off his ass."

34

Present Day

New York, NY

Kate Hampton sat by herself at a café table outside a small East Village coffee shop. Her cup of coffee sat on the table untouched. The caffeine, she decided, would only put her already jittery nerves more on edge. She pulled out the note that had been slid underneath her apartment door the night before. She read it again.

I believe your brother was murdered. Meet me tomorrow morning. 9am at the Coffee Shack. Corner of Avenue B and Seventh. Come alone.

She looked down at her watch and checked the time again. It was ten minutes past nine.

It had been a whirlwind week since the events in the Gila National Forest. She had long since removed the wafer-thin tracking device the Russian hit man had hidden inside the screw back case of her favorite watch. After a thorough search of her apartment, Matt had found two other transponders. One was hidden inside a pair of Kate's sneakers and a third tucked inside a seam of a favorite handbag. They were confident they had found them all, but remained on high alert just in case there were more bad guys trying to find them.

It had taken them almost two days to hike back from Canyon Creek to the Gila Hot Springs Ranch. Their ride out of the wilderness had been slowed considerably due to the additional load lashed to the backs of the pack mules—the dead bodies of Hal Billings and his Russian assailant. They gave matching, albeit untruthful, statements to the local sheriff, agreeing to keep the truth a secret until they could plan their next move.

They claimed a deranged man dressed in camouflage appeared out of nowhere and attacked them. There was no mention of the cave or Geronimo's Gold. Kenny Morgan was painted as a hero, having arrived back at their camp just in time to kill their assailant. The sheriff had no reason not to believe their story. According to him, this was not the first time something like this had happened inside the remote park. Just two years earlier a young couple was accosted by a drifter wielding a machete.

The mysterious Russian assailant was carrying no identification, so the sheriff explained it might take them some time to identify the man. In the meantime, he would arrange for Hal's body to be returned home. Buzz, his shoulder in a sling, flew on ahead to Arizona to personally break the news to Cora. The sheriff took their contact information so he could follow-up as necessary in the coming weeks.

Kate scanned the sidewalks outside the coffee shop. Still nobody approached her table. She was becoming increasingly nervous as the minutes passed. *Was this a set-up?* She and Matt had discussed the possibility. But they reasoned that if someone wanted to harm them, they wouldn't have chosen such a public venue. She looked across the street to where Matt had discreetly positioned himself at a bus stop. He had covered the bottom half of his face with a newspaper he was pretending to read, but kept his eyes fixed on Kate from the moment she sat down. He would be there in seconds if anything went awry.

At 9:20 a.m. man finally approached her table.

Matt spotted him first as he walked up the sidewalk. It wasn't hard. As he advanced toward the coffee shop he kept glancing over his shoulder to see if he was being followed. His skittishness made Matt immediately suspicious—and also uneasy.

Short in stature, the approaching man appeared to be in his late twenties or early thirties. Black framed eyeglasses adorned his slightly jowly face and his thick, curly black hair was a bit unkempt. If not for the way he was dressed, Matt might have mistaken him for an accountant. But instead of a suit and tie, he had on a pair of jeans and a ratty black T-shirt. A Nepali hemp knapsack with rope ties was slung across his back.

With one last look over his shoulder, the man sat down warily across from Kate. A moment later, Kate motioned for Matt to join them at the table. The man was caught off guard by his arrival. He became agitated and threatened to leave. But when Kate insisted she would not continue without Matt's presence, he reluctantly agreed to stay.

His name was Josh Reuben and he was a reporter for *The Pit*, a financial news website. *The Pit*, and Reuben in particular, had developed a reputation over the past couple of years for breaking major financial news stories before the mainstream media outlets. Reuben was one of their best reporters and his primary area of expertise was financial scandals. He was a relentless investigator and had a take-no-prisoners reporting style. This approach had secured him considerable notoriety, which is how Adam Hampton found him. But it had also earned him more than a few enemies along the way.

"So how did you know my brother?" Kate asked after Reuben finished his brief introduction.

Reuben answered while continuing to eye Matt suspiciously, "A couple of months before he was killed, Adam came to see me. It wasn't long after he uncovered the suspicious gold-trading activity taking place inside his firm, Morton Sinclair. He wanted someone to talk to who was an expert and who wouldn't pull any punches. I guess given my reputation for getting to the bottom of scandals, he came to me."

For the first time since he had sat down, Matt saw the confident side of Reuben. When it came to his abilities, Reuben was self-assured, if not downright cocky. His assuredness, however, was quickly replaced with paranoia when a waiter approached unexpectedly. Reuben nearly jumped out of his chair at the sound of the man's voice behind him.

As the waiter retreated from their table, Matt asked, "Are you okay? If you don't mind my saying, you seem pretty nervous for a guy who deals with corruption on a daily basis."

Reuben took exception. "Corruption, yes, but not *murder*," he snapped.

His behavior was becoming more animated by the second. He wiped perspiration from his upper lip and ran a shaky hand through his hair. His eyes were in constant motion, darting left and right. He reminded Matt of the black-and-white Kit-Cat clock that used to hang in the kitchen of his childhood home. The cat's round, plastic eyes shifted left and right with every tick.

Matt was on high alert. Kate, on the other hand, felt empathy for Reuben. She could tell he had been under a tremendous amount of stress.

"Believe me," she interjected, "I understand your anxiety. I mean, finding my brother's apartment burglarized was one thing, but getting mugged by the men involved in this conspiracy was terrifying."

Reuben went from being agitated to downright panicked. "You were mugged?" he croaked. "When?"

"A few weeks back," Kate said, taken aback by the urgency in Reuben's voice.

"Jesus," he said. "This is so fucked up," he muttered. He looked like he was going to be sick. He got up from the table abruptly. "This meeting was a mistake," he said.

Matt shot a hand out and grabbed Reuben firmly by the wrist. "You're not going anywhere, Josh," he said firmly, "until you tell us why you asked Kate to come here today." Reuben stood there frozen in place, unsure of what to do. "Look," Matt added, sensing his indecision, "we know about the conspiracy to corner the gold market, but it's obvious there's more you want to tell us. What else did Adam find?"

Matt could feel Reuben's body shaking beneath his grip. Finally, he sat back down. "What the hell, I'm probably a dead man anyway," he muttered bitterly.

"What do you mean by that?" Matt asked.

Reuben reached into his knapsack and removed a crumpled-up article. He laid it down and flattened out the creases before sliding it across the table to Matt.

It was a story from the *New York Post* about a reportedly random mugging in New York's Greenwich Village neighborhood. The victim was apparently robbed at gunpoint. In gruesome detail it told how the victim was taken back to his apartment where his neck had been slit open with a hunting knife. The article went on to say that among the items stolen from the man's apartment was a cache of sophisticated computer equipment. According to the police, the victim was a freelance computer programmer.

"Did you know this guy?" Matt asked, confused as to how this related to their situation.

Without looking up, Reuben answered slowly, "Yeah, I knew him. But to say he was a freelance computer programmer doesn't do him justice."

He cracked the knuckles on his left hand loudly before continuing. "He was a hacker. And not just any hacker—he was the best. I hired him off the books a few times in the past to help me get hold of sensitive files"—he paused—"from people who wouldn't part with them willingly, if you get my meaning."

"So he helped you steal them," Matt said bluntly.

"Pretty much." Reuben shrugged unapologetically. "It was justified, believe me. It helped us expose bad guys doing lots of illegal shit."

"So what does any of this have to do with Adam?" Kate asked.

Reuben took a deep breath before saying, "Adam hired my hacker friend to break into the mainframe computer at his firm."

"He did what?" Matt said, surprised at the extremes Adam had gone to in order to uncover the truth. "What was he thinking?"

Reuben looked back and forth between Kate and Adam as if they were missing the point. "Don't you get it? I introduced the two of them. There were only three people in the world who knew about the gold conspiracy...and now two of them are dead."

35

Present Day

New York, NY

Matt picked up the article and read it for a second time.

Two items jumped out at him. The first was the way the victim had been killed—his neck slit open with a knife. The image of a knife handle sticking out of Hal Billings's chest flashed through his mind. It was just too much of a coincidence. He trusted his gut and it was telling him the same man who killed Hal Billings also murdered the computer hacker—*the Russian.* The next image that came to mind was Kenny Morgan's arrow impaled in the Russian's neck. *Karma.*

The second item that jumped out at Matt was from the list of items stolen. "Sophisticated computer equipment," the article said.

Matt thought about it for a minute. He looked at Reuben and said, "They were after his hard drive, weren't they?"

Reuben nodded. "That would be my guess."

"What had Adam and this hacker friend of yours found that was so important—important enough to get both of them murdered?" Matt asked.

Reuben hesitated before answering. He once again turned and

studied the steady stream of pedestrians making their way along the busy sidewalk.

"It's a little late in the game to be getting cold feet, Josh," Matt said impatiently. "We're in this thing up to our asses now. So you need to focus and tell us everything you know. It's our only chance of stopping these guys."

Reuben stared off into the distance for a few moments, lost in his own thoughts. He unexpectedly turned to Kate. "I'm sorry about your brother," he said. "I should have already told you that. He seemed like a good guy."

"Thank you," she said. Then she reached across the table and gently squeezed Reuben's hand. "Please, don't let Adam's death be in vain. Will you help us?" There was desperation in her voice but also determination.

Reuben wrestled for a moment with his own mixed emotions. He feared for his life but he also knew he owed it to Adam to help his sister in any way he could. It didn't take him long to make up his mind. He sat up straighter in his chair.

"Okay," he said, "I'll tell you everything I know. But I have to warn you, it might be too late to do anything about it."

Matt had to give Kate credit. Her softer approach worked.

Reuben went on, "My hacker friend—he went by the name Slayer, by the way. He found a back door into the email system of Morton Sinclair. But he didn't stop there. He also hacked into a half dozen other Wall Street banks."

"A half dozen?" Matt said, surprised.

"Like I told you, Slayer was the best."

"Who were the other firms?" Matt asked.

Reuben rattled off the names from memory. They were some of the largest, most prestigious firms on Wall Street.

"My god, there are more people involved in this thing than we thought," Matt said.

"According to emails and other encrypted documents Slayer downloaded, the conspiracy involved an elaborate network of traders. The traders all placed buy orders for the same large confidential client. But since the trades were carefully timed and spread out across so many different firms, the scheme went undetected for years," Reuben said.

"This confidential client didn't happen to be Chinese, did they?" Matt asked even though he suspected he already knew the answer.

Reuben didn't hide his surprise. "How the hell did you know that?"

"James Sinclair told me."

Reuben leaned back in his seat and silently absorbed this new information. "Huh, Adam never told me" he muttered to himself while pushing the glasses up on the bridge of his nose, "but obviously, he had enlisted the help of Sinclair, too." He mulled the thought a moment longer before he changed gears, "So you must also know cornering the gold market isn't China's endgame."

"Yes, we know about their plan to replace the U.S. dollar with the renminbi as the world's currency," Matt said.

"And in the process kill two birds with one stone," Reuben added. "They become the dominant financial superpower while precipitating the collapse of the only other economy big enough to challenge them on the world stage—the United States."

Matt shook his head in amazement just as he had when James Sinclair first told him about China's audacious plan. It was financial terrorism on the largest possible scale. But he had to admit, it was also brilliant. He motioned for Reuben to continue.

"So Adam and Slayer were eventually able to trace the buy orders back to the largest sovereign wealth fund in China—the Shanghai Investment Consortium. The SIC is part of China's shadow banking community. They're responsible for investing the biggest chunk of China's currency reserves. We're talking trillions of dollars. But they operate in the shadows. Their investments are highly secretive and funneled through multiple shell companies to avoid international monitoring."

He paused a moment to make sure they were still following him. "But in order to corner the gold market, they had to establish a network of traders here in the U.S. These crooked traders not only executed the trades for China but they manipulated their respective firm's widely published commodities market forecasts—to help nudge the future price of gold in the direction they desired. That way China could acquire gold in the dips, so their buying wouldn't drive the price too high."

"So they killed Slayer to get to his hard drive and eliminate all the incriminating evidence he had compiled on them," Matt said shaking his head in disgust.

"I'm afraid so," Reuben said.

"That's why they broke into Adam's apartment," Kate suddenly blurted out, remembering her brother's burglarized apartment. "His laptop must have had copies of those files on it."

"Adam would have definitely had a copy of everything Slayer did," Reuben agreed.

"We're never going to catch these guys without those computer files," she said. Her eyes moistened with tears as the reality hit her. "My brother's death will be for nothing."

Kate held her head in her hands.

Matt smacked the table in frustration. "Damn it," he said. "We're too late."

Behind them, a taxi driver leaned on his horn. A city bus had just cut him off. The driver leaned out of his yellow cab and cursed in an unrecognizable language. The commotion went unnoticed by the three people sitting around the small café table.

"Maybe not," Reuben offered hesitantly.

He reached down into the knapsack lying at his feet. He pulled out a small flash drive, the kind used to back up files on a computer. "I received this in the mail a couple of days after Slayer's death," he said. "Evidently, he had put a contingency plan in place, in case something happened to him." He paused and said admiringly, "Like I told you, he was thorough."

Kate brushed aside her tears. "You mean," she said, looking wide-eyed at the little flash drive, "the files you talked about are all on there?"

Reuben nodded. "Everything—the entire conspiracy is laid out in explicit detail by your brother. I couldn't have written a better exposé myself. He connects names, he calls out the institutions involved, he details their covert trading strategy, everything. And there are hundreds of incriminating emails on there as well."

It took a few moments for Matt to comprehend the magnitude of the evidence sitting in front of him. This was a game changer. But he still had one more question.

"So, who was the point man for the Chinese here in the U.S.?" he asked, still trying to put together all the pieces of the conspiracy. "They had to have had a very well connected Wall Street insider," he guessed. Then he remembered their visit to Morton Sinclair. "It wasn't Barry Walker was it?"

Reuben smiled. "That douche bag?" He turned to Kate and apologized, saying, "Sorry, but that's how your brother referred to him."

Kate waved him off. "It's alright; it's what we thought of him, too."

Reuben turned back to Matt. "To answer your question, no, Walker and the rest of the insider traders were only in it for the money. They had no idea what the Chinese were really up to. But Adam and Slayer were able to track one man down. And you're right; he is *very* well connected—connected enough to put together a highly functioning trading operation inside some of the largest financial institutions in the country. One that went undetected for years."

"So who is he?" Matt pressed.

Reuben's paranoia seemed to have come back for a return engagement. He glanced quickly over both shoulders. Only when he was once again satisfied that nobody was eavesdropping on their conversation, did he continue. "The person in bed with the Chinese is a man named *Samuel Rothstein*—the chairman of Eight Ball Investments," he said in a hushed tone.

"Sam Rothstein?" Matt said surprised, "the junk bond trader who did time in prison?" He knew the name well from his own days as a bond trader on Wall Street. Rothstein was a legend for his meteoric rise and subsequent fall from grace.

"That's right," Reuben confirmed. "Adam found a preliminary and highly confidential prospectus filed by Eight Ball Investments as part of their initial public offering process three years ago. That's how he discovered Rothstein's connection to a certain sovereign wealth fund doing business out of mainland China."

"Shanghai Investment Consortium," Matt interjected.

"One and the same," Reuben acknowledged. "According to the confidential documents, SIC owns a twenty-five percent stake in Eight Ball Investments. But even though Adam had found the link he had been looking for, he still needed proof of Rothstein's involvement in the conspiracy. So with a little help from Slayer, he gained access to his home computer. What they found confirmed Adam's suspicions. The email stream between the Chinese and Rothstein left no doubt. Rothstein was China's man on the inside. And he had full knowledge of their intentions to bring down the U.S. financial system."

"That son of a bitch," Matt grumbled.

"At least the conspiracy now has a face," Kate said hopefully.

"Why haven't you gone public with what you know?" Matt asked Reuben. "*The Pit* is the perfect forum to take Adam's case directly to the American public."

"Are you serious?" Reuben asked incredulously. "First of all, the evidence compiled by Adam and Slayer was obtained illegally. But more than that, I'd like to go on living," he said with contempt. "This isn't just some run-of-the-mill conspiracy. Sam Rothstein is a very powerful and obviously very dangerous man. And my guess is his Chinese partners wouldn't hesitate to remove any obstacles in the way of their plans either. So if it's all the same to you, I'd prefer to lay low right now."

Reuben stood up to leave. "Here," he said, thrusting the flash drive at Kate. "This belonged to your brother. I think you should decide what to do with it. Good luck."

The second the flash drive left his hands, Reuben looked like a lead weight had been lifted off his shoulders. Without saying good-bye, he turned and hurried off down the street.

Kate turned to Matt with a look of dread. No words needed to be spoken because they shared the same thought. The responsibility for throwing the door wide open on China's terrorist plans to collapse the U.S. economy was in their hands now.

And Sam Rothstein was the key.

They should have been excited by the progress they had made that morning. But the reality was that the target already placed on their backs had just gotten bigger.

36

Present Day
New York, NY

Black-tie events were relatively commonplace in a city like Manhattan. But this one was different. Sam Rothstein did not throw ordinary parties—especially when the evening's honoree was Rothstein himself. The occasion was his sixtieth birthday and the event was by invitation only.

The guest list wasn't small, but it was exclusive. And since everything Rothstein did he did to excess, his Park Avenue triplex was decorated like a set from one of his favorite James Bond movies. Blackjack tables, roulette wheels, and craps tables had transformed his Upper East Side sprawling apartment into a Monte Carlo casino. As specified on the invitation, Rothstein was the only attendee allowed to where a white tuxedo. The diminutive host had to sometimes get creative to ensure he would be the focus of everyone's attention.

The all-female waitstaff had been hired from a local modeling agency. Their high cheekbones, ample cleavage, and long legs gave them away. Dressed in ultrashort gold lamé cocktail dresses, the girls strutted their way through the throng of guests. They handed out crystal flutes filled to the rim with bubbly two-hundred-dollar-a-bottle champagne. The girls did not go unnoticed by the men in attendance, particularly the married ones. More than a few of these men paid for their conspicuous ogling with a sharp elbow to the ribs, courtesy of their miffed wives.

Kate Hampton turned a few heads of her own as she entered the expansive room known as the Grand Salon. She was hard to ignore, dressed in a shimmering emerald green evening gown that augmented the curves of her shapely figure. The gown was accessorized by diamond earrings and a strand of pearls that had been gifts from her grandmother. She looked resplendent as she walked arm in arm with Matt.

"Stop fidgeting," she whispered.

"I can't help it," he said. "This bow tie is cutting off my oxygen."

"You look very handsome," she reassured him.

"Thanks," he said distractedly, "do you see him yet?"

"He's hard to miss." She nodded her head in the direction of an enormous fireplace on the other side of the room. Standing among a fawning passel of guests was Sam Rothstein. He stood out like a white exclamation point in a sea of black ink.

Just then, the music came to an abrupt stop. It was replaced by a breathy Marilyn Monroe–like voice. They spotted a woman with a handheld microphone sashaying her way through the crowd in the direction of Rothstein. One of the other guests informed them it was Rothstein's second wife—a socialite from a well-known and well-connected Manhattan family. She looked to be a good ten years younger than Rothstein. But looks could be deceiving. With the kind of money Rothstein possessed, the natural aging process could be reversed by a plastic surgeon's scalpel and an expensive dye job.

As wife number two dived into her prepared speech, one that undoubtedly had been approved by her obsessively controlling husband, Matt scanned the roomful of guests. He recognized the faces of a few local politicians but everyone else was unfamiliar. Even so, it wasn't hard to guess who the Wall Street money men were—with their graying hair, pot bellies, and entitled dispositions. There was a smattering of young traders in attendance as well. They were the ones with the enormous gold watches, slicked-back hair, and confidence oozing out of their pores. He wondered how many of them were in on the gold buying scheme. But at the moment, none of them mattered to Matt. He was searching for the more dangerous types—the men who stood out for different reasons, namely their jacket size and threat potential. After a few minutes he pegged three such candidates. The biggest bodyguard was standing only a few feet from Rothstein. The other two were on opposite sides of the room, by the exits.

This wasn't going to be easy.

A sudden round of applause interrupted Matt's ad hoc reconnaissance. He turned just in time to see a large sheet being pulled away from something hanging above the fireplace. As wife number two dutifully pulled the rip cord, a full-length oil painting of Sam Rothstein was dramatically unveiled—a special gift to her hubby on his sixtieth birthday.

"I think I'm going to throw up," Kate remarked.

"Wait until we're closer so you can do it on his shoes," Matt said with a smirk. "Come on," he said as he took Kate's hand and pulled her forward, "let's get this over with."

As they crossed the imported, custom-made Italian marble floor, Matt kept an eye on the bodyguards he'd spotted earlier. The good news was that two of the thugs hadn't moved from their posts by the exits. The bad news was that the third man hadn't moved from Rothstein's side either.

"Do you think they know what we look like?" Kate asked.

"I don't know," Matt said, "but we're about to find out," he added ominously.

The smile on Rothstein's face made it clear he thoroughly enjoyed being the evening's center of attention. A husband and wife had just finished their conversation with the guest of honor and moved on.

Matt seized on the opportunity. "Happy birthday," he said, stepping forward.

Rothstein looked quizzically at Matt, trying to place his face. "I'm sorry," he said. "But I don't believe I recall your name." It wasn't an apologetic admission, more of a challenge. Sam Rothstein prided himself on never forgetting a name or a face.

"Technically, we've never met," Matt said with a disingenuous smile. "My name is Matt Hawkins." He held out his hand.

Rothstein's hand was small but his grip firm. "Perhaps my friend's name will ring a bell," Matt said. On cue, Kate stepped forward. "This is Kate Hampton."

To his credit, other than a subtle flinch and the smile disappearing from his face, Rothstein kept his composure. "No," he said coolly, "I don't believe I know the name."

Kate gave Rothstein an icy stare. "How about *Adam Hampton*," she said. "Do you recognize that name? You murderous son of a bitch."

Rothstein's man was too far away to hear the exchange, but he had observed it. The tension in his boss's face was hard to miss. He took a step forward but Rothstein gave him a curt shake of the head. The man retreated but maintained his unwavering vigil.

"Another Russian friend?" Matt said, jerking his head in the direction of the fierce-looking brute.

Rothstein's eye twitched at Matt's "Russian" reference. But he didn't take the bait. "I have no idea what you're talking about," he said, glaring back at Matt.

"Yeah, well just in case you were wondering," Matt said, "the guy you sent to find us in New Mexico won't be able to attend this evening. I'm afraid Boris's partying days are over." Then he added coldly, "Forever."

Rothstein's eyes narrowed. The mystery as to why he hadn't heard from his hired gun in close to a week had just been answered—apparently he was dead. Inside, Rothstein was seething, but he remained remarkably calm on the outside.

"You've got some balls, I'll give you that, boy," he said condescendingly. "But," he continued, and leaned in so he was only inches away from Matt's face, "you're fucking with the wrong guy."

"Call me boy again and you'll find out just who you're fucking with," Matt said icily. "I don't care how many gorillas you've got protecting you."

A Barbie-looking waitress sauntered over. Her presence seemed to break the tension. Rothstein took a step back and casually plucked a flute of champagne off her tray. He took a small sip and smacked his lips loudly. As the waitress moved on, Rothstein said through a forced smile, "I eat chumps like you for breakfast."

Matt pulled a copy of the flash drive out of his pocket and tossed it at Rothstein. "Eat this."

Rothstein snatched it out of the air. For the first time, a glimmer of doubt showed in his eyes.

"What's this?" he demanded.

"That," Matt answered, enjoying the leverage the little flash drive had given them, "is a real problem for you."

Kate added, "It contains the names of all the banks involved, the network of crooked traders you assembled, your secret arrangement with the Chinese...everything. The entire gold conspiracy is flayed open like a dead fish. All compiled in painstaking detail by my brother, Adam Hampton." She paused to control her emotions. "You thought you had eliminated the trail of evidence when you murdered my brother and that poor computer programmer who helped him—but you didn't."

Rothstein's jaw went slack.

Kate added contemptuously, "That's right, you bastard, they made a copy of *everything*. We have it all." It took her all of her self-control not to scratch his eyes out.

Rothstein remained uncharacteristically silent for a moment.

Matt's curiosity finally got the best of him. "Why did you do it?" he asked. "Why did you help the Chinese? Don't you know what will happen if they succeed? The amount of suffering you'll cause? This country might not ever recover, for God's sake."

For the first time that evening, Rothstein's famous temper surfaced. "Suffering?" he said indignantly. Spittle flew from his mouth. "I spent six years in jail because of some bullshit government vendetta," he raged. "Don't you dare talk to me about *suffering*."

Matt shook his head. "It doesn't matter now anyway. It's over," he said. "When we go public with what we have, you and your pals will be finished."

"Finished?" Rothstein mocked. "I hardly think so."

Matt and Kate looked back at him in bemusement.

"You're too late," Rothstein explained. "You think this," he held up the flash drive, "is going to stop me?" His look turned wicked. "I wanted to start a war. And by God, a war is what I'm going to get," he seethed. "Don't you understand? The fuse has already been lit and the explosion is inevitable."

Matt couldn't tell if Rothstein was bluffing or telling the truth. The shrewd Wall Street dealmaker was tough to read. Either way, Matt knew it was time to move on and play his other card.

"Well, you better snuff out that fuse, because you're not going to corner the gold market," Matt said confidently.

"We already have, you fool," Rothstein replied while glancing down at his watch. "I think your time is up here..."

Matt pressed on. "What if I told you we've found the mother

lode of all gold deposits right here in America. And that it's a deposit so big you'll never be able to corner the world's gold supply?"

Rothstein took a measured sip of champagne. "I assume you're referring to the so-called Geronimo's Gold?" he replied offhandedly. Before he had departed for the Gila wilderness, the Russian had apprised Rothstein of Matt and Kate's search for Geronimo's Gold. "From my understanding, it's nothing but a legend. But even if it weren't, I doubt it's big enough to worry about."

"You sure about that?" Matt said, and then leaned in and added, "you smug son of a bitch."

Rothstein was not a man blessed with deep reserves of patience. And he had just reached his limit. He turned and signaled to his bodyguard. The man stepped forward with a menacing scowl.

"Help them find the exit," Rothstein ordered angrily.

The man reached out a beefy arm. "Let's go," he commanded.

Before Matt was ushered out, he looked up at the life-size painting of Rothstein just unveiled above the fireplace. "You know," he said, "you're a lot shorter in person."

He knew it was childish to say, but he also knew it would get under Rothstein's skin. And by the look on Rothstein's face, it had.

In the back of the cab on the way to Kate's apartment, Kate said, "Do you think we did enough to spook him?" She added skeptically, "He seemed pretty confident."

"He may have seemed confident, but, trust me, we rattled him," Matt answered.

He pulled out his cell phone and dialed a private number that only a handful of people in the world possessed. When the man answered, Matt said simply, "The bait's been set."

After Matt ended the call, Kate asked anxiously, "So now what?"

Matt continued to stare out of the cab window at the bright lights of the big city. He was deep in thought, replaying the events of the evening in his head.

"Now we wait," he said.

37

Present Day

New York, NY

They didn't return directly to Kate's apartment.

Matt asked the cab driver drop them off a few blocks away. He needed some fresh air to clear his head. After walking for a bit they ducked into a neighborhood tavern for a nightcap. By the time they reached Kate's building their edginess had eased and their spirits had improved considerably.

They trudged up the stairs to the top floor of the old brownstone. Matt commented that maybe it was time for Kate to move to a building with an elevator. Kate scoffed at the idea, insisting part of the historic building's charm came from the fact it was a walk-up.

"Come on, you're a big strong guy, can't you handle a few steps?" Kate teased.

"I'll show you what I can handle." Matt eyed her mischievously. She giggled uncontrollably as he chased her up the final flight of stairs.

Just as they reached the door to her apartment, a man stepped out of the shadows of the dimly lit top landing. Startled, Kate screamed and jumped back.

"Shut up," the man hissed.

Matt stepped in front of Kate, ready for a confrontation. But he stopped short when he spotted a pistol in the man's hand. The stranger stepped forward until he was directly beneath the solitary overhead light in the cramped corridor. Kate and Matt reacted simultaneously in shocked surprise.

The man was no stranger. It was Barry Walker, Adam's old boss from Morton Sinclair.

"Barry," Kate managed to say, "what are you doing?"

"I told you to shut up," Walker said nervously. He waved the gun in the air dangerously. He was wearing what looked to be an expensively tailored blue pin-striped suit. But it was rumpled so badly it was hard to tell.

"Easy now, Barry," Matt said, fearing he might fire the gun accidently. "What exactly do you want?"

He made sure to hold his hands where Walker could see them. He spoke in a calm voice—at least as calm as he could manage given the circumstances.

Walker ignored him. "Open the door," he told Kate.

When Kate didn't move fast enough, Walker raised the gun and hissed, "Do it now."

Walker stepped closer and, for the first time, Matt got a clear view of his face. It wasn't good. His pupils were so dilated Matt could barely see his irises. Matt remembered from his Wall Street days seeing the same thing in the eyes of some of the traders known to be addicted to cocaine. He knew he needed to tread carefully. Walker wasn't just holding a loaded pistol, he was one.

"Okay, Barry, we're doing what you asked, now point that thing away from us," he said angrily.

"Just hurry up," Walker barked. Kate fumbled for the key to her apartment and inserted it into the lock.

Matt thought he detected a trace of exhaustion in Walker's

voice. And the dark circles under his eyes gave him reason to believe Walker hadn't slept in days. It appeared to have been at least that long since he'd shaved.

Kate was shaking as she pushed open the door. They entered her apartment in a single file. Matt looked for any opening to go for the gun. But in spite of his harried state, Walker was careful to keep his distance. Still, he appeared afraid and confused, which was a bad combination for a man with a loaded gun in his hands.

Matt tried to keep him talking. "We know all about the gold conspiracy, Barry. And we know Sam Rothstein is the man behind the operation." He had no intention of enlisting the help of Walker at this point, but the guy looked like he could use a friend, so he added, "We're going to nail him and we could use your help."

"You think you can stop someone like Rothstein," he scoffed at Matt's suggestion. "Forget about it. He's too well connected."

"That's not true, Barry. We've found a way. He's going to go down." He paused. "And if you help us, we'll put in a good word for you, maybe help you cut a deal," he said, trying to convince Walker he still had options.

But Walker wasn't going for it. "I don't think there are any deals in my future," he said as he shook his head cynically. "And as for Rothstein, he'll be long gone before anyone gets close to him."

"What do you mean, long gone?" Matt asked.

"Don't you know, smart guy?" Walker said mockingly. "Rothstein is a Russian citizen."

Matt couldn't hide his surprise.

Walker continued, "That's right, both his parents were born there. He's even got a place on the Black Sea in some little resort town."

Walker looked exhausted. He wavered on his feet before barely regaining his balance. He blinked his eyes hard to try to regain his focus. "If he thinks the government is onto him, he'll just head to

New Jersey, fire up his private jet, and disappear. And you know what the beauty of his plan is?"

Matt shook his head.

"Russia has no extradition treaty with the United States." He laughed derisively. "So believe me when I tell you Sam Rothstein is most definitely untouchable."

"We can find a way, Barry. I promise you," Matt said hopefully.

"No, no, no, no, no," Walker repeated maniacally. "Shut up." He massaged his throbbing temples with the knuckles of his free hand. "No more talking, you're just trying to confuse me."

Matt inched closer but Walker saw him. He thrust his gun forward and warned, "Don't move or I swear I'll shoot." The man was teetering on the edge. He began muttering nonsensically to himself while continuing to wave the gun haphazardly in Matt and Kate's direction. Matt had no choice but to back off.

A few moments later, Kate spoke up in a soft voice. "This isn't you, Barry." Her voice was hesitant but strong. She recollected the framed pictures of Walker's wife and children from when she and Matt had visited his office. "You've got a family that loves you and you make a good living," she continued. "You're not a killer."

"Yes, I am," he said, in a voice that sounded more like a child's than a grown man's.

"No, you're not, Barry, this isn't who you are," she said soothingly.

"Yes, it is," he snapped. The unpredictable anger had bubbled to the surface once again. "You don't understand," he whined. He began to rock on the balls of his feet. "Oh God, what have I done?" he blubbered.

Matt and Kate could see he was wrestling with some inner demons. Tears began to stream down his face. They were running out of time. Walker's emotional state was reaching a breaking point.

Kate persisted. "It's okay, Barry." She took a hesitant step forward, then another. Only three feet separated them now. She held out her hand. "Give me the gun, Barry."

"Don't you hear me?" he cried. "I am a killer." He looked at Kate pleadingly. Snot bubbled from his nose. Finally, he said, "Rothstein didn't give me any choice. He told me to kill Adam...and I did."

Kate froze. *The man who had ducked behind the subway platform pillar was Barry.*

"That's right, it was me. I pushed your brother in front of that subway train. I killed him," he screamed. Tears flowed freely down his face and the gun went momentarily slack in his hands. He was sickened with what he had done. He hated himself for becoming Rothstein's lackey, but he also knew he'd kill again if it meant saving his own ass.

Possessed with a rage that had been building ever since she first suspected her brother had been murdered, Kate threw herself at Walker. "You bastard!" she screamed. She closed the gap and was on him before he could react.

She clawed at his face. Walker yelled out in pain. He was a large man and he managed to toss her aside, but not before blood streamed out of one of his eyes. Kate landed on the floor with a thud. Her eyes were wild and Walker could see she would not stop until she had her revenge.

Once again, he believed he had no choice. He would be forced to kill again. He raised the gun. But before Walker had a chance to fire, he felt the full force of Matt's two-hundred-pound frame slam against him. The impact sent the two men toppling over the couch.

Somehow Walker managed to hold on to the gun. He got to his knees and once more attempted to fire. But Matt's reflexes were too fast for the cocaine-impaired killer. He thrust his left hand out and grabbed hold of the muzzle. He twisted hard so that the gun was no longer pointed in his direction. Then he slammed his right fist into Walker's face. The gruesome sound of snapping cartilage could be heard as Walker's nose collapsed under the blunt force of the blow. A river of blood ran down his face.

Finally, Walker released his grip on the pistol and collapsed in a heap on the floor. His will to fight had been completely sapped. He began to sob uncontrollably.

Knowing Walker no longer posed a threat, Matt pocketed the gun and scrambled over to check on Kate. She was sitting with her back against the wall. She, too, was crying, but for a much different reason. He glanced back at Walker, who was still curled up in a ball on the floor.

"Adam probably never saw it coming," she sputtered. "Can you imagine the shock when Walker pushed him in front of that train? I just keep imagining the terrified look on his face before the train slammed into him."

He knelt down on the floor beside Kate. "Shh, it's over now," he said softly. "Walker isn't going to harm anyone else. And I swear to you, Rothstein is going to pay for ordering Adam's death."

Kate collapsed into his arms. "I don't know if I can take any more of this," she said.

A few minutes later, after Kate's crying had abated, Matt leaned back so he could look her in the eyes. "I can't do this alone, Kate," he said firmly. "We need to finish this together." He knew he needed to pull her back from the dark place she had entered and give her a reason to go on.

Finally, she looked up at him. But before she could speak, her eyes went wide in surprise.

"Matt," she screamed and pointed over his shoulder.

He pivoted around just in time to see Walker running toward the enormous custom plate glass window Kate recently had installed in her living room.

"No!" Matt shouted. He scrambled to his feet and chased after Walker. "Barry, don't!"

But it was too late. The window exploded as Walker hurtled through it. By the time Matt and Kate reached the shattered opening, Walker lay prone on the sidewalk four stories below. His neck was positioned at a ghastly ninety-degree angle to his body. Kate gasped and looked away in horror.

Matt shook his head in disgust; *another casualty of the gold conspiracy.*

38

One Week Later
Beijing, China

The news made headlines across the globe.

The Chinese government had just made the startling announcement they were going to back their currency, the renminbi, with gold. But it was the second part of the announcement that sent shock waves throughout the world's financial centers: China would no longer use U.S. dollars for their international trade.

Xinhua, the official news agency of China, said it was time for a "de-Americanized world." The news outlet made the Chinese government's disgust with Washington clear by printing with the following statement from Beijing: "The cyclical stagnation in Washington and their decision to raise the debt ceiling yet again has left many nations' tremendous dollar assets in jeopardy and the international community highly agonized."

The government-run publication went on to quote a highly placed official: "Politicians in Washington have done nothing but postpone the final bankruptcy of global confidence in the U.S. financial system." And the latest debt deal "was no more than prolonging the fuse of the U.S. debt bomb one inch longer." The official stated in no uncertain terms that China would no longer stand by and wait for that to happen. The time had come, he urged, for the world to reject the dollar as their default reserve currency.

The far-reaching announcement called for a return to the gold standard where all countries would be required to back their currencies with hard gold reserves. They asked the International Monetary Fund, which had morphed over the years to become the central bank of the world, to hold an emergency meeting to vote on reinstating the gold standard. They dropped yet another bombshell when they revealed their own gold reserves now exceeded 10,000 metric tons—a five-fold increase from where they stood just seven years earlier. And to eliminate any doubt that they possessed this staggering amount of gold, they would be willing to open their vaults to a transparent and complete international audit.

They boldly went on to accuse the United States government of lying about the amount of gold they had in reserve, and they called for an immediate and independent audit of all U.S. Treasury vaults. If the United States was found to have insufficient gold reserves on hand, then China would subsequently demand that the renminbi replace the dollar as the world's new reserve currency and that the international community transition to the renminbi as quickly as possible.

To hasten this process, China announced they had already entered into currency convertibility agreements with a dozen countries, including Australia, France, Russia, Switzerland, and Germany. This meant these countries could now trade with China without having to convert their currencies into U.S. dollars first. The unilateral move effectively cut the U.S. dollar completely out of the exchange process with these key trading partners.

In auspiciously timed press releases issued later that same day, Venezuela, India, Brazil, South Africa, and Iran all announced they would flatly refuse to buy or sell oil or any other commodity using

U.S. dollars. They would instead recognize the renminbi as their currency of choice. The stated rationale was that China's currency was less risky than the rapidly depreciating U.S. paper currency, especially since it was now fully backed by gold. It was expected more countries would follow suit—or run the risk of being cut out of the loop with the world's biggest trading partner.

The impact of China's midday announcement was immediate. The New York Stock Exchange lost twelve hundred points in less than an hour. In a highly unusual move, trading was halted and the exchange was closed two hours earlier than normal. The writing on the wall was clear. If the Chinese got their way, countries would not be required to carry millions of American greenbacks in reserve. So the United States could no longer resort to printing mountains of money with the confidence there would be a built-in demand for those dollars. World markets reacted swiftly. Demand for the U.S. dollar and U.S. debt dropped precipitously and the value of the dollar cratered on the international exchanges.

American news outlets seized on the story and forecasted catastrophic consequences. If the rest of the world followed China's lead and rejected the U.S. dollar, it would wreak havoc on the comfortable lifestyles many Americans had come to take for granted. When all those dollars from overseas were redeemed, the U.S. would experience hyperinflation—food, furniture, clothing, and, most importantly, gas and oil, would double or triple in price.

American news outlets warned that access to capital would dry up. Many U.S. banks would be forced to shut down because they would no longer be able to borrow money. In turn, both businesses and private citizens would not be able to get loans at reasonable rates. Because the country would be strapped for cash, many government services would be disrupted and some eliminated altogether. In short, the entire American way of life would change dramatically overnight.

People took to the streets in Washington, D.C., and other large cities around the country. They demanded answers. Was it true what the Chinese had claimed—that we no longer had any gold left in our vaults? Was Fort Knox really empty? People held spontaneous rallies and marches. They were angry, scared, and confused. The president put the National Guard on alert as the country prepared for the worst.

At his lavishly appointed multimillion-dollar uptown Manhattan apartment, Sam Rothstein prepared for his self-imposed exile. His bags were packed and he was busy tying up some final loose ends. He would leave the country in less than twenty-four hours.

He hadn't planned on leaving so soon, but his impromptu meeting with Matt Hawkins and Kate Hampton sped up his time-table. Rothstein had been more unsettled by his conversation on the evening of his sixtieth birthday party than he let on. If Hawkins had been telling the truth and there was even the slightest chance he and his friends had found Geronimo's Gold, it could throw a wrench in their carefully laid plans.

Rothstein had invested three years of his life and hundreds of millions of his own money stockpiling gold. He had socked away more physical gold inside a private vault in Russia than he could spend in ten lifetimes. So when the dollar eventually collapsed and the world returned to the gold standard, his net worth would increase tenfold. He would no doubt be one of the richest men in the world. There was more at stake, however, than his personal fortune—much more.

What he would take the greatest satisfaction in was the role he played in bringing the United States to its knees. With his help, China had cornered the world's supply of physical gold and was poised to become the world's preeminent superpower. This mattered little to Rothstein. He could care less which country dominated the world stage, so long as the U.S. was destroyed in the process. Only then would he have made good on his promise to make America pay for how it had wronged him. And pay it would.

Even he never imagined his retribution would take place on such a grand scale. Rothstein smiled inwardly as he recalled the day the Chinese had approached him. At the time, he had no idea how far they intended to go with their plan. Now, three years later, he was ready to taste his revenge—and it would be sweet. But all of it hinged on gold remaining a scarce commodity. Only then could China manipulate its price and hold the world hostage to its demands. That is why the morning after his unsettling meeting with Hawkins, Rothstein called his Chinese partners to Manhattan for an urgent meeting.

After Rothstein informed the Chinese there was a chance the United States could be on the verge of finding an enormous deposit of gold, they agreed to immediately launch the final phase of their plan. While China still held the upper hand, they had to force the international community to reenact the gold standard. They would have to release their intentionally incendiary announcement to the world months ahead of schedule.

As Rothstein prepared for his surreptitious exit, he thought about how his life was never going to be the same. He would most likely never set foot inside the U.S. borders for the rest of his life. He would have to make his new home in Russia—a country whose amenities and conveniences paled in comparison to what he enjoyed in America. He would also have to ditch his second wife. She would never leave her beloved Manhattan, even if she realized the extent to which the value of her family inheritance would decline once the dollar crashed.

But, of course, she had no idea what was coming. She had no

idea her husband was in bed with the Chinese or that his name would someday be synonymous with perhaps the greatest terrorist America had ever known. Their life together was over. Not that it really mattered to Rothstein. He had tired of her anyway. He made a silent vow that his next companion would be younger—he'd seen enough plastic surgeon bills for one lifetime.

After stuffing a few final files into his briefcase, he picked up his cell phone and dialed the number of a private airstrip in New Jersey. It was time to schedule the departure of his personal jet for the following morning.

39

The Next Morning
Washington, D.C.

The president of the United States held an unscheduled press conference the morning after China's shocking announcement. The event had to be moved to a larger briefing room in the White House to accommodate triple the normal amount of reporters in attendance from both the United States and abroad. The New York Stock Exchange had not yet reopened for business. The opening would be delayed until after the president's address.

As he stepped to the podium, it was estimated that more than a billion people around the globe were watching on television—including most every household in America. The preceding day had been filled with tension and building paranoia regarding the truth behind China's claims—and with them, the future stability of the American economy. In addition to the delayed opening of the stock exchange, the president had declared an emergency federal holiday for all U.S. banks. It was a necessary step to prevent panicked withdrawals from customers concerned about their financial institution's solvency.

Standing next to the president was an entirely unexpected guest.

Carl Lynch, the Libertarian nominee for the upcoming presidential election stood ramrod straight, looking equal parts contrite and irked. Sweat beaded on the Texas senator's brow from the white-hot lights of the television cameras. The president cast a withering sidelong glance at Lynch, and then went on the immediate offensive.

Although he stopped just short of calling China's announcement the day before an act of terrorism, he didn't mince words. He claimed their intentions were premeditated and a deliberate attempt to cause an international crisis by questioning the stability of the U.S. dollar. He further stated their ultimate objective was to collapse the value of the dollar so that the renminbi could ascend to the international reserve currency by default. He went noticeably out of his way, however, to absolve the president of China of any wrongdoing. Instead, he accused a rogue faction within the Chinese government of carrying out the plot.

Then the president switched gears. He turned to his left and revealed the reason Carl Lynch was asked to join him on the podium that morning. "As you know, one of the major claims of China's announcement yesterday was that our country's gold reserves are insufficient to back the U.S. dollar," the president said, "and furthermore, that our vaults, particularly at our Fort Knox facility, are empty."

The president paused and looked directly into the camera. "I stand before the American people today and assure you our vaults are not empty," he declared resolutely. "It is true there has not been an outside audit of our Fort Knox facility in more than fifty years," he admitted. "But as I'm sure you all can appreciate, security and logistical concerns make an audit of this nature a bit tricky, to say the least."

His expression softened a bit, and for the first time since the press conference began, the president allowed himself to smile. "Hell, yours truly wasn't even allowed near the place," he said to a few chuckles from the press corps.

"But that changed last night. Based on yesterday's events, I made a personal visit to Fort Knox to appraise the situation for myself. And I didn't go alone. I wanted to make sure I appeased all the conspiracy theorists out there who wouldn't take my word for it." He paused and looked directly at Carl Lynch. "To satisfy those who would insist that I was part of a cover-up, I decided to bring their most outspoken critic with me."

He motioned with an outstretched arm to the bombastic Libertarian candidate and said, "I'd like to hand the podium over to Carl Lynch. I'll let him tell you what we found inside Fort Knox."

After an awkward handshake, the two men switched places. Lynch was now at the lectern and the eyes of the world were upon him. He fumbled to adjust the microphone. As he did so, he looked nothing like a man who had conducted hundreds of press conferences over his extended political career. On this day, he looked more like a flustered freshman congressman.

"Good morning," he croaked.

He cleared his throat before continuing. "As the president said, he called me last evening and asked that I accompany him to Fort Knox." He removed a handkerchief from his pocket and wiped perspiration from his forehead. "I'm not going to lie to you. Given our past relationship, he was the last person I would have expected to ask me out on a date." Lynch smiled disingenuously. His attempt at humor fell flat.

"Uh, anyway, we arrived at Fort Knox shortly after eight p.m., at which time the president and I were given unfettered access to the most highly secured facility in the land." He digressed and said, "I'd like to take a moment to thank the men and women of our armed services who guard Fort Knox. I believe they do a tremendous job and deserve our highest praise."

The president coughed loud enough to be heard. The message

to Lynch was clear: move on. The president would not tolerate any attempt by him to utilize this particular press conference to score points in the polls. Lynch promptly returned to script.

"As many of you know, I've made some claims in the recent past that the amount of gold our government claimed to possess was overblown. I even went so far as to suggest the vaults in Fort Knox might be empty." He paused before continuing. "It's not often I admit this, but in this instance...I was flat out wrong. I'm here to tell the American people, and the world for that matter that, Fort Knox is not empty, not by a long shot."

Lynch waited for the flashes and murmurs to subside before adding, "But you don't have to take my word for it, I brought along some pictures to show you."

A slide show appeared on a large screen behind him. The images showed Lynch and the president standing in front of a series of enormous vaults. They were lined floor to ceiling with unmistakable rectangular-shaped solid gold bars. Military personnel pictured in the foreground and markings on the vault doors and walls clearly identified the location as the inside of Fort Knox. Additional photos showed Lynch himself drilling into bars of gold to prove they were not filled with tungsten.

The impact of Lynch's declarations and the accompanying photos was immediate. The press corps shouted hundreds of questions all at once. The president quickly stepped back to the podium and held up his hands to quiet the crowd. After a few moments, the room once again fell silent.

"I know you all have plenty of questions, and I promise we will get to them in time," the president said.

"But Mr. President," a senior correspondent from the *Washington Post* shouted out, "how do we know that visit wasn't staged?"

"I'm glad you asked that, Phil," the president responded quickly. "The short answer is you don't. But it's the best we could do on short notice. We thought bringing Mr. Lynch—the most outspoken skeptic regarding the extent of our country's gold reserves—to Fort Knox would go a long way to calming the world's fears."

Before a follow-up question could be asked, he added, "But we have no intention of stopping there. In the coming months, we plan on inviting prominent world leaders to tour our Fort Knox facility. They will be able to see the extent of America's gold reserves for themselves. We have nothing to hide.

"To that end," he continued, "just prior to walking to the podium this morning, I was on the phone with the president of the People's Republic of China. I invited him to tour Fort Knox as well. He accepted the invitation. In return, he assured me he would launch a full investigation into our charges that a subversive faction within his government conspired to collapse the dollar."

Other questions followed but the president ignored them. He talked above the shouts from members of the press. "But that's not even the most exciting development I have to share with you this morning," he said in a raised voice.

The intriguing proclamation had its intended effect. The latest uproar subsided. The president waited until the mechanical whir of the television cameras was all that could be heard in the room.

He said with a noticeably more confident tone, "Most Americans are probably not aware of this. But the fact is almost half of all the gold in this country has yet to be discovered." He paused for effect. "But that's about to change."

The president spent the next ten minutes briefing the world on the remarkable discovery of a new gold deposit on American soil. He explained that geological experts recently dispatched to the undisclosed site estimated the deposit didn't simply represent the largest gold mine ever found in the United States. If their estimates were correct, it would likely be the largest ever found in the world. At an estimated annual production of more than one hundred tons, this newly discovered deposit would surpass the annual gold production of the mammoth Muruntau mining complex in Uzbekistan. Again, the president stressed that independent gold experts from around the world would be brought to the site so they could verify not only the mine's existence but its estimated annual output.

To a stunned audience the president began to wrap up the news conference. "I want to assure the American people," he said emphatically, "your country is stronger than ever. And I want to assure the world that the U.S. dollar continues to be backed by the full faith and credit of the United States government, as it always has been."

He stared defiantly into the cameras. "And for those people who believe a country's currency should be backed by a sufficient amount of gold reserves, you can also rest easy. We have proven today that China's claims regarding our lack of gold reserves are simply untrue. You've heard it from Carl Lynch and you will hear it from other world leaders in the coming months.

"And if that weren't enough, we have recently discovered the largest gold deposit on the planet…right here on American soil. So rest assured, our country's future supply of gold will be guaranteed for years to come."

Before he left the stage, the president stated confidently, "When I leave this room, I am going to personally call the head of the New York Stock Exchange and tell him to open the doors of the exchange."

He concluded by saying, "And to everyone watching at home and across the world, you can be damn sure the United States of America is open for business as usual."

40

The Same Morning
Teterboro, New Jersey

The sleek blood-red Gulfstream G550 private jet was fueled and ready for takeoff. One of the reasons Sam Rothstein had purchased the sixty-million-dollar aircraft was because it could fly more than sixty-five hundred nautical miles without having to refuel. Rothstein would need all of that range on this day. His final destination was located halfway around the world. According to the unfiled flight plans drawn up by the pilot, the plane was scheduled to touch down in twelve hours in the tiny resort town of Gelendzhik on the Russian Black Sea.

Rothstein had built his lavish new home on a thickly wooded mountainside overlooking Gelendzhik Bay. Its temperate climate and impressive views made the southern coastal area a favorite of the Russian elite. And while many villas and mansions lined the picturesque coastline, none were quite as impressive as Rothstein's. It had taken him more than two years and close to one hundred million dollars to construct. Reminiscent of the country palaces the Russian tsars built in the eighteenth century, Rothstein's eighty-thousand-square-foot monstrosity included formal gardens, a private theater, two swimming pools, a landing pad with bays for three helicopters, and accommodations for an army of security guards.

The fortress was conceived shortly after he had entered into his illicit arrangement with the Chinese. He knew the day might come when he would have to flee the United States. And that day had arrived. He had chosen his location wisely, seeking asylum within the borders of the old Soviet Union, America's one-time Cold War adversary, and still a country where U.S. federal authorities could never touch him.

Even though the jet's spacious and luxuriously appointed cabin could accommodate eighteen people comfortably, Rothstein was the only passenger on board. As the Gulfstream began to taxi toward the runway, he took one last look outside. Beyond the tarmac and modest control tower at the edge of the small airport, he could see the famous skyline of New York City ten miles to the east. Memories flashed through his mind as if he were a man headed for the electric chair. And in a strange way, Rothstein felt condemned to a sort of death, as his life in the United States would soon be dead and gone.

His eyes scanned the horizon, searching in vain for the lower Manhattan building where decades earlier he had spent his very first days as an eager young trader. He remembered being stunned at the amount of money there for the taking on Wall Street—and how easy it was to be had, especially if you were willing to bend the rules. It hadn't taken him long to discover he was more than willing to do that.

Like a heroin user, once Rothstein experienced the high that came with the wealth, he realized there was no turning back. As with most addicts, Rothstein overreached and paid the price. During his stint in prison, the life to which he had become accustomed all but disappeared. In the end, it wasn't so much the money he missed, but the power. Power was the ultimate addictive drug. But even during those dark days, Rothstein knew he wasn't finished. He would find a way to return to the top of the mountain. And return he had, with a vengeance. Now, at long last it was his turn to play the role of punisher. It was his turn to sit back and watch people suffer as he had suffered.

His list of enemies was long—the Wall Street insiders who had turned their backs on him; his elitist neighbors on the Upper East Side who tried to evict him from his own home; his wife's blue-blooded family who fed on their bloated trust funds like infants suckling on their mothers' teats; and most gratifying of all, the politicians and bureaucrats who comprised the SEC, the FBI, and every other watchdog agency inside the federal government. He smiled at the thought of what was going to befall the lot of them over the coming weeks and months.

He was interrupted from his private musings by an unanticipated sound. The brawny Rolls-Royce BR710 turbofan engines that powered his Gulfstream abruptly began to power down. Alarmed, Rothstein got up from his seat and walked quickly to the front of the plane. He opened the cockpit door and stared wide-eyed out of the front windshield.

His worst fears had just been realized.

Blocking the runway was a line of government-issued black SUVs and a swarm of agents, all wearing blue windbreakers with *FBI* written in bold yellow letters across the backs. The agents raced toward the plane, automatic weapons drawn. The terrified pilot, who had no knowledge of the nefarious activities of his boss, raised his hands in the air in confused surrender.

Seconds later, the pilot was instructed to lower the stairway and the FBI men boarded the plane. The agents found Rothstein slumped in a plush leather chair toward the rear of the aircraft. After checking him for any concealed weapons and making sure the area was secure, they stepped aside and made way for their boss.

FBI director Stan Krueger cut an imposing figure as he lumbered down the center aisle of the top-of-the-line private aircraft. Krueger stood at over six foot four inches and weighed more than two hundred and fifty pounds. A large bald head and grim scowl completed the intimidating package.

He stood over Rothstein and waited patiently for him to look up. Finally, Rothstein raised his head and locked eyes with the director.

"Hello, Sam," the director growled, "we meet again."

Rothstein's eyes narrowed. He knew exactly who the man was standing in front of him, but he did not ever recall meeting him. "You better have a search warrant, Mr. Director, or I'll have your ass in a sling," he said in a futile attempt at keeping up the appearance of having the upper hand.

The director tried to smile but it looked more like a pained grimace. "I've got something better than a search warrant, Sam. I've got a direct order from the president of the United States."

"Fuck the president...and fuck you, too."

Krueger calmly folded his oversized frame into a matching leather seat facing Rothstein. He rubbed his bald head. "You don't remember meeting me, do you?" he said. "It was back in the early '90s during the government's investigation into your insider trading activity. I was just a wet-behind-the-ears lawyer working on the SEC's lead investigative team."

Rothstein's eyes registered pure hate at the mention of the federal agency responsible for regulating the securities industry and prosecuting white collar criminals.

"The first day of the trial, I met you in the lobby of the courthouse," Krueger continued. "You tried that same bullshit false bravado back then, too. Right up until we put your ass in jail. And now here we are again. But this time, you miserable son of a bitch, I'm going to put you away for good."

Rothstein remained silent and strangely calm. He'd been caught, that much was true. And he would probably spend the rest of his life buried deep inside a federal prison. But he hadn't lost. He had helped the Chinese corner the gold market and given them the leverage they needed to crush the U.S. dollar. America was about to suffer like it never had before. The imminent financial collapse he had helped precipitate would be ten times worse than the Great Depression. An evil smile spread across his face.

"You may have won this round," Rothstein said, motioning in the air with his hand, "but you've already lost the war." He sat back and confidently folded his hands in his lap.

Director Krueger shook his head slowly from side to side. "You still don't get it, do you? It's over, Sam. The Chinese backed down."

Krueger looked around at the latest technology inside the cabin of the jet. There was a sleek laptop computer, a wireless sound system, a high-speed local area network, and the best satellite communications equipment money could buy. He motioned for one of his agents to flip on the sixty-inch flat-screen television mounted to the cabin wall.

The president's press conference was not hard to find; it was playing on every channel.

They watched for a few minutes. Rothstein's jaw dropped as he listened to Carl Lynch elaborate on his personal trip to Fort Knox and expound on all the gold he found there.

"That's bullshit!" Rothstein cried out.

They continued to watch as the president went on to disclose the news of a discovery of a mammoth gold deposit on U.S. soil. Rothstein knew he was referring to Geronimo's Gold. But the reality that the widespread conspiracy had failed didn't hit Rothstein until the president described his private conversation with the president of China. Rothstein was crestfallen when the leader of the free world claimed the president of China had given him his personal assurance that he would ferret out the perpetrators of the conspiracy within the Chinese government.

Krueger got up and switched off the television. Then he walked slowly to the doorway and waved to an agent outside. Seconds later, Matt and Kate ducked into the cabin.

"You two?" Rothstein said bewildered.

Kate marched directly over to Rothstein and, without hesitation, punched him hard in the face. "That's for what you did to my brother."

For the first time all day, Director Krueger smiled.

Surprised by the blow, Rothstein's face turned crimson. He stood up angrily and, remarkably, appeared ready to strike back. Before he had the chance, Matt stepped forward and said, "You might want to rethink that idea."

Defeated and humiliated, Rothstein sat back down. In a voice barely above a whisper, he said, "You were working with the FBI?" He was trying to piece together the events that had culminated with the FBI's raid on his plane.

"The director and I go way back," Matt said simply.

The truth was Matt had met Stan Krueger only a couple of years earlier when he helped derail a plot conceived by a pair of antigovernment billionaire brothers designed to covertly seize control over the U.S. government. The director had given him his personal cell phone number during that time. Matt had held on to it even though he never thought he would have cause to use it again—especially after finding out that the director was also a member of the Ring. But after his meeting with Josh Reuben, he knew he had to call Director Krueger and enlist the help of the FBI. That's when the two men hatched the plan to entrap Rothstein and his Chinese partners.

Krueger said, "Even after Matt came to me with Adam Hampton's flash drive we knew it wasn't enough to stop the conspiracy.

We needed to get the Chinese on video for the world to see. And we knew the only way to do that was through you."

"So we came to your sixtieth birthday party and set the bait," Matt said matter-of-factly. "We hoped revealing the evidence Adam had compiled on you and the Chinese, along with the news of our discovery of Geronimo's Gold, would be enough to make you panic."

"And panic you did," Kate added with a contemptuous smile. She was rubbing the throbbing fingers of her right hand—the hand that had connected with Rothstein's jaw moments earlier. It hurt like hell but she had no regrets.

"You blinked, Sam," Director Krueger said bluntly. "The very next morning, you called your Chinese contacts and arranged an emergency meeting with them. You thought the meeting took place in a secret and secure location. But we were there watching and listening. We recorded and filmed the entire thing. Pretty damning stuff, I've got to tell you."

"So you wanted us to accelerate our timetable?" Rothstein asked in confusion.

"That was the risky part," Krueger allowed. "The downside of sending Matt and Kate to see you that night was it would accelerate your plans. But we also knew there was a good chance the Chinese wouldn't agree to do so without a face-to-face explanation from their point man in America—you. Once we had the video and audio in hand, we had what we needed. All we had to do was sit back and wait for them to go public with their intentions."

"But we have all the gold!" Rothstein shouted in frustration.

Krueger shook his head at Rothstein. "You've got to understand how world diplomacy works, Sam. And the power of back channels." He winked. "After China went public with their announcement yesterday we knew there would be a shit storm. But we were ready. The president ordered the stock market to close early and banks not to open until he had a chance to speak to the American people directly. Then last night, we worked our back-channel contacts within the Chinese intelligence community. Eventually those back channels led to a series of conversations between the president of the United States and the president of China late into the evening. We offered the Chinese president an out—blame the conspiracy on a rogue faction. He either was going to take the deal or risk losing face with the world. He opted to take the deal."

"But why would China back down?" Rothstein croaked. "They had the U.S. by the balls."

"That brings us back to the world diplomacy part," Krueger explained. "Reputations and integrity matter when it comes to international trade relations."

"I think you're talking to the wrong guy about integrity," Matt chimed in, unable to resist the jab.

Krueger nodded. "Good point. But as for the Chinese, they understood the consequences of what we had on them. Once we threatened to expose their treachery to the world in high-definition sound and color, including all the evidence on Adam's hard drive, China knew their credibility as an international trading partner would be destroyed—no matter how much gold you and your little Wall Street elves had helped them squirrel away," he said to Rothstein.

He continued, "But just in case, we still needed to sow seeds of doubt that their plan would succeed—even if they still decided to go through with it. They had to believe or at least think there was a chance they were going to fail anyway, because maybe we had more gold in our vaults than they thought we did. That's where Lynch's tour of Fort Knox came in, and the announcement of the discovery of Geronimo's Gold."

"But the key to the whole operation was getting you to call that emergency meeting with your Chinese partners in crime," Matt said.

Rothstein put his face in his hands and slumped back in his seat in defeat. There was nothing more to say.

It was over.

As Kate and Matt made their way to the exit, Matt, as usual, couldn't resist one last shot. He turned and said with a crooked grin, "I guess you won't be eating any more chumps like me for breakfast, eh, Rothstein?"

41

The Same Morning

New Jersey

"Ride with me," Krueger said to Matt. It wasn't so much a request as it was an order. Krueger turned and headed toward a massive black SUV with tinted, bulletproof windows.

Matt looked over at Kate but she waved him on. "It's alright," she said, "I'll catch a ride with one of these fine-looking young agents." She winked at him teasingly.

"Keep your hands to yourself, young lady," Matt said with a sideways grin. He leaned in and gave her a kiss. "I'll see you back in Manhattan."

As they pulled out of the airport, Krueger said, "It looks like our country is indebted to you once again, son."

"I guess I keep finding myself in the right place at the right time. Or is it the wrong place at the wrong time?" Matt said with a wry smile.

Krueger said, "Either way, I'm glad you're on our side."

"Whose side are we talking about, Mr. Director?"

The large man gave Matt a mischievous look. "Speaking of which, have you made up your mind yet? You've certainly proven your worth. The Ring could use someone like you."

"But I like my quiet life in Savannah," Matt said dryly.

Krueger chuckled. His baritone laugh sounded like runaway boulders tumbling down a mountainside.

"Shit, your life is about as quiet as mine these days," Krueger scoffed.

Matt turned serious. "How the hell did you convince Carl Lynch to stand next to the president at the news conference this morning?"

"He volunteered," Krueger replied, sounding like an innocent schoolgirl.

"Volunteered, my ass."

"Alright, maybe he volunteered after I put his nuts in a vice."

"And I was under the impression torture had been outlawed in this country," Matt replied sarcastically.

"Actually, torture wasn't required in this case," Krueger said. "All I had to do was show him some of Rothstein's emails from Adam Hampton's flash drive. They proved Lynch was colluding with Rothstein to put pressure on the government regarding the extent of our gold reserves at Fort Knox. That's when he offered up his services."

"Those emails between Rothstein and Lynch were fairly tame as I recall," Matt said. "Besides, we both know Lynch had no knowledge of the conspiracy Rothstein and the Chinese had concocted. My guess is the only reason he volunteered was because you threatened to ruin any chance he had at the presidency or any future political office, for that matter. You threatened to expose his role in the conspiracy—even though he really didn't have one. Am I close?"

"Pretty close. Do you disagree with my methods?"

He thought to himself, *Hell no, everything is fair game as far as Lynch and Rothstein are concerned. They deserve whatever they got.*

The end justifies the means—Buzz's words echoed in his head.

Matt stared out the window in silence.

His mind was preoccupied with all the men he and Buzz, with the help of the Ring, had prevented from harming the institutions that kept America's democracy functioning. He remembered the frantic days during the search for Washington's surrender letter. He had no doubt that Charles Metcalf and Chuck Conrad, the two men who had tried to use the presidency for their own financial gain, deserved what they received in the end. Next he thought back on Landon and Oliver Spates' attempt to overthrow the U.S. government. They sure as hell got what they deserved, too. And now they had prevented Rothstein and his band of corrupt bankers from hijacking the international monetary system and wreaking havoc on the U.S. economy in the process.

He felt no guilt about any of it.

The end justifies the means.

Then another thought occurred to him.

"You staged that audit by Lynch, didn't you?" Matt said evenly.

"Sometimes you're a little too smart for your own good, Matt. Let's just say candidate Lynch saw what he needed to see," Krueger said cagily.

"So how much gold really is inside Fort Knox?" Matt asked, unwilling to let it go.

The director turned his massive body in the seat to face Matt. The leather-covered interior squeaked loudly under his considerable weight. "Just enough, evidently," he said evenly.

"Guess we'll never know, eh?" Matt said.

"No, you will not," the director said definitively.

Matt knew the subject was closed.

As they entered the Lincoln Tunnel the car was thrown into darkness. "So how did you really get the Chinese to back down?" Matt asked, changing the subject.

"It happened pretty much the way I told it to Rothstein back on the plane," he began. "After you set the bait with Rothstein at his little party, we obtained a special federal warrant and began tracking his every move. We used bugs in his apartment and offices, wiretaps, surveillance—the whole nine yards. When the Chinese delegation came to town, we filmed and recorded everything they said and did."

He continued, "We had them dead to rights. We had senior officials within the Chinese government on tape planning a financial attack on the United States."

As the intermittently spaced lights on the sides of the tunnel flashed by, Director Krueger looked like an actor in an old black-and-white movie. His face flickered eerily in and out of view.

"And that was enough to make the Chinese back down?" Matt asked.

"You bet it was. Like I told Rothstein, it goes back to confidence and trust. The dollar has value as the world's international currency because the world *believes* it has value." He paused. "Think about it this way. We all work for little green pieces of paper because we have confidence we'll be able to exchange those slips for food and shelter and whatever else we need to get by, right?"

Matt nodded.

"It's the same on an international scale. Countries trade in U.S. dollars because they have confidence they are backed by the government of the United States of America. People can say what they want about us, but America still has the world's faith and trust."

"Agreed," Matt said.

"Now imagine the world found out about China's terrorist plot to collapse the U.S. dollar. All the gold in all the vaults in China wouldn't be able to repair the damage to the Chinese government's reputation. They would have lost the world's confidence and trust. And without that, the renminbi would have never ascended to the position as the world's new reserve currency."

Matt shook his head at how close the Chinese and Rothstein

had actually come to pulling it off. He said, "What about that nonsense about all this being masterminded by a rogue faction inside the Chinese government? You really expect me to believe the president of China had no idea what was happening?"

Krueger had to smile at Matt's keen instincts. "We had to come up with an elegant solution that allowed the Chinese to save face. One might surmise the president of China knew what was going on. But in the end it didn't really matter, we still had to give him an out."

"Why? Why not throw him under the bus with the rest of the bastards?"

"Because that's not how the world works, Matt. As much as we distrust China, we need them. They are an economic behemoth *and* our biggest trading partner. And don't forget, they buy a hell of a lot of U.S. Treasury notes, without which we couldn't keep our economy afloat," Krueger admitted.

"Jesus Christ. It's like a junkie and his drug supplier. The trouble is, I don't know which one we are," Matt said cynically. He shook his head in disgust. "So we just continue on as if nothing ever happened? They tried to destroy us—it would have been like an economic Pearl Harbor, for God's sake."

"I said we gave them an out, Matt, not a free pass. We've got some newfound leverage with them, and believe me, it will be used."

Matt ran a hand through his hair and took a deep breath. "The whole thing stinks, Stan," he said, unable to hide his distaste for the backroom maneuvering that took place on both sides.

"Unfortunately, in this business, we all get a little stink on us."

Matt wasn't sure if he was referring to FBI business or Ring business—probably both.

The two men fell silent. When they emerged from the tunnel onto the island of Manhattan, the sun was shining brightly. It helped improve Matt's mood, if only slightly.

He said to Krueger, "What about Geronimo's Gold?"

"What about it?"

"The president claimed in his speech that it was the highest grade, highest ounce deposit ever discovered—was that just more spin, too?" Matt said, unsure of who and what to believe anymore.

"Actually, that's the truth. We sent our gold experts to New Mexico. It turns out, you guys made a remarkable discovery."

"Yeah, so where's my cut?" Matt asked with a sly grin.

"Sorry, but any gold found on government land is the property of the United States government," he said in an official-sounding voice. "But, of course, you have our undying gratitude," he added blithely.

"Yeah, that and fifty cents will buy me a cup of coffee," Matt said cynically.

Then a thought occurred to him and he asked, "You're not going to mine that gold are you? That would destroy the Gila National Forest."

"The government has no plans to mine Geronimo's Gold...at least for the time being."

"At least for the time being?"

"Let's just call it our ace in the hole—in case we ever need it," Krueger added with a wink.

"You mean in case you ever need the stuff our government claims is not a monetary asset?"

"That's correct, wise guy."

42

Present Day

New York, NY

It wasn't until a few weeks after the president's press conference that stock markets around the world finally returned to normal. Even after the president's personal assurances, the international community's confidence in the dollar had been badly shaken. True to his word, however, the president invited the leader of China for a special visit to the United States. The two world leaders purportedly toured Fort Knox together, although no members of the press were allowed to accompany them inside the facility. After the tour, the president of China released a statement announcing he was satisfied the United States had more than enough gold reserves on hand.

A contingent of international gold experts was escorted to the secret location of the New Mexico gold deposit. They emerged from the visit astonished at the size and quality of the lode. They confirmed it had the potential to be the largest gold deposit ever discovered. The combination of the president of China's announcement, and the validation by international gold experts of the enormous gold deposit, further eased the nerves of the international community. The dollar slowly began to regain strength on foreign exchanges. All talk of a return to the gold standard subsided.

As the world's confidence in the dollar began to return, demand for gold dropped precipitously. The value of China's gold hoard was halved in a matter of weeks. The value of their stash was further diminished as the executive board of the International Monetary Fund levied stiff penalties against them for their illicit attempt to corner the gold market. The United States requested that China's fines be paid in gold bullion. It was a curious demand, especially given the U.S. government's continued public stance that gold had no value as money.

A shake-up within the Chinese government was quietly announced. An unnamed senior Commerce Minister was relieved of his post along with the director of the Shanghai Investment Corporation. Although the two accused men had yet to be made available for comment, it was widely speculated that they were the leaders of the so-called rogue faction responsible for the conspiracy. According to a somewhat vague official news release from Xinhau, the government-controlled news agency, they were being held at an undisclosed location for questioning.

While news filtering out of China regarding the alleged gold conspiracy was limited, that was not the case in the United States. Newspapers, television networks, and online news outlets had been fixated on the crisis for weeks—and with good reason. The country had barely averted a colossal financial disaster. The FBI quickly announced the arrest of Samuel Rothstein. According to several reports, his palatial estate in southern Russia had already been seized by the Russian government. Rumors had it that the president of Russia had his eye on it—as the perfect retreat for him and his poorly kept secret of a mistress.

The FBI had also arrested close to a dozen commodity traders involved in the gold scheme. Even though these men had no knowledge of the larger conspiracy to collapse the American economy, they had been labeled as traitors just the same. Most of them would spend years behind bars. Not only would they never get close to working in the financial sector again, they would most likely spend the rest of their days living as pariahs in their own country.

Josh Reuben's daily column in *The Pit* had gained an enormous following since he first broke the story. In as much detail as the FBI would allow him to share, Reuben outlined the conspiracy from start to finish using information obtained from Adam's flash drive. The American public was shocked out how many banks had been unwittingly duped by Rothstein's gang of corrupt traders.

The FBI would not, however, let Reuben share the true story of Geronimo's Gold and Roosevelt's role in covering it up. They were afraid the story might give away the gold's secret location and tarnish the image of the revered former president. The world would never know about Theodore Roosevelt's private meeting with Geronimo in the White House or the map that was the key to unlocking the now-famous mother lode of gold. As such, the Gila National Forest would remain undisturbed just as Roosevelt intended when he made it a national park more than a hundred years earlier.

Adam Hampton was accurately portrayed as a hero in Josh Reuben's articles. Though Adam's dogged pursuit of the truth had cost him his life, it had also saved his country. Sam Rothstein would not be charged with ordering Adam's murder. There simply was not enough evidence. After committing suicide, Barry Walker, the man who had implicated Rothstein, was not around to testify. Even so, *The Pit* published a personal statement from FBI director Stan Krueger. Krueger made it clear it was his agency's belief that Adam had been murdered by the men behind the conspiracy. The New York City Police Department was told to officially change the cause of death from suicide to murder.

Kate Hampton would be forever grateful to Stan Krueger for going out of his way to make his statement about her brother, and to Josh Reuben for printing it. At least the world would know how Adam had really died.

Krueger further showed his appreciation to Matt's friends by helping Buzz make good on his promise to Hal Billings. The director arranged for the government to pay a generous lump-sum death benefit to Hal's wife, Cora, for the special sacrifice her husband made for his country. It would enable Cora to live comfortably for the rest of her life.

As for Kate and Matt, the memory of Adam proved too much of a strain for their budding relationship. Try as she might, when Kate looked at Matt she couldn't help but think of her brother. And the same was true for Matt in regard to Kate. There was simply too much painful history between them. After talking late into the evening at Kate's apartment one night, they reached the same conclusion. As difficult as it would be to separate, it was the only thing to do.

After saying their good-byes, Matt returned home to Savannah—a bachelor once again.

Epilogue
Present Day
Ruidoso, New Mexico

Matt hadn't planned on returning to Ruidoso. About a month after the crisis ended, a package was delivered by messenger to his shop in Savannah. There was no return address listed. The package was about the size of a shoebox and was not particularly heavy.

Before opening it, Matt paused for a moment to consider the crazy idea that it might contain a bomb or some other incendiary device sent by a pissed-off associate of Sam Rothstein's. But then he remembered that at his request, Director Krueger had left him out of the official investigation report and Josh Reuben had kept his name out of the papers. Matt had already achieved his share of fame in the past. He preferred anonymity this time around.

He grabbed a pair of scissors and sliced through the packing tape. Inside was something that had been wrapped tightly in brown packing paper. And lying on top of the unmarked item was a handwritten note.

Congratulations Matt, it began.

You did it, you won. You stopped the bastards. I know Adam would be very proud of you, as am I. And your country surely owes you a debt it can never repay. You are a good man, Matt, and your selfless actions made this old man pause and take stock of his life. As I said to you when we met at the Buckhorn Saloon, I have done some things for which I am not very proud. If I could go back in time and live my life differently, there would be things I would no doubt change. But, alas, that is not possible. However, there is one wrong I can right. After speaking with my fellow Bonesmen, we agreed it was time to return the enclosed to Geronimo's descendants. It has been sitting in the Tomb, the Skull and Bones headquarters on the campus of Yale University, for the last century. That's quite long enough. I hoped you would do us the honor of delivering it to Kenny Morgan. Thank you in advance for your help.

Respectfully,

James Prescott Sinclair

As Matt drove his rental car through the little resort town tucked away in the New Mexico Mountains, he turned up the speed on his intermittent wipers. The annoying mist swirling around outside had turned into a steady rain. The crappy weather only darkened Matt's already gloomy mood. His thoughts turned to the note from James Sinclair. *You won,* he had written. Only Matt didn't feel like a winner. In fact, he wondered if there were any winners at all at the end of the day.

It all seemed so surreal. Matt still had a hard time reconciling the crazy sequence of events—from Geronimo's Gold to Roosevelt's map to the clandestine activity of the Skull and Bones society. He was grateful, of course, that history had once again revealed just enough of her secrets to help stave off a modern-day crisis. And he took pride in the role he had played in preventing the financial collapse of the American economy and the untold pain and suffering millions of people would have experienced if Rothstein and the Chinese had succeeded. Still, he couldn't shake the empty feeling he had inside. *Had anything really changed?*

Sam Rothstein would never be seen or heard from again, that much was true. But neither would Adam Hampton—or Hal Billings, for that matter. *Was that a fair and just trade-off?* And as much as Director Krueger told him China hadn't received a free pass, Matt had a hard time reconciling that with what he knew to be true. The United States was more than willing to have a short-term memory with regard to the conspiracy, as long as China continued to buy Treasury bills to help finance America's snowballing debt and keep the U.S. economy afloat. *Was that a fair trade-off?*

Matt knew now there was no such thing as a fair trade-off. There never would be. There are only decisions and actions. And noble causes.

Now that he had made his own decision he knew it would come with a price. He believed in the Ring's endgame—the preservation of the democratic institutions that comprised the heart and soul of the United States. But he vowed to never stop questioning their means—because he also believed in checks and balances.

It was late afternoon by the time he pulled off the main road. The parking lot of the Wooden Indian was relatively empty.

As he shut off the engine and removed the key from the ignition, the sun suddenly burst through a fissure in the thick cloud cover. Its rays shone through the windshield like a beam of light through a prism. Matt looked down at the shoebox sitting on the passenger seat next to him. It was bathed in the colors of the rainbow.

He had never removed the item inside from its brown paper wrapping. He didn't have to. He knew with certainty what it was. And besides, it didn't belong to him.

As he picked up the box, a thought occurred to him that immediately lifted his spirits. Maybe one thing was about to change.

A man was about to be reunited with his family—albeit more than a hundred years after his death. He wasn't all the way there yet, but at least his journey back had begun. For Matt had little doubt Kenny Morgan would someday soon return his great-grandfather to where he had so desperately wanted to be at the end of his life—his ancestral home by the foot of the Mogollon Mountains.

It was time to right a wrong, indeed.

Matt grasped the car door handle. "Welcome home, Geronimo," he said quietly.

And for the first time that day he had something to smile about.

###

Author's Note

While the story of Geronimo's Gold and its subsequent cover-up by President Theodore Roosevelt is entirely fictional, many of the historical places, dates, and events in this book are factual.

❖ Geronimo was born near the headwaters of the Gila River, within the present-day boundaries of Gila National Park. He was believed by many to possess supernatural powers, the most noted of which was that he could not be killed by a bullet.

❖ In the mid-1880s more than a quarter of the U.S. Army was hunting for Geronimo. After an extended chase across the deserts and mountains of the Southwest, he finally surrendered to General Nelson A. Miles at Skeleton Canyon, Arizona. After his surrender, he spent the rest of his life in the custody of the U.S. government. The majority of that time was spent at Fort Sill, Oklahoma.

❖ Remarkably, Geronimo did, in fact, ride his horse down Pennsylvania Avenue in Roosevelt's inaugural parade in March 1905. Later that week he met with the president at the White House. He pleaded with Roosevelt to allow him to return to his homeland so he could live out the final years of his life. He was denied. He died four years later and was buried at Fort Sill. His remains are still interred there in the Apache Prisoner of War Cemetery.

❖ Geronimo's Winchester rifle and bowie knife were taken from him after his capture in 1886. They are currently on display at the museum at the U.S. Military Academy in West Point, New York. (However, there is no map etched into the knife's sheath).

❖ While Geronimo's Gold is fictional, a 1998 U.S. geological survey stated that 40% of all U.S. gold deposits had yet to be discovered. The Southwest, including New Mexico and Arizona, is considered a high potential area for undiscovered gold.

❖ The Skull and Bones society is a secretive organization still in existence at Yale University. According to a number of accounts, in 1918, four Bonesmen robbed Geronimo's grave. They allegedly stole Geronimo's skull and brought it back to the Tomb—the name of the Skull and Bones society's building on the campus of Yale. One of the alleged members of the tomb raiders was Prescott Bush, father of George H.W. Bush and grandfather of George W. Bush. In 2006, a group of Geronimo's descendants sued to get the skull back. They were unsuccessful.

❖ Other notable members of Yale's Skull and Bones society include Gifford Pinchot (1889), first chief of the U.S. Forest Service; Harold Stanley (1908), cofounder of Morgan Stanley; W.A. Harriman (1913), cofounder of Harriman Brothers & Company, which later became the highly successful Wall Street firm Brown Brothers Harriman & Co.; George H.W. Bush (1948), 41st president of the United States; and George W. Bush (1968), 43rd president of the United States.

❖ In March 1900 Congress passed the Gold Standard Act. It was signed into law by President William McKinley. It established gold as the only standard for redeeming paper money, stopping bimetallism, which had allowed silver in exchange for gold. The gold standard remained in existence off and on until 1971 when President Nixon finally abolished it. Since that time the U.S. dollar has replaced gold as the basis for the international monetary system.

❖ President Theodore Roosevelt created the United States Forest Service in April 1905. The Gila Forest Reserve was indeed expanded in July of that same year by more than 200,000 acres. Two years later, the Gila Cliff Dwellings were designated as a National Monument.

❖ Many believe China's gold reserves are much higher than China claims, due to the following: They export none of the gold from mines on mainland China; they have taken ownership stakes in a number of large mines around the world from which they take direct shipments (allowing them to effectively bypass the London and Hong Kong exchanges); and they have been a net buyer of gold on the international gold markets for years. While there is much debate as to the exact size of China's gold reserves, everyone agrees their reserves have increased dramatically over the past decade.

❖ Some contend the motive for China's alleged gold hoarding is to prepare for a return to the gold standard. At that time, it has been argued, China will make a play for the renminbi to become the new dominant world currency, effectively dislodging the U.S. dollar from its current reserve role.

❖ The largest sovereign wealth fund in China is the China Investment Corporation. It manages a significant portion of China's $4 trillion foreign exchange reserves. In the recent past they took minority ownership stakes in two large U.S. investment firms—Morgan Stanley and The Blackstone Group.

❖ There has not been an audit of Fort Knox since 1953. At that time, U.S. gold reserves stood at more than 20,000 tons. That amount is now believed to be less than 8,000 tons. But without an audit, nobody is certain how much gold is really there. Some have claimed the reason for the government's refusal to allow an audit is because the vault at Fort Knox is empty.

❖ The Buckhorn Saloon is exactly as described in the book. If you ever visit Pinos Altos, New Mexico, make a dinner reservation. You won't regret it.

After more than twenty-five years as a business professional, Richardson finally parlayed his fascination with American history and love of a good mystery into writing his own works of fiction. *Geronimo's Gold* is the third installment in the Matt Hawkins historical mystery series. His first novel, *Imposters of Patriotism* was released in June 2014 to enthusiastic reviews. *Abolition of Evil* followed in June 2016.

Visit him on Facebook at:
www.facebook.com/AuthorTedRichardson
Or his website:
www.AuthorTedRichardson.com

74978620R00175

Made in the USA
San Bernardino, CA
23 April 2018